T0148498

REECE WINNER
FOR THE WIN

The Making of a Teen Humanitarian

by Kevin Armes

authorHOUSE®

AuthorHouse™
1663 Liberty Drive
Bloomington, IN 47403
www.authorhouse.com
Phone: 1-800-839-8640

© *2013 Kevin D. Armes. All rights reserved.*

No part of this book may be reproduced, stored in a retrieval system, or transmitted by any means without the written permission of the author.

Published by AuthorHouse   2/7/2013

ISBN: 978-1-4817-1335-1 (sc)
ISBN: 978-1-4817-1336-8 (hc)
ISBN: 978-1-4817-1337-5 (e)

Library of Congress Control Number: 2013902277

Any people depicted in stock imagery provided by Thinkstock are models, and such images are being used for illustrative purposes only. Certain stock imagery © Thinkstock.

This book is printed on acid-free paper.

Because of the dynamic nature of the Internet, any web addresses or links contained in this book may have changed since publication and may no longer be valid. The views expressed in this work are solely those of the author and do not necessarily reflect the views of the publisher, and the publisher hereby disclaims any responsibility for them.

With love to my wife for her patience, my son for inspiring me and my baby daughter for making me realise that the time was right.

With grateful thanks to everyone else who has offered advice, given their opinion and provided encouragement.

Chapter One

The sound of a bottle shattering against a wall yanked Reece Winner's eyes from their glued-together sleep. A door slammed and the wall next to his bed shook. The rattle of someone fumbling with a bolt, told him his mother had locked herself in the bathroom.

'NAOMI. I'M TIRED OF YOUR GAMES!'

His dad's foot punctuated the statement with a kick to the bathroom door. Reece heard the crack of splintering timber as the bolt was torn from its anchor. His mum screamed and Reece strained his ears to distinguish if he could make out the sounds of a scuffle. His parents had argued a lot recently, but their verbal abuse of each other had never deteriorated into physical violence.

'GAMES? PLAYING GAMES MEANS HAVING FUN AND THERE'S BEEN NO FUN IN THIS MARRIAGE FOR A LONG TIME!'

Reece took comfort from his mum's yelling. At least while they were shouting at each other, they weren't killing each other.

'NO, BECAUSE YOU'VE BEEN GETTING YOUR FUN ELSEWHERE WHILE I STAYED HOME LOOKING AFTER OUR SON AND KEEPING THIS BUSINESS AFLOAT!'

His dad's voice was guttural, but the emphasis of each word hissed through teeth clenched in obvious loathing.

The flat fell into an uneasy quiet. Reece held his breath, frightened by the lull. His mind raced and produced images of his dad choking his mum's taunts into silence with his bare hands, or her standing over him clutching a bloodied knife. He slid out of bed, hurriedly tiptoed across the bedroom and eased a crack into the door. He was relieved to see both his parents standing at the end of the corridor. His mum had her back to him and held bags in each hand. Reece couldn't tell if her stooped shoulders came from the weight of her baggage or the weight of the decision she was about to make.

His father was facing her, his eyes displaying the pain of someone keeping vigil over a loved one on their deathbed. The tension was palpable. The two people Reece loved stood poised, like gunslingers each waiting for the other to reach for their weapon.

His mum finally looked up and straightened her back with resolve. 'Tell Reece I'm sorry.' Her voice broke into a sob as she disappeared down the stairs.

'YEAH, LEAVE ME THE CRAP JOBS AS USUAL!' his dad shouted after her, before shuffling into the kitchen and closing the door.

Reece wanted to go after his mum, but he was already shivering in his pyjamas and was sure she'd be gone by the time he was dressed. Besides, he didn't want to give his dad the impression he was taking Mum's side. He wondered if he should go to console him, but slamming noises coming from the kitchen told him this was not the time. He gently closed his bedroom door and got back into bed, hoping that his parents would sort it all out the next day once they had calmed down.

He pulled the quilt over his head, in the same way that a younger child might hide from the Bogeyman. He squeezed his eyes tightly shut, until troubled sleep eventually regained its hold over him.

Chapter Two

It seemed that no time had passed before shrill bleeping from his Harry Potter alarm clock, prised his eyes open again. Reece groaned from the dull headache throbbing behind his eyes and he rolled over, burying his face in the pillow. A tangible gloom hung in the air and he wished he could stay in bed rather than face it. The memory of his parents' row hammered on the door of his consciousness to dispel any hope that it had been a dream.

Everything had seemed fine when his mother had come upstairs to say goodnight to him. He had asked her why she was all dressed up and she'd replied that she was having a girls' night out. He'd assumed this to mean with her friend Elaine; a loud, fat woman whom he always found to be quite excitable, yet funny, in a childish sort of way. He knew his dad disliked her though, because she often got drunk in their pub and Reece had heard his dad say that he thought she was 'two-faced'. Reece had imagined Elaine as a female version of the Professor Quirrel character in his Harry Potter book, with a second, evil face hidden under her clothes that only his dad had ever seen. This would also explain why his dad had once accused her of 'talking from her backside.'

He peered at the clock on his bedside table but struggled to read the time in the half gloom of the bedroom. The dawn sun had poked only a scrawny finger of light through the triangular gap in the curtains, so he tapped the head of the Voldemort figure on the top of the clock to illuminate the face. It was seven o'clock.

He'd checked the time earlier when his parents' fight had woken him and it had been a little after three. He tried to recall what the row had been about, but couldn't remember being awake at the start of it. The flat was

3

above the pub that his parents ran and was a huge, five-bedroomed affair, so he probably wouldn't have heard anything if the argument had started in their bedroom at the far end of the corridor.

His own room was on a seaward facing corner of the first floor and had large, panoramic windows on two sides. It was bigger than most sitting rooms and had its own en suite bathroom. He had particularly chosen it when they had moved to Cornwall a few months ago because it was like having his own apartment and he had always liked his privacy. His parents had allowed him to have it because their long working hours downstairs in the pub would mean them having little time to enjoy the views, which were spectacular.

The front window framed the majestic, granite cliffs of the north Cornish coastline, with their rugged, primitive structure that only the seagulls could surmount. Through the side window, he could see the estuary, with its myriad of yachts and leisure boats bobbing alongside the timber jetties of the marina. Beyond lay the working fishing harbour of the neighbouring village where they had holidayed last spring. That was when his dad had first spotted the 'To Let' sign projecting from The Smuggler's Watch pub. Six months later, they had left their pub in London and moved to a new life in Trevarnick.

He always felt better looking out at the ocean, so he put on his dressing gown and went to open the curtains in his bedroom. The room flooded with bright, spring sunlight, which made him squint and instinctively create a visor with his hand. Beyond the cliff top, across the road beneath his window, stretched the cobalt blue ocean. It was tranquil for April, yet still interspersed with white horses, which caught the early sunlight and glistened like diamonds in a sea of sapphires. Through the side window, the serenity of the marina was interrupted by a solitary fishing boat, chugging out of the harbour beyond on the morning's rising tide.

It made no difference that he enjoyed this magnificent view every morning. It was still more dramatic than the curtain up at the opera his dad had once taken him to see in Covent Garden and never failed to lift his spirits.

Reece sat on the windowsill watching a Red Setter cavorting on his leash while his owner tried to stop it playfully grabbing the newspaper he had bought from the newsagent at the bottom of the hill. The annoyance of the man yelling 'No!' at the dog focused his thoughts on his parents' argument the night before. What had been the cause of it and why did he have a feeling in the pit of his stomach that this morning, everything was different?

It was only then that he noticed the absence of the usual morning noises of the house; the radio playing in the kitchen, the kettle whistling its reminder, the sound of teaspoon against cup as his dad made his first coffee of the day. All these sounds would usually be Reece's subconscious countdown as he performed the daily routine of preparing to go to school. Reece listened harder, holding his breath to eliminate even that sound. The flat was silent.

His mind raced while he considered the unlikely possibility that he was all alone in the building. He never for a moment thought his parents would leave him by himself, but the silence worried him. He replayed in his head the argument that had got him up in the early hours of the morning. The shouting had been more violent than usual and his dad kicking the bathroom door open had been so out of character it had shocked him. His mum had been holding two bags when she left and now he recalled hearing the sound of the front door slamming, followed by the distinctive engine note of her car as it accelerated down the road under his bedroom window. Yes, that was it; his mother had stormed out and his dad had probably overslept, having been up most of the night wondering where she'd gone. He headed to his parents' bedroom to see if he was correct. He knocked on the door but there was no answer.

'Dad must still be asleep,' he whispered to himself, as he opened the bedroom door and peered round the frame towards his parents' bed. The bed was empty and didn't look like it had been slept in.

With panic beginning to rise within him, he raced to search the rest of the flat. His parents' office overlooked the two spaces in the car park reserved for his mum's sports car and his dad's people carrier. He snatched back the curtains and wiped the condensation from the glass with his dressing gown sleeve. His dad's car was in its usual place but his mother's had gone, adding credibility to his theory that she had driven off after the argument, perhaps to spend the night at Elaine's. At least now he was reassured that his dad must be in the building somewhere and he concluded that he had to be downstairs in the pub.

He went back to his room to put on his slippers, remembering the years of warnings from his dad about the danger of bare feet finding broken glass on the pub floor. Downstairs he turned the combination latch that prevented uninvited staff or customers from wandering into the flat. Only the dim lights of the beer pumps lit the vast room of the Public Bar, making it look eerie and deserted. Once again, the fear of possibly being alone in such a large building began to well up inside him.

'Good morning.'

He jumped as the sound of his dad's voice cracked the silence like a pebble breaking glass. He spun round to look in its direction and caught his elbow on one of the tall, granite-topped tables that ran down the centre of the room.

'Bugger!' he hissed and then instinctively waited for the chastisement he always got from his dad whenever he let a swear word slip. He rubbed his elbow, the numbing sensation in his funny bone making him feel ever so slightly sick. 'Sorry Dad,' he volunteered, even though his dad had said nothing. 'Is everything okay? Where's Mum?'

He crossed the room to where his dad was sitting next to the fruit machine, in the corner furthest from the windows. He stared back at him from the shadows and Reece saw a picture of despair that shocked him.

His dad clearly hadn't slept and it was obvious that he'd been crying, something that until then, Reece had not thought him capable of. He waited for his dad to respond to his questions, knowing he wasn't going to like what he heard.

'Your mum's gone,' he murmured.

'What do you mean she's gone? Gone where?'

'I'm not sure,' he sighed, his face tired and grey and looking like it might never again show happiness. 'Sit down, Son. There's something I need to tell you.'

Reece stood rooted to the spot as though trying to put off what he was about to hear. He found himself counting the stripes on his dad's sweater which he remembered him wearing the same one the day before, confirming his suspicion that he hadn't been to bed. Even his greying hair, which was always cut short, looked flat and unkempt and he hadn't shaved. He was a tall man, over six feet in height with broad shoulders, but this morning he looked stooped and slightly shrunken, like the patients Reece had seen recovering from operations when he'd visited his granddad in hospital. His normally bright, dark-brown eyes, that Reece had inherited, were red and watery, peering through the slits that his eyelids were grudgingly conceding.

'Mum will be coming back, won't she?' he asked, slumping into the chair that his dad had moved towards him with his foot.

'No, Son. I'm afraid your mum and I aren't going to be living together anymore.'

'You're splitting up?'

David Winner cleared his throat, as if trying to summon a more optimistic tone. 'Yes, but I promise, it won't change anything between you and me, or you and your mum. We both love you very much and this is not your problem or your fault.'

'So where's Mum now and where's she going to live?'

'I don't know yet. She has a lot to sort out, but I'll tell you everything, as soon as I know myself.'

'And where do I get to live, or don't I get a say in any of this?' snapped Reece.

'Of course you do, Son. What would you like to happen?'

'I'd like things to stay the way they are! I don't want to be another broken home kid with parents who hate each other!' He saw his dad wince from the pain of his words and softened his voice. 'I'm sorry dad. I know it's not your fault. I bet it was Elaine getting Mum drunk again, wasn't it?'

'No, Son, it's not Elaine's fault. It's much more complicated than that, but I don't expect you to understand.'

'Dad, I'm almost thirteen. Don't treat me like a baby!'

His dad half smiled. 'I'm sorry, Son, you're right; I shouldn't patronize you.' He spent a few seconds pondering, as though coming to terms with the realization that his son was old enough to deal with the unpalatable truth that life was sometimes cruel. 'You know things haven't been good between your mum and me for a while now don't you? You've heard the constant rows and noticed your mum spending more time out with her new friends.'

'I didn't realise things were *that* bad,' Reece muttered.

'We tried to hide it, for your sake and the sake of the customers, but it has been that bad for some time and last night we finally faced the inevitable truth that it was time to go our separate ways.'

'So, will I stay here, or go with Mum?'

'You can stay here, of course; in fact I'd love you to if that's what you want. Then later, when your mum is settled, you can have a room at hers too. I don't want you to feel you have to take sides.'

'Most of the kids I've met from broken families have parents who hate each other.'

'That may be true, Reece, but in our case I think it's simply that we've both realised we want different things in life. You knew your mum didn't want to move to this pub, didn't you?'

'No, I didn't. I thought she liked it here.'

'Oh, she likes being in Cornwall, but she didn't want us to buy another pub. She said she'd had enough of feeling like we had customers in our home twelve hours a day, seven days a week. But I persuaded her to give it another few years in the hope that she'd enjoy the slower pace of life down here. Sadly, the recession meant we couldn't afford as many staff as we had in London and she's grown sick of the long hours. So have I, to be honest, but I've got to pay the bills somehow.' He gave a weak grin but it didn't hide the stress etched into his brow. 'Anyway, what I'm trying to say is, I don't want you to worry, because we'll do everything we can to ensure that you don't suffer too much upheaval. Okay, Son?' He stood to stretch limbs stiff from his sleepless night and ruffled Reece's hair. Reece knew he was waiting for him to respond.

'Okay, Dad but promise I won't have to move schools again. I've only just started to make new friends and haven't got many.'

'I promise I'll do everything I can,' he said. 'Now let's get some breakfast and get you off to school. I've still got a pub to run and I'm going to have to find staff to replace your mum.'

'So Mum won't even work here anymore?' Reece asked, as the enormity of what his dad had just told him began to sink in.

'No, Son, I've fired her.' There was a lilt in his voice, to suggest he was trying to inject some humour into a miserable situation.

'Then I hope you're going to employ a new cook.'

'Yes, of course I am. Why?'

'Because making me eat your cooking could be classed as child abuse!'

His dad pretended to cuff him. 'Well if that's what you think, *you* can make breakfast this morning!'

Chapter Three

On his first day as a member of the broken home club, Reece felt he had a perfectly good excuse not to go to school. His dad though, had disagreed and told him that he needed to try to keep everything normal and avoid having too much spare time to dwell on things. Reece thought that his dad just wanted him out of the way, which he accepted was understandable, given that he had a lot to deal with.

He left the pub late and had to run for the number five bus, which was already signalling its intention to pull away from the bus stop as he turned the corner of Seaview Rise.

He waved and shouted and caught the eye of his classmate Kara Steigers who was sitting on the back seat and happened to be looking back in his direction. He saw her stand and apparently call to the driver and Reece was relieved to see the orange indicator stop flashing as the driver waited for him to approach.

He reached the bus and the door hissed open, allowing him to clamber breathlessly up the steps. He reached in his pocket for the fare, struggling to keep control of his rucksack, which he had only thrown over one shoulder before beginning his sprint for the bus. He was scanning his palm for the required coins, when the bag slipped from his shoulder and jolted his arm. The coins bounced from his hand, rolled down the steps and out of the open door. Reece turned to see the coins drop into the drain that was inconveniently located directly below the bus steps.

'Oh bugger!' he exclaimed.

The bus was full of fellow pupils and some of those near the door, exploded into a roar of laughter at his misfortune and Reece, though normally mild-mannered, yelled an obscenity at his tormentors.

'Oi!' snarled the driver. 'I'll have none of that language on here. You'll be walking if you don't watch it.'

'Sorry,' muttered Reece. 'I'm having a bad day.'

He fumbled in his empty pockets, hoping that the driver would take pity on his plight and let him off the fare. From the driver's scowl, no such kindness was looking likely. He was still frowning in annoyance at Reece's bad tempered outburst.

'I've no more money,' he finally admitted, while trying to put on a face that he hoped would extract some mercy from the grumpy driver.

'Looks like you're walking then, doesn't it?' The driver's voice was so sarcastic, Reece couldn't be sure if he was serious or not. He felt the hairs on the back of his neck bristle and was about to blow his top at the unpleasant driver, when a girl's voice asked how much he needed. It was Kara Steigers, who had walked from her seat at the back of the bus, to offer him a lifeline.

'Forty pence!' snapped the driver, holding out his hand for the fare. She had a purse full of copper coins and proceeded to count them laboriously into the hand of the driver who was clearly getting more and more impatient. By the time she reached twenty-six pence, the driver was making no attempt to hide his annoyance and Reece detected, with mild amusement that Kara was going deliberately slowly just to wind him up.

She eventually reached forty pence and announced the amount to the driver triumphantly, with a disarming smile. He grunted something unintelligible and pressed a button to issue the ticket. Kara threw Reece a sideways smirk and a swift wink. Reece thanked her and returned her smile, then realised the whole bus was watching his clumsy attempt at flirting.

When she turned to walk back to her seat at the rear of the bus, Reece was unsure if he should follow her, seeing how she had come to his rescue, but the rows of faces staring and sniggering at him from behind the headrests, compelled him to drop quickly into the first available seat. Unfortunately, a little too late to change his mind, he found himself sitting next to Robert Fathaby, an unpleasant boy, whose dad owned a rival pub in the next village.

'Hello Loser!' he sneered.

'The name's Winner,' Reece retorted, trying to muster some courage. Fathaby was bigger than he was and would probably win if it came to a fight, but Reece didn't think he would try anything on the bus and there would be teachers on duty around the school gates when they arrived.

Robert Fathaby glared at him and threatened through clenched teeth to tear his head off if he gave him any more lip. Reece chose to ignore him and decided to play a game on his mobile phone.

'Ha! Call that a phone, Loser?' jeered Fathaby, as Reece produced the mobile phone his dad had bought him three years ago on a trip abroad. Then it had been one of the most up-to-date available, but now it looked quite out of date. 'Still, I suppose having a crap pub with hardly any customers, means your dad can't afford to buy you a decent phone like mine.'

Reece once more felt the anger building inside him. He hated to hear his dad, being criticised, especially by a moron like Fathaby. It was true that The Smuggler's Watch had been quieter lately. He had heard his dad say that the takings were down, but that it was due to him barring some of the local troublemakers. His dad was sure things would pick up once nicer people realised that rowdy customers were no longer welcome and soon the summer months would bring in the tourists. One of the short-term consequences though, was that most of the people his dad had barred had started going to Fathaby's pub, *'The Ship'* as it was the next nearest. This had given the impression that, for the time being at least, Fathaby's pub was more popular.

He tried to ignore Fathaby's goading, but the morning's events had fractured his usual composure. His eyes moistened involuntarily, forcing him to blink back the faintest of tears. Fathaby took this to be a sign that his intimidation was having the desired effect and like a lion calculating the weakness of an isolated zebra, he moved in for the kill.

'Even your mother knows which pub is better,' he taunted. 'She was in ours last night with her fat friend. They got totally drunk and left with a couple of men. Did she come home last night, Loser?'

Reece suspected that Fathaby might be using blatant lies mixed with a hint of truth, to rile him. Maybe his mother and Elaine had been in The Ship last night and maybe Fathaby's dad had mentioned it this morning. He doubted Fathaby would have still been up and in the bar late enough to see his mum and Elaine leave, but Reece couldn't be sure. What if his mother had been with a man last night in Fathaby's pub? Reece could feel the rage building inside him as he considered the possibilities. He didn't only wonder if his mum could have been cheating on his dad, but also how, if she had, she could do it in Fathaby's pub of all places.

'Well, did she come home last night, Loser?' His interrogator was being persistent.

Reece squirmed uncomfortably. He searched the rows of gleeful faces peering over the tops of the bus seats. He hoped to find an ally; someone who would come to his defence and get Fathaby to be quiet, but he saw no one with whom he was especially friendly and the driver was still busy at the front of the bus, counting and bagging up the loose change Kara had just handed to him.

Reece felt vulnerable and facing two choices. He could move to another seat or stay and possibly end up in a fight. He was sure that running to the back of the bus wouldn't shake off the bully's attention. It would simply hand him a reason to call him a coward. That left fighting as his only option and Reece hated fighting.

The bully continued to grin at him and Reece was sickened by his disgusting teeth. They still had bits of breakfast cereal stuck between them and were the colour of custard, which reminded him of the nickname he had devised for Robert Fathaby a few weeks earlier.

Reece's dad was a crossword fan and had often tried to teach Reece how to solve cryptic puzzles. His dad's love of words had rubbed off on him and Reece had shown a talent for solving anagrams. One of his hobbies was to find anagrams of people's names, which he had done for some of his friends, most of his teachers and one or two of the bullies he hated, which included Robert Fathaby. He had never divulged any of them to anyone else though, because he was afraid that the other kids might call him a geek, but he had always thought the one he had found for Robert Fathaby was quite funny. Now might be a good time to test its insult value.

'Fathaby?' he asked, fighting the quiver in his voice that came from knowing that what he was about to say would be like lighting the touch paper on a damaged firework. 'Can you fart through your mouth, because it sure smells like it?'

The effect was immediate. Robert Fathaby's face turned pink and then crimson as the rest of the bus laughed loudly. The laughter bolstered Reece's bravado. He sniggered at his own joke while Fathaby fumed, struggling to find words in retaliation. Reece didn't notice the bully's right fist slowly tightening into a ball.

'Loser, you're dead meat!'

'Loser?' retorted Reece. 'Is that the cleverest name you can come up with Fathaby, something that's simply the opposite of my real name?'

'And you think calling me Fathaby is smart?' snarled the bully, who spat the words so violently, that a bit of cornflake flew from between his teeth and stuck to Reece's face.

'Oh no,' Reece said, removing the cornflake particle from his cheek in disgust. 'I have a much better nickname for you than that. It's an anagram of your real name and now I've sat next to you, I think it's perfect. Did you know that Robert Fathaby is an anagram of *Fart Breath Boy*?'

Reece held his breath while Fathaby absorbed what he had said. Meanwhile, some of the passengers on the bus continued to laugh loudly, while others took it upon themselves to check if the anagram was, in fact, accurate. One boy, a couple of years older than Reece, had quickly written *Fart Breath Boy* on the back of his hand and then ticked off the letters of Robert Fathaby to check that the anagram worked. It did, of course and within seconds, he was yelling down the bus.

'Hey! *Fart Breath Boy*. He's right you know!'

The bus now erupted into raucous laughter and Robert Fathaby sat mortified. He wasn't the sharpest mind in the school but he had been a bully long enough to know that nicknames could often stick. He knew that he could be facing the next few days, weeks, or even the rest of his school life labelled *Fart Breath Boy* and when the reality of it sank in, his temper erupted. He sent the clenched fist, that he had so far managed to restrain, hurtling towards Reece's face. Reece didn't have time to see it coming. The fist landed fully on his nose and blood immediately trickled from his nostril. He turned towards the aisle and bent forward to allow the blood to drip on to the floor of the bus, rather than on his clothes. He remained in that position while he composed his thoughts and fumbled for a tissue from his pocket.

He was surprised that the punch had not felt particularly powerful and that he was not experiencing any real pain. If that was Fathaby's best punch, maybe he wasn't as hard as he liked to pretend; 'All mouth and no trousers,' as his dad would say. He was steeling himself to smack Fathaby right back when Kara Steigers was at his side again, asking him if he was all right and offering him a drink of her cola. Before Reece had chance to answer her, Fathaby tried to reinforce his authority by snarling again that Reece was a loser. Kara's response surprised Fathaby even more than it did Reece. She calmly turned to the bully and fixed him with a cool stare.

'*Fart Breath Boy*,' she sneered, to more sniggers of approval from several of the onlookers. '*You* are a bully and if I see you picking on Reece, or anyone else again, I'll personally post your new nickname to everyone on the school network.'

'Get lost, Steigers!' spat Fathaby. 'I'm not scared of a teacher's pet like you!'

'Well, I think you should be,' replied Kara. 'Because with oral hygiene like yours, you really don't want the entire school calling you *Fart Breath Boy*, do you?'

'Steigers, I'm warning you. You don't want to make me—'

His threat was cut short by the shock of Kara Steigers calmly emptying the remaining contents of her cola can into his lap. For a second, Fathaby could only sit there stunned while Kara took Reece's hand and led him back to where she'd been sitting at the rear of the bus. A livid Fathaby leapt from his seat, intending to follow them and exact his revenge, but by then the bus driver had decided he had heard enough and was walking down the aisle of the bus. He met Robert Fathaby as he was launching himself from his seat.

'What do you think you've been up to?' barked the driver. 'Why is there cola all over the seat of my bus? I'll have to clean that up when I get to the depot!'

'It wasn't me,' spluttered Fathaby. 'It was—'

'Don't lie to me boy, I can see it all over your trousers. Now stay in that seat until I tell you to move and when we get to school, wait there until I've had a word with a teacher and shown him this mess!'

Robert Fathaby wanted to argue, but the grimacing face of the bus driver told him that it would do him no good. He might even be ejected from the bus, forced to walk almost three miles to school and then get a detention for being late. Petulantly, he slumped back into his seat and spent the journey to school imagining what he would like to do to Reece Winner.

Reece meanwhile, was being comforted by Kara Steigers. His nose had stopped bleeding and was displaying little evidence of Fathaby's punch. Kara removed a spot of dried blood from his face by licking her handkerchief and giving his cheek a firm rub like his Aunt Debbie always seemed to do whenever she saw him.

Reece could be quite an extrovert when dealing with adults; his dad had once commented that this was probably because he had always lived in a pub and mixed with the regular customers. Yet Reece found people his own age more difficult to weigh up, which often made him shy and awkward with them. There was something about Kara though, that told him she was more understanding than most her age and he felt unusually comfortable with her.

While she was dabbing at his face with her hankie, Reece noticed, for the first time, that she had the deepest blue eyes. When she had been displaying her contempt for Robert Fathaby, those eyes had seemed cold and piercing, but now they were warm and kindly. Her hair was mostly blonde, yet up close, he could see it was interwoven with variegated strands of white, gold and titian, which he guessed was evidence of natural bleaching from the sea and the strong Cornish sunshine. He wondered why he had never looked beyond her apparent plainness to realise that she was naturally pretty. She had a neat, shoulder-length hairstyle and, unlike most of the other girls, such as Belinda Sopers, who all the boys seemed to fancy, wore no make-up. She had a sprinkling of freckles around her nose and very white, though slightly irregular teeth.

Reece also noticed that, as usual, her school uniform was pristine and worn completely in the regulated fashion. Most pupils tried to individualise their appearance by adapting the uniform in some way. The girls would try to get away with non-regulation blouses, with enormous knots in their school tie, unlike the neat Windsor knot his dad had taught him to tie. Skirts would often be too short, while boys would wear their trousers so loose they would appear ready to slide from their hips and the hems would become ragged from dragging on the ground.

Reece's dad had always been a stickler for getting him to comply with the uniform regulations, but even Reece would occasionally fail to fasten the top button of his shirt and leave his tie hanging loosely round his neck. But not Kara; she was the epitome of the Headmaster's vision of perfect school attire.

After making sure that he was showing no signs of his skirmish, Kara produced a book from her bag and to Reece's disappointment, continued the journey reading in silence.

As soon as the bus came to a stop outside the school gates, Robert Fathaby tried to make good his escape by being first up to the opening doors, but just as his freedom appeared imminent, the driver shot his arm out across the aisle to block his path.

'Not you, Sunshine! You go back to your seat and wait, like I told you!'

Turning to go back to where he'd been sitting, Fathaby was annoyed to see Reece standing in the aisle, waiting for him to return to his seat. He paused to glare at Reece and hissed something about seeing him later. Reece shuffled past him, happy to take the opportunity that the bus driver had given him to get away from his antagonist.

Kara followed him from the bus and immediately hurried towards the school entrance as though afraid of being late. A glance at his watch told Reece that there were still ten minutes to go before the bell and so he called after her, 'What's the rush?'

She turned her head, hardly slowing and said that she had to hand in some homework, before disappearing through the doors.

'See you later then,' he called, unsure whether his words reached her before she vanished.

Reece glanced back at the bus to see Robert Fathaby stood in front of the driver and the sports master Mr Poutril, who was the teacher on gate duty that morning. Fathaby was trying, without success, to proclaim his innocence but Mr Poutril appeared to be having none of it and Reece heard him issue the bully with a detention. Reece decided to make himself scarce as he didn't particularly wish to be around when Fathaby was allowed to go on his way. He entered the main school building and was walking along the corridor to his tutor room when he heard the voice of Mr Bierce, his history teacher, calling his name.

'Damn!' hissed Reece under his breath, suddenly remembering he'd left his history homework on the desk in his bedroom. He disliked history and had failed to hand in the previous week's homework. Mr Bierce had given him until today to submit it and he was annoyed that having spent over an hour doing it last night, he'd forgotten to put it in his bag this morning.

Anton Bierce was not a bad teacher, but Reece often found the subject he taught, boring. The fact that Reece had discovered that the teacher's name was an anagram of ***Ancient Bor***e, seemed to reinforce his reasons for disliking the subject.

'Hello Sir,' he said, in a voice he hoped sounded confident and friendly. 'I have done the homework, it's in my bag.'

He swung the bag from his shoulder onto the floor and rifled through the books and papers, pretending to search for the history book he knew couldn't possibly be there. He could feel the eyes of ***Ancient Bore*** boring into him, probably hoping that he would fail to produce the homework, so that he could issue him with a detention.

'I'm sorry, Sir. I seem to have left my history book at home, yet I'm certain I put it in my bag last night,' he lied.

'Nice try, Mr Winner, but I can see it from here. It's the bright orange one.' He swooped down and with hawk-like accuracy and fingers like talons, he plucked Reece's history book from between all the others.

'Forgot to do the homework again I suppose?' sneered Mr Bierce, who was now thumbing through the pages searching for proof of his accusation.

'I have done it, Sir,' Reece said, still wondering how the book came to be in his bag when he was certain he hadn't put it there.

Mr Bierce arrived at the correct page and quickly scanned through it. He seemed surprised to find the homework and stared hard at Reece, as if wanting to chastise him, but unable to find a reason. He grudgingly thanked him for doing the work and warned him of the consequences of being late next time.

He abruptly closed the office door creating a draught which blew loose sheets of paper from Reece's open bag. They floated across the floor to be kicked and trampled underfoot by hordes of students scurrying to their classrooms. Reece scrambled on all fours trying to retrieve them without getting his fingers trodden on. As he scooped them up and turned to cram them back into his bag, a foot was thrust into the small of his back, spread-eagling him across the corridor floor. Robert Fathaby had caught him up and was now leering down at him.

'You'd best keep out of my way Loser, or I won't be responsible for what I do to you.'

Reece quickly scrambled to his feet, fearful of getting another kick while he was down on the floor. 'Get lost, Fathaby! Touch me again and I'll do what Kara said and tell the entire school that your name is an anagram of *Fart Breath Boy*!'

'What did he just call you, Rob?'

Reece turned to see Belinda Sopers watching from the sidelines and it was obvious whose side she was on.

'You're not going to let him talk to you like that are you?' she demanded, clearly trying to provoke Fathaby into more violence.

Reece's spirits sank. Why was the girl he had often fantasized about asking out, goading a thug like Fathaby to beat him up? What had he ever done to her to cause her to dislike him?

'Come on, Bel,' Fathaby said, ignoring her question. 'The boy's a loser.' He put his arm around her shoulder as if to indicate his ownership of her and the two of them sauntered off down the corridor laughing.

Reece took some comfort from believing that Fathaby had let him off lightly, because he didn't want his girlfriend to hear the nickname he'd given him. His dad had said that most bullies were insecure individuals who used intimidation and threats to hide their own sense of inadequacy and Reece was pretty sure that Fathaby was no different. But what was

Belinda Sopers' problem? How could the girl, considered by many boys to be the most attractive in their year, have such an ugly personality and turn out to be such a bitch? How could someone he had fancied from his first day at the school, enjoy watching him get a kicking from Fathaby, even if she was going out with him?

As he trudged towards his tutor room, despondency gripped him so tightly that it took all of his will power not to run from the building and go home. The problem was, thinking about home simply reminded him that it no longer offered the sanctuary he craved either. It too had become a place of disharmony and instability and so he decided reluctantly that he'd be as well to stay at school and tough it out. He felt trapped in his situation and fingers of depression slowly tightened around his heart, making him wonder if things could possibly get any worse.

Chapter Four

After school, Reece decided to take advantage of the fine spring weather and walk home. He still had no money and he didn't want to trouble his dad by asking him to collect him in the car. Most of the few friends he had, lived close to the school and so he cut a lonely figure as he traipsed along the narrow country lane. The events of the day played through his mind and he wondered if there would be any new developments at home. Would his mum and dad have seen sense and decided to stay together? He decided to ring his dad and use the pretext of letting him know that he'd be late home, to find out if anything else had happened.

'Hello, The Smuggler's Watch. How may I help you?' His dad answered the phone as businesslike as usual.

'Hi Dad, how's things?'

'Not too bad, Son. I've managed to find a new chef already, so it looks as if we'll be able to keep the restaurant open. She starts next week and your Aunt Debbie has agreed to come down and help until then. So that's good news, isn't it?'

'Yes, that's great news,' Reece lied. His dad's words had actually sounded like nails in the coffin of his parents' marriage. 'Listen, I'll be late home because I lost my money down a drain this morning, so I'm walking. I'll see you later.'

'I can pick you up if like,' his dad offered. 'Peter's on the bar at the moment and the place is quiet.'

Peter was the only full-time barman his parents had employed since buying the pub and they often trusted him to look after the place during quiet spells. However, Reece wanted to be alone with his thoughts.

'No, don't bother, Dad. I fancy a walk along the beach from Trevarnick Point seeing as it's low tide.'

'Okay, Son,' his dad replied with a hint of hesitation. 'Is everything all right? Did you hand in your history homework I put in your bag this morning?'

'Oh, that explains it. I wondered how it got there. Thanks, Dad, you saved my life. What's for dinner later?'

'Well I had a late lunch and probably won't eat again. Why don't you grab some fish and chips from Tom's and tell him I'll settle up when he comes in later for a pint?'

Reece cheered up at his dad's suggestion. Tom's Fish Restaurant served the tastiest fish he had ever eaten and Tom himself was a great guy who always made him laugh. 'Okay, Dad. I'll probably be home around seven o'clock then.'

'Do you have homework?' questioned his dad, in his supposed stern voice, which Reece knew was anything but.

'Yes, more history. We have to find out if there were any famous smugglers or pirates round Trevarnick. I don't normally like history, but this project might be interesting. I was going to look on the internet, but maybe I'll ask Tom if he knows any local history. He's lived here all his life, hasn't he?'

'I believe he has, but don't pester him if he's busy, Reece.'

'I won't, Dad. See you later.'

He was about to hang up when he heard his dad add, 'Ring me every hour so I know you're safe.'

'Okay, Dad, I will. Bye.'

He hung up and decided he would try to enjoy the rest of the walk to Trevarnick Point. The country lanes were narrow, with no pavements and bound on both sides with high hedges on top of steep banks, which gave them a tunnel-like appearance in places where the foliage was densest. The long, spring shadows danced on the tarmac before him, as Reece walked on the right-hand side of the road, facing the oncoming traffic for safety.

He climbed the hill towards Trevarnick Point, anticipating the stunning view across the bay. He had seen it many times before, but it still never failed to enchant him. He quickened his pace, eager to escape the gloomy, arboreal subway. It reminded him of the Greenwich Foot Tunnel under the Thames in London, which he had once walked through with his dad. He'd had a minor panic attack from the claustrophobic fear of having a river inches above his head. He felt a similar sense of foreboding now, being alone under the chilling mantle of branches, which attempted to barricade the sun's rays like an army of pikemen. When he finally reached the top of the hill, he emerged from beneath the trees to the sun's applause. The emotional lift he had hoped for energised him and he realised how lucky he was to have on his doorstep this visual narcotic, which could chase away depression faster than anything yet discovered by medical science.

A bench, bearing a plaque as a memorial to a loved one, stood on the large grass verge leading to the cliff edge. Reece imagined that someone had placed it there to remember a deceased relative who had been similarly awestruck by the view; someone who wanted their legacy to include a comfortable seat, where others could sit and enjoy it. He decided he would take advantage of their generosity and sit a while. He didn't bother to look closely enough at the plaque to read the name of his late host, but he did notice their age when they had died. Forty-two was too young, he thought. It was younger than his dad was.

The breeze coming off the ocean was cool and refreshing after his long climb up the hill. He inhaled deeply, enjoying the saltiness, which gave the air a taste of purity, so unlike the polluted atmosphere he remembered from his years in London. Ahead of the bench, daffodils had already pushed their yellow buds through the grass, ready to replicate on Earth the colour of the spring sun. Reece had the briefest impulse to pick some for his mum and then stopped as he remembered that she wasn't coming home.

And that made him cry.

Self-consciousness made him dart his eyes to check he was indeed alone. When he had assured himself that no one was around, he wept unashamedly and allowed the tears to wash away the scum of his dreadful day. He sat for several minutes, until eventually his sobs abated. Inwardly he felt better, but his tear stained face was tight and sore from the salt on his cheeks.

The sound of a car changing down a gear to power up the hill he'd just climbed, intruded on his self-pity. He guiltily wiped his face with his hands to remove evidence of his crying, in case the car stopped or the driver recognised him. He feigned nonchalance, staring out to sea without turning his head towards the road behind him. The car slowed to take the sharp left bend that steered the road away from the precipitous cliff edge and safely down the hill towards Jasmine Cove which lay south-west of Trevarnick Bay. He wanted to look to see what car it was, but he didn't want to risk exposing his tear stained face to whoever was in it. When it had passed, he quickly stole a glance in its direction and saw the brake lights come on as it slowed to a stop.

'Damn!' he muttered under his breath and quickly turned away again, hoping he didn't know the occupants. He heard a door open and a young girl say something about walking home. He recognised the voice, but embarrassment wanted him to pretend otherwise. He considered hurrying on his way but decided that would look silly and a part of him was pleased to hear the footsteps getting closer as the car drove off again. He continued to look away as if hoping that the longer he did so, the less evident his crying would be.

'Hi Reece, I thought it was you. Are you all right?' Kara Steigers asked.

'Of course,' he replied, turning his face towards her just enough to avoid appearing rude. 'Why shouldn't I be?'

His words sounded unfriendly even as he spoke them and he wished he could retrieve them before they reached her. To his relief, Kara seemed not to notice.

'Can I sit with you?' she asked, her voice calm and soothing.

'It's a free country,' he said, again with unintentional sarcasm which he instantly regretted. He muttered a one-word apology, aware that his posture and lack of eye contact with this pleasant girl who had befriended him earlier, was giving his bad mood away.

'I've often sat here and cried,' Kara announced coolly.

Reece wanted to make it clear that he most certainly had *not* been crying, but he knew such a protest would be unconvincing with this intuitive girl. He also believed he could trust her not abuse his present vulnerability.

'How come you didn't catch the bus?' he asked.

'Mum had been shopping in town and decided to pick me up.'

'So what made you stop and get out here?'

'I saw you and thought you looked sad,' replied Kara, simply.

There was a long pause, which Reece was afraid to fill. He didn't want to give her the impression that he preferred to be alone, when he really wanted her to stay. Eventually Kara broke the silence.

'This is my dad's seat,' she said.

'Your dad's?' asked Reece, finally turning his face towards hers. 'How come?'

'My mother had it put here after he died three years ago.' She spoke matter-of-factly and Reece struggled to find an appropriate response.

'I'm sorry,' he murmured, immediately sensing the inadequacy of the words to acknowledge the depth of her loss. He swivelled on the bench to look at the plaque that he had earlier ignored and read the inscription.

'In memory of John Steigers, aged 42.
A loving husband and father.
With heartfelt remorse.

Reece felt guilty for crying. What right did he have to indulge in childish self-pity when Kara had suffered the grief of losing her dad forever? At least both his parents were alive, even if their marriage was dead. He wanted to know more but didn't know how to proceed. Should he simply ask, or would that make her upset?

As if hearing the turmoil in his head, Kara continued. 'He committed suicide.' She paused before pointing to where the stretch of grass came to an abrupt end directly in front of them. 'He came up here and jumped off the cliff, right just there.'

A shiver played an arpeggio down his spine. He'd stood on the edge of that precipice a few times and been genuinely terrified of toppling over.

'You're kidding,' he whispered, again regretting the inappropriate choice of expression. Kara though, had learnt from past experience that most people struggled to articulate their true reaction to such horrendous information. He paused, unsure if his next question was appropriate. 'Why did he do that?'

'My mother walked out on him,' she said, in the same casual tone. 'And he never got over it.'

Her words were like a bang to the head. His neurons conjured up a vision of his own despairing father, standing at the cliff edge in front of him, turning his head to say goodbye, before leaning forwards for gravity to wrench him from his life forever. The horrific imagery of his dad's suicide was seemingly reflected in Kara's deep blue eyes and suddenly he realised that she was staring back at him unblinkingly, as though allowing him to use her eyes as windows to his own personal nightmare. He felt his cheeks redden and he hurriedly averted his eyes.

'So what's gone wrong in your life?' she asked.

'My mum walked out last night, too.'

'I thought it was something like that,' she replied.

She put an arm around his shoulder and gently pulled him towards her. He slipped an arm around her waist and their heads rested on each other's. Together they stared across the vastness of the Atlantic Ocean, each engrossed in their own private thoughts.

Several minutes later, his mobile phone began to play Monty Python's *'Always Look on the Bright Side of Life,'* the tune he had selected as a ring tone when life was good. Kara laughed and Reece couldn't resist smiling at the irony. The screen flashed 'David Winner'.

'It's my dad, probably checking up on me,' he joked.

'Hi, Dad,' he said, trying to sound cheery. 'What's up? ... Yes, I'm fine ... I'm with a friend ... Kara ... Oh, just a friend!' he laughed at Kara who had crossed her arms and cocked her nose indignantly. 'Oh thanks, Dad. I'll ask her.' He held the phone to his chest while he asked Kara if she fancied going to Tom's with him if his dad paid.

'That would be nice. Tell your dad thanks, I'd love to.'

He put the phone back to his ear. 'She said yes, Dad, thank you. Shall I bring you some home too? ... Okay, if you're sure ... I'll see you later then.' He switched off the phone and put it in his pocket.

'He sounds nice,' Kara said.

'He's the best,' Reece replied, again feeling a twinge of sympathy for Kara's loss. 'I'm sure he'll like you too.'

'Oh, so you're already planning to take me home to meet him are you?' Kara teased.

He realised he had sounded presumptuous and hurriedly backtracked. 'Sorry,' he blurted. 'Only if you'd like to, of course.'

Kara laughed. 'Don't be so serious Reece, I'm only teasing. I'd love to meet your dad sometime.' Reece heaved an inward sigh of relief. He was enjoying this new friendship and didn't want to say something to spoil it before it had barely started. 'When I do meet him, shall I call him Dave, David or Mr Winner?' she asked.

'How do you know his name's David,' Reece asked.

'I saw it on your phone just now when he rang,' she replied, smiling.

'Do you miss anything?'

'Nope, not much!' she quipped, clearly enjoying the look on his face.

'Well most people call him David or Dave. He doesn't like being called Mr Winner.'

He got up from the bench and turned to face her. 'So, Miss Steigers are you ready to go to dinner?' He was putting on his pretend, posh voice and he bowed, offering her his arm.

'Fish and chips sounds delightful, Mr Winner. With tartar sauce I hope,' she replied in a similarly formal voice, sharing his joke.

'But of course, Miss Steigers and I'm sure my father's budget might even stretch to that delicacy common people call mushy peas, if one would like some.'

'Oh stop it, you sound daft,' Kara laughed, her voice returning to its subtle West Country twang. 'Shall we walk across the beach to Trevarnick?'

'I was planning to, if there was still enough time to beat the tide?' He checked his watch. It was 4.30pm. 'Low tide was about an hour ago I think.'

'Good, we've just enough time to get under the bridge,' she said. 'I'll race you to the steps!' Then like a hare, she was away across the cliff top, leaving Reece to call after her as he tried to catch her up.

Chapter Five

A footpath ran along the cliff top and followed the coastline back towards Trevarnick. However, at Seagull Island Bay a flight of primitive steps had been cut into the blue-grey rock to allow access to the beach below; but only for the fit and sure-footed. Kara was certainly both. She skipped down the steep, irregular steps like a mountain goat, unlike Reece who knew that he would probably end up on his backside if he tried to go so fast.

As he had got older, he had begun to feel more self-conscious about his poor physical coordination. When he was younger, he had often fallen over, bumped into things and had endless accidents, causing his parents to be concerned that outsiders might think the bruises were the result of domestic violence. His doctor had eventually done tests and confirmed that he had a condition called dyspraxia. Reece had only recently asked questions about it because he had noticed that he was not particularly good at sports and was usually the last boy left when football teams were picked. He suspected it was a contributing factor in the bullying he suffered, as well. His dad had explained that the condition made it difficult to put actions into the correct sequence. He had compared it to dyslexia, which could cause a similar confusion with the order of letters within words.

Apparently, the paediatrician had said that Reece would probably never ride a bicycle, but no one had told Reece. When he was six, he had asked for his first bike and his dad hadn't hesitated to buy him one, despite his mum having reservations about it. His dad had then spent hours running after him, holding the saddle while he pedalled, until eventually letting go to watch him wobble his way across the park before hitting the only tree around for a hundred metres. Reece had been so euphoric at the achievement that he had laid on the grass in fits of giggles while his dad ran to his aid. When he was sure Reece was unhurt, his dad had joined in the laughter before helping him get back on the bike for another go. Reece had fallen off the bike many times after that, but he'd always had the determination to get straight back in the saddle no matter how bruised or bloodied he was.

Running down steep, damp, rocky steps was different to riding a bike though and carried the very real danger of falling a long way if he slipped. Therefore, he picked his way carefully, holding on to the rusty handrail that had been crudely bolted to the rock many years previously. By the time he jumped from the bottom step onto the freshly washed sand of Seagull Island Beach, Kara was already writing her name in the sand with a discarded fishing net cane.

'You took your time,' she said. 'Have you got dyspraxia or something?'

Reece frowned. Was there nothing this girl couldn't identify about him? 'Is it *that* obvious?' he asked.

Kara looked up from scrolling her name in the sand in one-metre-high letters. 'Don't be embarrassed about it. It's not like it's your fault, is it?'

'How do you know about dyspraxia,' Reece asked, still surprised by Kara's frankness, which, although abrupt, carried no trace of nastiness.

'My younger brother has it,' she replied. 'But he has mild autism too, and dyslexia. You can't have dyslexia though, because I've seen you in English lessons and you're good at anagrams. That one for Robert Fathaby was brilliant.' Reece relaxed once more and smiled at her. It seemed nothing she might say could upset him. 'Have you worked out an anagram for my name yet?' she asked.

'No I haven't,' replied Reece, hoping that she wouldn't be offended by his apparent lack of interest in her before today.

'There's a rather good one, actually,' she said.

'Reece stared at the sand where she had scrolled 'Kara Steigers – Aged 13' and adopted a studious pose. Unfortunately, as he mentally rearranged the letters, the only word that leapt out at him was 'geek'. He didn't want her to think he shared the opinion of some of their classmates, that her good behaviour and regulation school uniform meant she was a 'geek' and so he lied and said he couldn't see one.

'I need to scribble it on paper,' he said. 'But I'll try to find a good one later.'

'Well if you can't get it, you might never get to find out if it's true.'

He could tell she was teasing again and he frowned, wondering what she could mean, but before he could press her further, she was running away across the beach shouting for him to hurry up because she was hungry.

He caught her up at the pass between Seagull Island and the mainland. The island itself was nothing more than a large rock, the same height as the adjacent cliffs to which it had once been attached, before a trillion angry waves had amputated it from the mainland. Above the pass was a wooden bridge that allowed walkers access to the island when the rocks below were submerged beneath turbulent seas. At high tide, the rollers from Seagull Island Bay and Trevarnick Bay could collide with such force underneath the bridge, that the resultant deluge could engulf anyone standing on it.

Reece and his dad had once walked to Seagull Island when the sea had been spectacularly savage. His dad had said he wanted to take a picture of Reece on the bridge, with the waves crashing beneath him. His dad had shown him where to stand, before continuing onto the island to get into position for the best shot. Reece had been apprehensive about standing alone on the seemingly flimsy bridge, waiting for the surges from each direction to get their timing just right to create the eruption his dad was hoping to capture on camera.

There had been a couple of less-dramatic collisions first. These had thrown up lots of spray, which had created rainbows below him in the sunlight. Then his dad had shouted for him to look out. He had been looking towards his dad at the time; even smiling for the camera and had seen the huge wave rushing towards him. But he hadn't seen the even larger one coming from behind. After shouting the warning, his dad had raised the camera, just before the waves met like two charging Sumo wrestlers, directly beneath Reece's feet. In a millisecond, a wall of water had risen ten metres into the air, engulfed the entire bridge and thrown Reece against the opposite handrail like a stuffed toy in a washing machine. The receding cataract had left his clothes clinging to him as grimly as he had clung to the bridge.

When he had opened his eyes and wiped the water from his face, his dad had been creased double; wracked with hysterics at his son's reaction to his practical joke. Reece, although shocked, had been forced to join in; laughing at his own misfortune, while berating himself for being so gullible.

His dad had hurriedly joined him on the bridge to pick him up and carry him back to the mainland before another pair of waves struck. He had pulled Reece's shirt from his shivering body and wrung the water out of it, both of them giggling like naughty schoolchildren behind a teacher's back. His dad had removed his own sweatshirt and given it to him to wear. Then they had run, with Reece's water-filled shoes squelching rhythmically, back to where they had parked the car, before driving home to warm towels and hot drinking chocolate.

When he reached Kara, she was trying to climb onto a tall rock that guarded the entrance to the pass. Reece ran around the rock and used another simpler route his dad had shown him. Enclosed within the rocky floor of the pass was a huge rock pool, a good metre deep and the only way round it was a narrow ledge on the left side. Kara had planned to get to the ledge by jumping down to it from the rock she was struggling to climb. Reece, however, knew there were natural foot and handholds just below the ledge and he used these to beat Kara to her goal.

'Okay smart alec!' she exclaimed, conceding defeat. 'Give a girl a hand then.'

Reece smiled, partly at his success and partly out of amusement that Kara had called him smart alec, when most other kids their age would have substituted a swear word.

He reached down, gave her his hand and pulled her up to join him on the ledge. Together they edged their way along the narrow shelf with their backs to the rock. Reece was disappointed when she released his hand to feel her way along the rock face.

'Look at that,' exclaimed Kara, pointing into the rock pool below them. 'Look at the size of that starfish.'

Reece looked to where she was pointing at a very large, orange starfish lying at the bottom of the clear pool. 'Wow, it is big,' he enthused. 'Do you think I could reach it?'

'No it's too deep. You'd need to be wearing a swimsuit to reach that. Besides, we couldn't keep it, it would die of hunger. Like I will too if we don't eat soon!'

Reece laughed at her mock nagging. 'Okay, okay! I didn't realise I was dating a glutton!'

He instantly regretted his choice of words, fearing her reaction to his name-calling and the suggestion that their chance meeting had evolved into a 'date'.

The awkward silence lasted several seconds and Reece began to panic.

She looked at him as though enjoying his dilemma, before replying. 'Well you are!'

The butterflies in Reece's stomach tingled alarmingly and he wondered if Kara was feeling them too. She was awakening within him feelings that he had never experienced before, yet he was scared to exhibit them in case she thought he was silly.

He knew he was blushing, but was compelled to look into her eyes for some sign that she was experiencing the same emotions. Their eyes met for the briefest of moments before she coyly averted hers, leaving them both knowing the answer to the other's unspoken question.

Reece clambered along the rest of the rocky ledge and jumped down onto the sand of Trevarnick Beach. He turned to offer her a hand, sure that she would indignantly refuse his assistance, but she didn't. She jumped down from the ledge holding both his hands which sent a spark tingling down his spine.

Trevarnick Beach was a vast expanse of golden sand from which grew giant rocks that resolutely stared out to sea despite the ravaging effects of the tides. It was popular with surfers who even in the depths of winter would don their wetsuits and venture out to ride the ice-cold rollers. Reece spotted several, about a hundred metres offshore, sitting astride their surfboards, waiting for the Atlantic to throw up an elusive wave, capable of carrying them shoreward.

'They must be mental,' Reece said, nodding his head in their direction.

'No they're not,' Kara retorted. 'I love being out there.'

'Really? I didn't realise you were a surfer.'

'I've been surfing for about four years. My dad started to teach me a year before he died. I gave it up for a while afterwards, but then decided he would have wanted me to continue. He was once a county champion you see and I suppose I wanted to follow in his footsteps.'

'You still miss him, don't you?' Reece said, feeling inadequately equipped to deal with someone else's emotional luggage.

'It's strange. I do miss him. I think about him every day of my life. But a part of me hates him for what he did.'

Her use of the 'hate' word upset him and for the first time he felt disillusioned with her. It wasn't especially momentous, more like the disappointment that came when something failed to measure up to expectation, like the free toys he used to get with a burger meal.

'How can you hate your dad?' he asked.

'You wouldn't understand,' she replied calmly.

'I just don't think I could ever hate my dad, especially if he was dead.' He knew his words might have sounded critical, but he felt he needed to let Kara know his honest opinion if they were to be true friends.

'But he didn't just die, did he?' she snapped. 'He *chose* to die and I understand how he could feel that way, because I've felt like killing myself more than a few times since. But even though he said he loved us and even though he knew we loved him, he still chose to leave me and my brother just to get revenge on my mum and that was selfish whichever way you look at it. Even my mum didn't deserve the guilt she's suffered ever since.'

Just then, a wave, that had not quite lost all momentum, crept silently up the beach, in a surreptitious attempt to wash their feet. Kara spotted it and grabbed his hand to pull him out of its way. This time she did not let go and they continued along the beach hand-in-hand.

'Try to look at this way,' she resumed. 'How would you feel if your dad died?'

'Well I'd go mad I think,' Reece said, the image of his dad standing on a cliff top hauntingly reappearing.

'Now imagine how you would feel if he suddenly decided, without telling you, that he was leaving you and you'd never see him again.'

'But my dad would never do that. And even if he did, I'm sure I'd find him eventually.'

'I'm sure you'd try,' Kara reasoned. 'But remember, my dad left no forwarding address. I know I can never find him and that I'll never see him again. In one act of self-pity, he destroyed everything. He left me feeling that all those days we spent surfing together, all those moments when we laughed and played together, every happy minute we ever spent together, were not enough for him. He didn't just die. He killed himself and he didn't stop to think how much of me he was killing at the same time. For that, I don't think I'll ever forgive him, even though I wake up every morning and wish he'd come back to us.'

Reece tried to imagine a loved one simply disappearing and leaving no forwarding address. He thought of his mother's absence and wondered what he would do if she never came back or told him where to find her. It wasn't a pleasant thought and slowly he gained an understanding of what Kara had suffered when her dad had chosen death over his family. He conceded that it had been a selfish act but having seen the despair in his own dad earlier that day, he could also understand how extreme sadness could drive someone to do it.

He didn't know how to tell her that he understood, so he simply squeezed her hand. She squeezed his back in silent acknowledgement, before playfully tugging him in the direction of the road at the far end of the beach, where the distant fluorescent lights of Tom's Fish Restaurant were flickering into life.

Chapter Six

Hello Kara. Hello Reece,' greeted Tom, his round, ruddy face beaming as he spoke. 'Nice to see you both.' Tom's nature was always one of spontaneous affability that made Reece feel like he was basking in the warmth of it.

'Hi Tom,' Reece responded. 'My dad wondered if you'd mind if he paid you for our meal when you call in the pub later.'

'Of course I don't mind,' Tom replied. 'I'll be calling in for my usual half of shandy when I've shut up shop.'

He winked at Reece, who winked back, knowing that 'half of shandy' actually meant two or three pints of ale followed by a couple of whiskies.

'So what can I get you? Some nice fish and chips?'

'Yes please and the same for Kara too. My dad's paying for both, if that's okay. Can I have mushy peas as well?'

'Certainly Reece,' he replied. 'What about you Kara? Would you like mushy peas?'

'Oh, yes please Tom. Where do you want to sit Reece?'

Half of Tom's Fish Restaurant was kitchen and servery and the rest was a simple dining room with a scattering of tables with plastic tablecloths. The tables were pre-laid with cutlery and paper napkins and each had a matching set of glass cruets.

'Let's sit in the window?' suggested Reece, who never missed an opportunity to survey the coastline, such was his love of it. Kara took a seat at a table for two in the window.

'What would you both like to drink,' asked Tom. 'They're on the house.'

'Thanks Tom, can I have a latte please?' They had spoken in unison, which made them both laugh.

'Great minds think alike,' Reece said.

'Fools seldom differ,' Kara retorted with a grin.

Reece joined Kara at the table while Tom immediately set about dipping two large fillets of haddock into his secret recipe batter mix, before dropping them gently into the hot oil of the fryer. Soon the most delicious aroma accompanied the sound of the bubbling oil. Tom made two mugs of coffee topped with freshly steamed milk and delivered them to their table.

'Your fish and chips will be five minutes,' he said, before bustling back behind the stainless steel counter. A few minutes later, he was chasing the chips around the fryer with a basket, like a young child frantically trying to catch fish in a rock pool and Reece and Kara listened expectantly to him tossing the chips into the draining compartment. Soon he was by their table again, holding two plates heaped with hand-cut, chunky chips, fish in crispy golden batter and bright green mushy peas. On each plate was a wedge of fresh lemon and a small ramekin filled to the brim with tartar sauce.

'This'll sort you out,' he said, grinning from ear to ear at their faces when they saw the feast he had prepared for them. 'You get that inside you.'

'Wow, thanks Tom.' Kara snatched up her knife and fork. 'This looks gorgeous.'

For a few seconds Reece watched her tucking hungrily into the meal, silently thanking his dad for having the good idea of inviting her to join him. He took the lemon wedge and squeezed the juice from it over the huge piece of battered fish overhanging both edges of his plate. Then he shook vinegar all over the hot chips until the acidic fumes hit the back of his throat and made him cough.

He picked up one of the fattest chips on the plate with his fingers and used it to scoop tartar sauce from the little glass dish. It tasted delicious, but then he remembered his companion and decided to use the knife and fork. He didn't want Kara thinking he had no table manners. After a minute or two, Kara broke the silence.

'What are you planning to write for the history homework?' she asked.

'I'm glad you reminded me. I was going to ask Tom if he knows any interesting local history. He's apparently lived here all his life.'

'That's a good idea. Do you mind if we collaborate?'

'Erm, what do you mean,' Reece asked, not wanting to admit that he didn't know what 'collaborate' meant.

'I mean, can we work together if he comes up with a really good story?'

'Oh, of course. Let's call him over while he's not busy?'

Reece turned to look over his shoulder. 'Tom, do you have a minute or two?'

Tom looked up from the newspaper he was reading on the counter. 'I've got all the time in the world for my favourite customers,' he replied cheerily. 'What can I help you with?'

'We have a history homework project,' began Reece. 'We need to write an essay about a local pirate or smuggler. Have you ever heard of any around Trevarnick?'

'Heard of any?' laughed Tom. *'Heard* of any? According to my family tree, which I researched a few years ago, I'm related to one!'

'Really?' exclaimed Reece, his eyes widening in excitement. 'Who was he?'

Reece glanced towards Kara who was also staring at Tom attentively. He was pleased that she was sharing his interest and he was already looking forward to producing an excellent project now that the brightest pupil in his class would be assisting him. He turned back to Tom who was pulling a chair up to their table, clearly intent on making himself comfortable for a lengthy tale.

'Now you know my surname's Coppinger, don't you?' he began, the twinkle in his eye keeping both Reece and Kara enthralled in what they hoped was going to be an intriguing story. 'Well, in the late seventeen hundreds, an evil man named Coppinger was shipwrecked on the North Cornish rocks and legend has it that he dived overboard and swam through the worst of storms to dry land. He was a giant of a man, said to be a Dane.'

'What's a Dane?' interrupted Reece.

'A Dane's someone from Denmark, isn't it?' Kara offered.

'You're absolutely right young Kara. Therefore, Coppinger was a Viking, which is another name for a Scandinavian pirate. Anyhow, Coppinger settled in these parts and married a local girl. After her dad died though, Coppinger began to show his true, evil nature. The story has it that he bullied his newly widowed mother-in-law into handing over all her late husband's estate. It's said that he used to tie his wife to the bedposts and threaten to whip her with a cat-o'-nine-tails if her mother refused to give him money.'

'Sounds like a bloke you wouldn't want to meet down a dark alley,' Reece exclaimed, warming to Tom's story.

'Quite!' Tom said. 'But he did much worse things than that. Coppinger was also the leader of a villainous gang of cutthroat sailors and owned a ship called 'The Black Prince'. Anyone who crossed him would be kidnapped by his gang, taken aboard the ship and forced to join the crew on their murderous expeditions.'

'I bet he didn't get invited to many parties!' Kara said, trying to inject a little light-heartedness into the gruesome tale.

'On the contrary, Coppinger became a very rich man and accumulated vast treasures and a ready supply of rum and exotic foods from around the world, so he threw some pretty wild parties.'

'But surely people wouldn't attend a party knowing that their host was a murderer who had stolen what everyone was eating and drinking, would they? I certainly wouldn't!'

'Well Kara, you have to remember those were very different times and there was much more lawlessness then, than there is today. People were much poorer too and the chance of a free banquet was probably just too good to pass up.'

'Well I'm glad I don't live in such savage times. It sounds horrific!'

'Oh it was Kara,' Tom enthused, delighted that his storytelling was capturing the imaginations of his young audience.

'Coppinger was such an evil man he was nicknamed Cruel Coppinger and was one of the most feared men in Cornwall. You'd never guess I'm probably a distant cousin, would you?' chuckled Tom.

'No, you're far too nice,' Kara replied, with a sincere smile.

'Where did he used to live?' Reece asked.

'It's hard to say, with any certainty. The legend has it that he came ashore at a place called Gull Rock and some believe that might be our own Seagull Island. There's also an ancient myth that when he lived here, he used to come ashore into a cave near Gull Rock where he'd stash his contraband until he could get his men to collect it.'

'How did his men get it out of the cave?' Reece asked. 'Was there a secret tunnel up to the cliff top?'

'Well sometimes there are tunnels leading up from caves,' Tom replied. 'Have you ever seen a blowhole along these cliffs?'

'Yes. My dad's taken me to a few when the sea's been really high. They're like huge fountains of sea blasting out of the cliff tops.'

'Well, those blowholes are created by the sea crashing into caves over thousands of years and slowly eroding the rock until it creates a passage out on to the cliff above. When the tunnel is still quite small, the pressure of the sea driving up it is enough to create a blowhole like the one you described. However, eventually a passage can be created that is big enough for someone to climb down into the cave from the cliff above. Coppinger's gang might have used a tunnel like that to carry their loot from their secret cave.'

'Wouldn't it be great if we could find Coppinger's cave and get a photo of it for our project?' Kara suggested.

Reece was thrilled with her suggestion. 'It would be even better if we found his secret cave and it still contained hidden treasure.'

'Now forget any daft ideas like that.' Tom's voice was unusually stern. 'These cliffs and caves are treacherous and blowhole caves are nearly always inaccessible by foot because usually the tide doesn't go out far enough. Trying to get into one by boat is extremely dangerous because you're likely to be smashed against the rocks by the waves or get trapped inside the cave, that's if you're lucky enough not to drown first. And only experienced climbers, with all the right equipment should try to explore a blowhole from the cliff top. I used to be a coastguard volunteer years ago and I've seen too many accidents on this coast, so promise me you won't go doing anything daft.' Tom looked so serious that Reece and Kara both assured him that they wouldn't do anything dangerous. Tom looked relieved at the sincerity of their promise.

'So, did Cruel Coppinger ever get caught?' asked Kara.

'Nope, he never did,' announced Tom, with a note of satisfaction that suggested he was just the tiniest bit proud of his evil ancestor. 'The legend has it that he was responsible for the murder of a customs officer who had tried to arrest him. They found the officer with his head missing. Later, Coppinger was tipped off that more officials were planning to raid his house and so one dark and stormy night, he set sail for Europe and was never seen on these shores again.'

'Wow! How exciting it must be to have an ancestor like that in your family tree,' exclaimed Reece.

'Well, remember, it could all be myth and legend,' grinned Tom, clearly enjoying the effect his story had had on the two of them. 'But I'm sure if you look it up on that interweb thingy, you'll find that Coppinger really did exist.'

Reece and Kara stole a glance at each other and smirked. They both thanked him for his time and said they would look the story up as soon as they got home. They had continued munching their way through Tom's fantastic fish and chips while he was telling his story and were both completely full. They gulped down the last of their coffee and thanked Tom again before saying goodbye.

'How much does my dad owe you?' asked Reece, as he held the door open for Kara.

'Well, seven pound sixty is the total,' replied Tom. 'But seeing as you've both been delightful company, we'll call it seven quid.'

'Okay Tom, I'll tell him when I get home, although you should be charging us more, not less, for your brilliant story telling.'

'Get away with you, young Reece,' he laughed. 'Flattery will get you nowhere!'

Walking up the hill towards The Smuggler's Watch, Reece and Kara discussed Tom's story. Reece was captivated by the idea that Cruel Coppinger had possibly come ashore onto their very own Seagull Island Beach and might even have hidden his treasure in a local cave.

'I'd love to find that cave,' he admitted to Kara, even though he was worried she might think him a little childish for holding out any hope of doing so.

'That's just what I was thinking,' she said with a smile.

'Have you any idea where it could be?' Reece asked, pleased that she was sharing his hope that Coppinger's hiding place could indeed be nearby and that they might be able to find it.

'Well, there are a couple of caves on Seagull Island that are only visible from the sea.'

'How do you know that?' Reece asked.

'I've seen them when I've been surfing,' she explained. 'But I've never seen them close up because, like Tom said, it's very easy to get thrown onto the rocks if you venture too close.'

'Hmm,' Reece pondered, deep in thought. 'I wonder how Coppinger could have got into them.'

'If he was the giant Tom said he was, perhaps he was strong enough to row against the currents and manoeuvre a small boat in,' Kara suggested.

'Do you know if those caves have tunnels up to the cliff top?'

'If they do, I've never seen them. Although, it's never really occurred to me to look for a tunnel on Seagull Island, so I guess it's possible.'

'Why don't we go and explore up there this weekend?'

'I thought you'd never ask,' she joked and once again, the butterflies rose in Reece's stomach.

They arrived at The Smuggler's Watch and Reece could see through the windows that it was typically quiet for a Monday evening. He was sad for his dad, knowing that the lack of customers would be piling extra worries on top of dealing with his mum's leaving. He looked at his watch and saw it was only six thirty.

'I don't feel like going in yet,' he confided. 'Can I walk you home?'

'I thought I was going to meet your dad. Or are you ashamed of me?' She was grinning so Reece knew she was only teasing him again, but he genuinely wanted her to like his dad and didn't want to spring a surprise meeting on him and risk her catching him in a bad mood.

'Do you mind if we leave it until he's feeling a bit better?' Reece asked, hoping she would understand.

'I'm sorry, I wasn't thinking. Maybe later in the week?'

'I'd like that,' Reece said.

'That's a date then! In the meantime, of course you can walk me home.' She took his hand and this time his stomach turned more somersaults than an Olympic gymnast. They strolled silently down Seaview Rise to the main road, which they crossed before turning left into Sunnyside Crescent. This led to the small estate of neat semi-detached houses where Kara said she lived.

'I didn't know you lived down here,' remarked Reece. 'We're almost neighbours.'

'It's nothing special,' Kara replied dismissively. 'I only wish we could move to a place like yours, with gorgeous views across the bay. You're so lucky to live there.'

'I know. The view from my bedroom is amazing.' He hoped he didn't sound as if he was bragging, but Kara didn't appear to think so.

'You'll have to show me sometime. I'd love to see it.'

She steered him around a corner into a quiet cul-de-sac, called The Nook. They sauntered diagonally across the street towards a pair of semi-detached houses both painted white.

The one on the left was in pristine condition with a newly painted exterior, which accentuated the neglect that was evident in its neighbour. Its lawn was a chessboard of flawless yellow and green stripes, edged with borders of variegated green shrubs highlighting an almost-gaudy display of multicoloured flowers. In the middle of the lawn, a circle of earth had been surgically cut, from which grew a stout palm tree bearing a magnificent umbrella of leaves resembling polished, green plastic.

In contrast, the adjacent house appeared sad and unloved. The grey-white exterior drew a sharp line where it joined its neighbour. The wooden window frames were scabbed with flaking paint, dried-out by a good few seasons of inclement weather. The lawn was threadbare in places and overgrown with moss in others. The borders lacked definition as they gave up the fight against the encroaching grass and marauding weeds. Reece speculated which one was Kara's, but the slightly embarrassed demeanour of his friend as she stopped outside the rickety gate of the forlorn house on the right gave him his answer. He glanced at the number on the gate.

'So you live at number sixteen, The Nook,' he declared, trying to disguise his surprise that his impeccably turned-out friend lived in a rather tatty house.

Kara frowned briefly, before following his eyes directed at the number on her gate. Then she smiled and spun the number six, which was hanging by a single screw, back into its correct position.

'Nineteen actually,' she said, with an awkward grin and Reece sensed that she was a little ashamed of the house's condition.

He wanted to say that where she lived was of no importance to him, but thought it better not to comment at all.

'Since my dad died, we've had no one to keep on top of things like repairs and maintenance,' she continued. 'The place is falling apart. My mum tries her best, but she works full-time and she's not exactly skilled at DIY.'

'It must be difficult for her, being on her own,' Reece said, thinking about how busy his dad would be, running the pub and looking after the house without his mum there.

'Well she was very ill for a long time after Dad's death. She blamed herself you see, because he made it pretty obvious that it was her leaving that drove him to kill himself.'

'How? Did he leave a suicide note?'

'Sort of. We found a poem, which we think he may have written the day he died. It's clear from the poem how depressed he was about Mum leaving and how he couldn't sleep. A part of me wishes I could have stayed with him, but Mum gave my brother and me no choice but to leave with her, so I guess Dad felt like he'd lost his entire family. His poem still makes me cry sometimes.'

'I'd like to read it,' Reece said, thinking it might give him some insight into his own dad's state of mind.

'My mum keeps it framed on the lounge wall, which is a bit morbid if you ask me. I keep my copy here,' she said, sombrely tapping her head. She glanced at her watch. 'Have you got time for a drink before you go home?'

'Go on then,' Reece replied. 'Tom's mushy peas have made me dead thirsty.'

'My mum and brother have gone to his school for an open evening, so they won't be home for a while yet.'

She led the way through the gate to the front door and lifted the mat to retrieve the key that was hiding there. She smiled at Reece as if reading his thoughts about their poor attention to security and jokingly assured him that they had little worth stealing. She showed him into the hall and then opened the door into the lounge and switched on the light.

'Make yourself at home.'

Reece stepped into the room. It was extremely neat and tidy, in direct contrast to the neglected exterior and much more in keeping with the usual meticulous appearance of his hostess.

'Is lemonade okay?' she asked, once more sounding relaxed and self-assured.

'Yeah, cool,' he replied, sensing his attempt to sound 'cool' had come across as fake. She left him standing in the lounge and headed towards the kitchen. He cast his eye around the room, taking in the various photographs mounted in frames sitting on the mantelpiece and the top of the television. One showed a picture of a younger Kara standing next to a man on Seagull Island Beach. Both wore wetsuits and carried surfboards. He assumed the man was Kara's dad. He was tall and athletic looking, with the same sea-bleached blonde hair and piercing blue eyes of his daughter. They looked ecstatically happy and he once again experienced the cold finger of sadness down his spine as he was reminded that he could never meet this man in the flesh.

The photograph made him think of the poem Kara had mentioned and he searched the room for it. There was a small frame in the alcove to the left of the fireplace and Reece could see that it contained something hand-written, on paper that looked yellowed with signs of having been crumpled.

He was apprehensive about going over to read it, in case Kara returned and thought he was snooping. However, he was curious and sidled towards the alcove. The title of the poem was written at the top in calligraphic scroll, suggesting to Reece that the author had taken great care while writing it, perhaps in the hope that his words would live on after he'd gone. The two verses were written in perfectly straight lines, a skill which Reece, as a left-hander, had never mastered. He began to read.

The Key

Last night I prayed that sleep would take me,
Back to days when love was mine,
It closed my eyes in welcome slumber,
And in my dreams, we lay entwined,
Like perfect lovers locked together,
Holding tight the only key,
For fear that when the daybreak came,
The lock would turn and set you free.

Alas the sleep that brought me comfort,
Failed to greet the rising sun,
My eyelids rose to find you stolen,
Long before the birds had sung,
My heart cried out with pain so strong,
A pain my mind could not subdue,
Sleep had left me all alone,
The key was gone and so were you.
Goodbye. I'll always love you.

Reece read the poem several times, trying to get inside the author's head. He concluded that Kara's dad had been a man who loved deeply, but lost badly. He tried to imagine his own dad writing the poem, but couldn't. While the obvious sadness of the poem depressed him, he also felt angry with this man, whom he had never met, for manipulating his emotions and he began to understand how Kara could feel hatred for what her dad had done.

He suddenly became aware he was no longer alone in the room and turned sharply to find Kara standing immediately behind him. His sudden movement startled her and she jumped, spilling some of the lemonade she was holding. He spluttered an apology: partly for startling her, but mainly for being caught reading the poem without her permission, but she looked unconcerned by it. She reached for a tissue from an ornate box on the coffee table and mopped the few drips of lemonade from her hand before offering the drink to him.

'Do you like it?' she asked, looking over his shoulder at the poem he had just read.

'It's, er, very moving…,' he replied.

'But?' she asked, picking up the clue in his intonation.

Reece frowned. Sometimes her intuition could be unwelcome and he felt under pressure and uncomfortable with her question.

'Well, it's just a little…'

'Morbid?' she volunteered. 'Yes, I agree, but I've often wondered if it's good enough to be published. What do you think?'

'I think it is,' he replied, glad to get a question that he could answer truthfully. 'Have you ever tried?'

'No. I'm not sure if Mum would allow it.'

'I can understand that,' he said, before gulping down the lemonade she had brought him. He looked at his watch. It was almost seven o'clock, the time he had told his dad he would be home. 'I'd better go Kara,' he said. 'I don't want my dad worrying. I'll see you on the bus tomorrow morning and we can talk about our homework project some more then, okay?'

'Okay,' she replied. 'Listen; say thanks to your dad for me. Tell him I had a really lovely supper.'

'I will,' Reece replied, placing his empty glass on the coffee table. He paused as if to compose himself for that embarrassing moment when a goodbye becomes awkward. Kara took the initiative, holding her arms out in the offer of a hug while turning her head to one side to signify that a kiss was not on the agenda. Reece accepted her invitation and even though it was stilted, he was glad of the opportunity to feel her closeness again.

'I'll see you tomorrow then.'

Reece sensed a hint of finality in her words. He wondered if he had done something to displease her, but she was smiling as she pulled away, making him annoyed at his paranoia.

'Good night,' he replied rather weakly, before plucking up the courage to tell her that he had enjoyed her company.

She followed him to the front door and yanked the handle, explaining that it often stuck and needed some force to open it. Reece stepped outside and turned to face her for a final goodnight. As he did so, she leant forward from her vantage point on the doorstep and kissed him on the cheek. It was too fast for him to reciprocate and by the time he had realised it had happened she had stepped back into the doorway and was smiling at him through the gap in the door as she began to close it.

Reece returned her smile, his heart thumping against his ribs. As she waved her fingers at him through the slowly narrowing gap in the door, Reece wished her a final goodnight before the door clicked shut.

Chapter Seven

Reece almost skipped home, until turning into Seaview Rise where the lights of The Smuggler's Watch reminded him that his home life was still in turmoil. He trudged into the pub through the customers' entrance, rather than using the private back door, because he knew his dad would be working. Jake and Mervin, a couple of elderly regulars, were chatting at their usual table in the Bar.

'Hello young Reece, how are you this evening?' Jake was a retired schoolmaster who was always friendly, but tonight his greeting was more exuberant than usual.

'I'm good, thanks Jake. How are you?'

'Oh, not so bad for a geriatric,' he replied, in his well clipped, public school accent.

'Have you been out anywhere nice this evening?' the grin on Mervin's face and the gleam in his eye suggested that he already knew where Reece had been and with whom.

His dad had finished serving a customer in the Lounge and had appeared behind the bar. He grinned mischievously at Reece.

'Dad! Have you told *everyone*?'

'Told them what?' he joked. 'I don't know what you mean.'

'Yes you do!' Reece cried, in mock exasperation.

Mervin continued the joke. 'Have you been on a hot date, young man?'

'No I have *not*!' Reece retorted. 'She's just a friend.' His smirk, however, told the true story.

'So,' Mervin continued. 'What's she like? You can tell us,' he teased.

'She's my homework buddy, that's all,' Reece said, being economical with the details.

His dad joined in the teasing. 'So when are you bringing her home to meet your old man?'

'Maybe sometime this week, as long as you promise not to embarrass me.'

'Hmm...' His dad looked up at the ceiling as though making a mental note. 'I'd better get the baby photos out.'

'You dare!' exclaimed Reece, glad to see his dad's good mood. He seemed to be coping well with the present situation. His dad returned to the Lounge to serve another customer. 'Can I get an apple juice?' Reece called after him.

'No! Stop drinking the profits!'

'Thanks,' Reece replied, as he disregarded the remark and helped himself to an individual carton of apple juice from the fridge.

He sat himself down at Jake and Mervin's table and heaved a deep sigh like a man forty years his senior at the end of a tough day. As usual, Jake and Mervin were happy to let him join them.

'So, young man, your dad's been telling us about your mum leaving,' Mervin said. 'We're both very sorry to hear it.'

The comment caught him off guard and he was unable to respond. He looked down at the floor silently and Mervin put an arm round his shoulder in an uncharacteristic display of affection.

'Don't you worry young chap, everything will turn out for the best. It always does.' Reece nodded but gave no other indication that he shared his optimism. Mervin changed the subject. 'So, tell us about Kara,' he said in a kindly tone, releasing his grip on Reece's shoulder. 'Is she pretty?'

'*I* think so,' he replied, realising that just talking about Kara gave him a warm feeling inside.

'Well I'm sure she is and she obviously has very good taste in boys.'

Reece playfully ducked away as Mervin ruffled his hair, causing Jake to spill a little of his beer on the table.

'Oops, sorry Jake! I'll mop that up.' He dashed behind the bar to get a cloth, which he was rinsing at the under-counter sink, when the telephone rang. He snatched it up, before it had finished its first ring.

'Hello, The Smuggler's Watch,' he chanted into the receiver, mimicking the receptionist at his school who always seemed to find it necessary to sing when answering the phone. He walked to the table and mopped up Jake's spilt beer, while listening to the caller's response. The voice had a foreign accent but was businesslike and Reece suspected it was a telesales call; one of those uninvited nuisance calls which his dad usually dealt with abruptly.

'Is that Meester Veener?' the caller asked.

'Yes, this is Mister Winner,' Reece replied. He wasn't strictly lying, but he knew the caller undoubtedly wanted to speak to Mister Winner Senior, not Mister Winner Junior. However, Reece thought he might be able to reject the nuisance call without troubling his dad.

'It's about your loan arrears Meester Veener. Ve need to know ven you vill be making a payment.' The call was clearly not just a telesales call and Reece regretted telling the caller that he was Mister Winner. 'Meester Veener, ve need to know vot you plan to do about this loan or else ve vill begin legal proceedings for the full thirty-five thousand pounds.'

Reece panicked; worried that his dad would be angry with him for telling the caller he was Mister Winner. He decided to own up. 'I think you need to speak to my dad,' he blurted. 'Hang on a minute.'

He left the handset on the counter and went through to the Lounge where Peter was pulling a pint of beer for a customer.

Peter was a friendly, but quiet young man who had applied for a job the day they had moved into the pub. He had studied art at college, but found the qualification useless in Cornwall's challenging job market. David Winner had taken an instant liking to him and he had proven to be a hard worker who had become like a member of the family.

'Where's Dad?' Reece asked.

'He's down in the cellar, Reece, changing a barrel.'

Reece went into the kitchen from where a door, at the top of the stairs, led down into the cellar. Opening the door, he saw the lights were on and heard the sound of barrels clanking on the stone floor. The cellar was deep and had been cut from the rock of the cliff over a hundred years earlier, to provide cool storage for beer in the days before refrigeration. The first few stairs were of brick but these soon gave way to natural stone steps, primitively cut by hand and polished shiny by decades of foot traffic.

Reece stood at the top and called his dad. He got no answer, probably because his dad was tapping barrels and couldn't hear him over the hammering. He went downstairs, holding on to the rope handrail that ran the length of the steep stairwell. His dad was crouching beside a barrel, drawing off beer into a glass and checking it was clear. He took a swig and raised his eyebrows in appreciation of how good it tasted. Beer tasting was one of the few occasions Reece saw him drink.

'What's up Reece?' his dad asked, pouring the remaining dregs of beer down the sink before rinsing the glass under the tap.

'There's a phone call, Dad. It sounds important.'

'Why, what did they say?' His dad washed his hands at the sink.

'It's some foreign-sounding guy saying they want thirty-five thousand pounds or else they'll take you to court?' He intoned the sentence like a question as if hoping his dad would simply say there had been a mistake and they must have meant someone else. But his dad's face turned ashen and Reece could see the worry etched into his forehead.

'They told you that over the phone?' he asked, now showing the unmistakeable signs of anger. 'They had no bloody right to discuss this with anyone but me!'

'Sorry Dad, that's my fault. They asked if I was Mr Winner and I said yes. I thought it might be a telesales call and –'

'Okay Reece, say no more. It's not your fault. They're supposed to do security checks before they talk to people and I'll bloody well remind them of that in a minute! Which phone are they on?' He was already breathing heavily and Reece knew that whoever was waiting on the phone was about to be on the receiving end of one of his dad's rants.

'It… it's on the phone in the Bar,' he stuttered.

His dad dried his hands on a paper towel, which he screwed up and launched in the general direction of the bin, before stomping up the cellar stairs. Reece followed, eagerly anticipating listening to his dad tearing a strip off the man who had intimidated him minutes earlier.

By the time Reece reached the top of the steps, his dad was already in the Bar snatching up the telephone. Jake and Mervin had both finished their drinks and gone, leaving the room empty. David Winner took full advantage of the privacy by booming into the mouthpiece considerably more loudly than he would have been able to had customers been present.

'This is David Winner, who am I speaking to? … I know which company you're from! I want your name! … No, I will not answer your stupid security questions until you give me your name. I've given you mine and now I expect you to extend the same courtesy to me.'

There was a pause while David listened to the man at the other end. Reece watched as his dad's face slowly contorted into disbelief followed by rage. The rage finally exploded.

'Listen here you moronic little man! You have just divulged private information about me to a twelve-year-old boy and breached the Data Protection Act. Now either you give me your name so that I can report you to your managers, or you can go and tell those scum-sucking, bottom-feeding parasites to go to hell!'

Reece listened slack-jawed. He knew his dad had a temper, but he almost felt sorry for the man on the receiving end his tirade.

'Are you still there?' his dad demanded. He stared incredulously at the receiver. 'You cheeky...' he didn't bother to finish the insult. The caller had clearly hung up.

David Winner walked round to the other side of the bar counter and sat on one of the bar stools. Reece joined him. 'That'll make them think twice before making that mistake again, won't it?' he said with a grin.

'You were a bit hard on him, Dad,' Reece said, still shocked at his dad's outburst. 'Do we really owe them thirty-five thousand pounds?'

His dad stared at him for a second or two, as if assessing whether it was better to lie to protect him from further harsh revelations, or to tell him the truth. 'Sadly, we do, Son,' he finally conceded. 'We were short on the money we needed to buy this place and this firm were the only ones willing to lend to us. Trouble is it seems they're not the nicest people to deal with if you fall behind with the repayments.'

'Will they ring again?'

'Oh, I'm sure they will,' laughed his dad. 'But if I'm not around, just tell them I'm out and to send me an email. That'll shut them up for a bit.'

'What if they don't believe me? Can I call them names like you just did?' Reece joked, relishing the idea of copying his dad's rant.

'No Reece, you mustn't. Just tell them I'm not in and if they continue to hassle you, take their full name and a telephone number and say I'll call them back.'

'Okay Dad. I will.'

Reece went over in his mind some of the things he'd heard his dad say on the phone.

'Dad?' he asked, with a mischievous grin, 'What's a scum-sucking, bottom-feeding parasite?'

His dad laughed. 'Google it son, but don't say it to a teacher unless you want detention for the whole term.'

'Can I say it to Robert Fathaby?'

'Is that the boy whose dad's got The Ship?'

'Yes,' Reece replied. 'And he's a right pain in the arse.'

His dad playfully tweaked his ear. 'There's no need to swear.'

'Sorry Dad, but he is. He's always picking on me.'

'What sort of stuff does he do?'

'It's not so much what he does. It's more what he says. For instance, he said his dad's pub is much better than ours and that even Mum thinks so because she was in there last night with Elaine and two men.'

'Oh, I see,' said his dad. 'He sounds like a typical bully. They try to find your weak spot and then use it to wind you up. So what if your mum and Elaine were in his pub last night talking to a couple of men? I often talk to women in our pub. It doesn't mean I'm chatting them up does it?'

'I suppose not,' Reece said, sounding unconvinced. 'But do you think Mum could have been seeing someone else?'

His dad sighed. 'I'm sure she wasn't. And even if she was, your mum wouldn't be daft enough to make it that obvious to people round here. I reckon this kid, Fathaby's got hold of an insignificant scrap of information and he's using it to try and wheedle more out of you. Don't rise to his bait and he'll shut up. His sort always does.'

'Hmm, well I hope you're right Dad, I came very close to smacking him in the mouth today.'

'That's not like you. He must have really provoked you for you to feel like fighting. What did he do?'

'Well he punched me in the face and gave me a nose bleed on the bus this morning.'

'HE DID WHAT?' his dad bellowed, leaping off the stool, as if wanting to march to The Ship that instant. 'I'll have him done for assault!'

Reece was touched by his dad's reaction but laughed at how over-the-top it was.

'Calm down Dad, you'll give yourself a heart attack! It was nothing. I got my own back on him anyway and Kara embarrassed him by pouring her drink over him.'

His dad sniggered. 'How did you get your own back?'

'I told everyone on the bus that his name was an anagram of *Fart Breath Boy*.'

'Is it really?' His dad closed his eyes as if mentally rearranging the letters. 'You're a proper little smart-arse for finding that out, aren't you? That's a much better way of dealing with a moron, than using violence. You should always leave the hitting to those who are too stupid to think of a better way of making their point. I'm proud of you son. But let me know if he hits you again because he can't be allowed to get away with it.'

'I don't think he will, to be honest. Kara told him she'd post his anagram on the school network if he touched me or anyone else again.'

His dad laughed. 'I like the sound of this Kara already. She doesn't stand for any nonsense and she sounds much brighter than Belinda Sopers.'

Reece frowned. 'How do you know about Belinda Sopers?'

'Well I did see her name doodled inside your homework diary, but she's a bit of an air-head isn't she?'

'What makes you say that?' Reece asked, wondering how his dad even knew Belinda Sopers.

'Her parents own the off-licence in town where I sometimes go if I run out of anything for the bar and I've seen her helping to stack the shelves. Last week, when I was in there, her dad was telling her off because she had put loads of cartons of milk into the freezer instead of the fridge.'

Reece giggled.

'Her dad noticed her mistake when a customer brought one to the counter and there was so much ice on it that it slipped through his fingers and almost broke his foot. The air was blue I can tell you. As I left, I could hear him yelling at her to get it all out of the freezer and chuck it in the dustbin. Poor Belinda was throwing a tantrum and yelling how was she meant to know that milk didn't go in the freezer and her dad was bawling that he'd serve her cornflakes on a brick of solid milk and see if that helped the penny to drop.'

Reece laughed and slapped the bar. He hadn't forgiven Belinda Sopers for trying to provoke Fathaby to hit him and so he was delighted to hear his dad describing how stupid she was.

'She's going out with **Fart Breath Boy**,' Reece declared.

'Well, then I rest my case. She'd have to be a total idiot to choose Robert Fathaby over a handsome, intelligent chap like you.'

Reece grinned. He knew his dad was only trying to cheer him up, but it was still good to hear. 'What are you after? A cup of coffee, I suppose?'

'Well, if you're offering,' his dad replied with a wink.

Reece jumped off the bar stool and went behind the counter. He placed a large cappuccino cup under the nozzle of the coffee machine, hit the button and waited as the machine spurted and spat coffee into the cup. He added sachets of sugar and a teaspoon to the saucer and shakily, put it on the bar in front of his dad, before re-joining him. His dad was doodling on a food order pad and Reece could see he had written 'Belinda Sopers' and was crossing out letters as he mentally re-arranged them. He looked up at Reece with a smug grin before triumphantly putting the pen down.

'What have you found?' asked Reece.

'A little something you might want to remember if Belinda Sopers bugs you in the future.'

'Come on then, tell me!' Reece tried to grab the pad to see, but his dad snatched it out of reach.

'Guess what Belinda Sopers has for an anagram?'

'Go on then, tell me,' demanded Reece.

'Belinda Sopers just happens to be an anagram of ***Brainless Dope***, so what further proof do you need that she was never the girl for you.'

Reece burst out laughing. 'I wish I'd known that earlier when she was being such a bitch. Haha, who'd have thought it; ***Fart Breath Boy*** and ***Brainless Dope***. What a lovely couple they make.'

'They certainly do,' said his dad. 'But anyway, enough about them, tell me about Kara. What's her surname?'

'Steigers,' replied Reece, not noticing that his dad was scribbling the name down as he spoke. He then proceeded to tell his dad about Kara; where she lived, what she was like at school and eventually her parents' split and her dad's tragic suicide. Reece felt his throat tighten as he told of John Steigers' memorial bench. He hoped his dad didn't notice as the words caught in his throat like a hem on barbed wire. He didn't want him to know that the idea of him doing something similar had even crossed his mind.

He described John Steigers' poem. He was even able to recite some of it from memory and then wished he hadn't when he saw his dad's face. Was that moisture in his eyes? Was it evidence that he was guilty of considering the same drastic course of action? He ended the story abruptly and a chasm of silence yawned between them.

'She has a great anagram by the way,' said his dad, suddenly lightening the mood again.

'Who, Kara?' asked Reece.

'Yes,' his dad said with a smirk. 'You mean to say you haven't seen it yet?'

'Kara said her name had a good anagram, but she wouldn't tell me what it was. What do you think it is?'

'I don't think I should say. If Kara doesn't want you to know yet, it's hardly my place to tell you, is it? Maybe she wants you to solve it before she'll let you find out if it's true.'

Reece's exasperation elevated his voice. 'That's almost exactly what she said.'

'Then I reckon I've found the same one,' said his dad deliberately torturing him. 'I think she's setting you a challenge.'

'Well I bet I can find it,' said Reece, pretending to be in a huff in the hope his dad would tell him.

Instead, his dad changed the subject by asking him how he had got on at Tom's with his homework research and Reece was soon carried away telling him the story of Cruel Coppinger. He told him of his and Kara's plan to try to find Coppinger's cave later in the week.

'I think if there was a secret cave, someone would have found it long before now,' his dad said. 'But it won't do you any harm to look I suppose, as long as you're careful not to go into any caves at low tide and get trapped.'

'Well we think that Coppinger's cave probably had access up to the cliff top so we intend to see if we can find an entrance up there, rather than on the beach,' said Reece, worried his dad was about to object to their plans. However, at that moment, Peter came through from the Lounge to ask for some change.

'What do you need?' asked his dad.

'We could do with a bag of fifties and a bag of twenties,' Peter replied, handing him a twenty-pound note.

His dad jumped off the stool to get the change from the safe upstairs. Reece decided to go up to his room and shouted a goodnight after him. He heard a mumbled reminder about cleaning his teeth as his dad hurried away.

In his room, Reece sat at his desk and switched on his laptop. He hadn't heard from his mum since last night and he was hoping she might have contacted him on Facebook. His Inbox showed three offline messages. The first was from his mother. He opened it and was pleased to read that she was fine and had rented a caravan on a nearby holiday park for the next month while she decided what she was going to do. Her temporary address was Number Two Trevarnick Caravan Park and she went on to ask him to come to tea tomorrow night after school, but to make sure he told his dad where he was going so that he wouldn't worry if he was late home. The message gave Reece a glimmer of hope that Mum still had some feelings for his dad.

The next message was from Belinda Sopers. It seemed she'd decided that her boyfriend had not been hard enough on Reece earlier and that she should also try to stick the boot in from the safety of her computer. It was a pathetic attempt at intimidation, consisting of childish name-calling, so he replied by bluntly pointing out that an anagram of Belinda Sopers was **Brainless Dope** and that her email was evidence of this suiting her.

The third message cheered him up even more than his mum's. It was a single line from Kara which simply read, *'Night, night. Sweet dreams X.'*

He enjoyed the warm glow her message gave him and typed *'U 2! X'* and hit the reply button. As he prepared to go to bed, his face ached from the smile she had put there and that night he would spend twice as long as usual cleaning his teeth.

Chapter Eight

Reece trudged along the dark, deserted road towards Trevarnick Caravan Park, shivering in the damp, night air. His feet cut a swathe through the low-lying mist as he walked, his arms folded and his head down to protect against the cold.

At the entrance to the park, he was shocked to see it was in a bad state of disrepair. It looked deserted and showed no signs of life except for a solitary lamp, lighting the sign, which with its flaking paint, made the name 'Trevarnick Park' almost illegible. He paused at the gate, reluctant to enter, but the chill of the night was eating into him and all he wanted was to be in the warmth of his mother's caravan. He told himself the ominous desolation of the place was probably because it was low season, when people generally only visited their caravans on occasional weekends. That was why it looked like a graveyard, with the swirling mist moving palpably between the rows of caravans like an evil entity.

He thought that number two ought logically to be near the entrance. He ventured cautiously through the gate, straining his eyes to see if there was a number on the first caravan he came to. He thought he could see one stuck on the glass door, but in the mist and the darkness, he couldn't be sure. He wished he'd brought a torch, but for some reason he couldn't recall planning the visit at such a late hour. It had been a completely spontaneous decision to come.

He edged closer to the door to try to see more clearly. It looked like a number one, but the darkness was so dense he reached out with his hand, hoping to feel the outline of it. The glass was icy cold and wet from condensation, which ran in rivulets down the glass as he traced a finger round the vinyl number. Without warning, a large black shape launched itself from the other side of the door. It snarled and clawed at the glass in a desperate bid to reach him and he stumbled from the step in shock. He scrambled to his feet, the freezing dampness from the wet grass causing his jeans to cling to his legs. He cursed under his breathe and hurriedly tiptoed back to the main path. The barking stopped as abruptly as it had started and Reece composed himself, expecting the occupier to turn on the caravan lights and come outside to see what had spooked the dog, but the caravan remained eerily dark and silent. He crept away until he reached the next caravan, which, as he had hoped, was number two.

He knocked lightly on the door, afraid of disturbing the neighbour's dog once more, but there was no answer. Where could his mother have gone? Through a small gap in the curtains, he glimpsed what looked like a flickering candle inside. He wondered if a power cut had perhaps plunged the whole site into darkness. He knocked again and this time when there was no answer, he tried the handle. It turned and the door opened outwards with a long, sighing creak.

'Mum,' he whispered. 'Are you there?' He was worried that if his mother were asleep she'd be terrified to wake up and discover someone creeping in on her, so he proceeded cautiously, softly calling her.

The main room of the caravan was an open plan lounge and kitchen. A candle was flickering on the table and from the sparse light Reece could see that there was no one there. To his right he could see three doors, which he guessed led to a bathroom and two bedrooms. He knocked on the first door and again called softly to his mum, but there was no reply. He pulled the door open, but in the darkness it was difficult to see if there was anyone there or not. He paused silently, waiting for his eyes to adjust to the blackness. He eventually decided he could make out the shape of an unoccupied bed with a neat pile of blankets at the end nearest to him.

He moved to the second door which he pulled open to reveal a larger room containing an empty double bed. His thoughts about where his mum might be were interrupted by a single cough coming from behind the third door. It sounded masculine and Reece panicked, questioning if he was in the right caravan. What would the man do when he came from the bathroom and saw him standing there? Reece backed towards the outside door ready to make a run for it, but the bathroom door was already beginning to open. Reece held his breath trying to think of something to say to explain why he was standing in the dark in the stranger's caravan. The man emerged and showed no sense of alarm at Reece's presence. He was dressed in a grey shirt with grey trousers. His face was gaunt and his pallor suggested his face seldom saw sunshine.

'Hello young man. How nice it is to have someone for company.'

'He...hello,' Reece stammered. 'I'm sorry; I must be in the wrong place. I'm looking for my mum. She's just moved here.'

'I'm sure she's not far away. I'll help you find her if you like,' said the man, who Reece thought looked vaguely familiar.

'Thank you,' said Reece. 'But I'm sure I can manage on my own. I'm sorry to intrude.' He felt uncomfortable and edged towards the door, keen to get away.

'Please don't be in such a hurry to leave. I never get any visitors. Not even my family have time for me anymore.'

'Why is that?' asked Reece, now sensing the man's attempts to make him stay were out of loneliness rather than a threat of menace.

'I abandoned them and I know they can never forgive me,' he replied.

'That's sad,' said Reece. 'Have you tried visiting them?'

'Of course I have, many times, but number nineteen's no longer there.' He stared hard at Reece with penetrating, black eyes. 'My daughter would probably be about your age. What are you, thirteen?'

'Almost,' said Reece, a sense of unease beginning to creep over him once more. 'I'm sorry Sir, but I really must be going because I have a long walk home. I'll probably come back tomorrow when the site office is open, to ask which caravan my mum's renting.'

'Why don't you take the bus? The number five will be along soon,' said the man in a voice that rattled from his chest.

'I've only got a twenty pound note on me and the drivers never have change,' Reece replied, desperate to counter any argument the man might come up with to make him stay.

'Here, I have some change. Hold out your hand.' The man lurched towards him, fumbling in his trouser pocket.

'No it's fine, really. I don't mind walking.'

The man ignored him and took his wrist in an icy, vice-like grip. Reece involuntarily opened his hand and the man slowly began counting copper coins into his palm. A sense of foreboding overwhelmed Reece as he recalled the incident with Kara on the bus. He watched the scrawny, malnourished fingers slowly and deliberately placing the individual coins into his imprisoned hand and was gripped with an increasingly unnerving sense that he seen the man before; standing in a photograph next to Kara.

As he finished counting, the man announced the total and slowly raised his head to stare into Reece's eyes. He grinned with mouldy, yellow teeth through thin blue lips from which a cockroach crawled and scuttled across his face into his matted hair. Reece gasped and snatched his hand free from the clutches of Kara's dead father and fumbled for the door behind him, scattering the coins across the floor in his panic.

He twisted the handle and stumbled from the caravan, sprawling himself on the wet grass. He scrambled to his feet and ran as fast as his clumsy gait would allow, towards the park's exit, glancing back to see the ghoul coming after him. Reece sprinted through the gate and turned left towards Trevarnick. When he next looked back, the ghost of John Steigers had turned right and was walking away from him towards Trevarnick Point. Reece turned to continue his escape, but his morbid curiosity urged him to stop. He cursed his compulsion to follow the ghost, but he knew he could not, for Kara's sake, simply run away without trying to stop John Steigers from repeating the rendezvous he had kept years previously.

Reece called to him, but it was as if the sound of his voice was powerless to cut through the dense fog. He cupped his hands around his mouth to direct his voice and with his next scream, emptied his lungs. 'JOHN, STOP!'

The ghost appeared not to hear and continued to stride away from him. Reece gave chase, seemingly incapable of closing the widening distance between them. John Steigers strode ever more purposefully up the hill towards Trevarnick Point and Reece's sense of dread grew ever stronger, driving him on until his heart was pounding from the effort. The trees rustled in the evening breeze taunting him with whispered ridicule, while on the road, their shadows drew spine-chilling limbs, which seemed to claw at him as he ran and ran, shouting for John Steigers to stop. He emerged from beneath the mantle of haunted branches, to see the silhouette of Kara's father standing against the moonlit ocean ahead. He broke his stride and walked breathlessly towards him. His lungs ached from the exertion and he could barely speak, but he forced himself to gasp a final request for John Steigers to stop.

The ghost paused and fondly stroked the seat bearing his name before approaching the edge of the cliff. He looked back at Reece once more, his face impassive, but his intention still terrifyingly obvious.

'John, listen!' called Reece. 'Your family still loves you. They only hate that you did this!'

'Then where have they gone? Why can't I find them to make my peace with them?'

Reece recalled what the ghost had said about the house no longer being there and remembered the broken number on Kara's gate. 'John, try looking for number sixteen; I think you may find them there.'

'Thank you Reece. You have a good heart so I know you'll look after Kara for me. Tell her I'm sorry and that if I could change history, I would.'

He turned to face the precipice and raised his arms to each side like an Acapulco diver waiting for a wave surge. Reece attempted to run the last few metres between them, but his actions were heavy and laboured and he moved in slow motion like he were wading through treacle. His face contorted in a silent scream as he watched Kara's father steel himself for his final leap.

Reece was almost there now and with a final lunge was able to grab a wrist with both hands as John Steigers calmly stepped into the abyss. Reece fell to the ground on the cliff edge and his arms threatened to dislocate from their sockets as the full weight of John Steigers swung violently into the rock face. The burst of supernatural strength that had infused him was short-lived and he could feel John's arm inexorably slipping through his fingers. He was lying on his stomach, digging his toes into the earth in a desperate bid to stop himself being dragged over the cliff edge, but he knew he was losing the battle; he could feel the almost imperceptible shift of his own body on the ground telling him that if he didn't let go, he too would plummet with John Steigers to his death. Forced to make the grim decision in favour of self-preservation, he consciously began to release his grip, wracked with guilt at the selfishness of his deed.

The ghost looked up as though to bid him a final farewell but the face Reece saw made him cry out in shock. It was no longer John Steigers who stared up at him, but his own father, begging him to let go of his arm in order to save himself. Reece's muscles tautened once more, striving to find new reserves of strength in order to save them both, but his father's arm continued to slip through his fingers. He could hear himself screaming, 'DON'T LET GO! I'VE GOT YOU. I'VE GOT YOU. I'VE GOT YOU...'

Then, as the echoes of his own voice faded, another calmer voice took over his cries.

'I've got you. I've got you, Son'

Reece's hand was clamped onto his dad's arm when he opened his eyes and focused on his face leaning over him in his bed. His voice was quieter now and slowly his mind came to terms with reality and pushed the nightmare out of his consciousness. He clung to his dad for several seconds before finally releasing him when his terror gave way to relief, followed by embarrassment.

'Wow! That was one hell of a nightmare,' he finally exclaimed, letting out a long sigh as his head slumped back into his pillow.

'Would you like to talk about it?' his dad asked.

Reece didn't feel right discussing his dad's death with him and so declined his offer.

'Okay, Son, if you're sure. I'll leave your bedside lamp on for you. Shout if you need me, okay?'

'Thanks Dad,' Reece replied gratefully. 'Good night.'

Alone once more, Reece recalled the nightmare. He had read somewhere that everyone dreamt several times a night, but he had always doubted this was true because usually he could never remember dreaming at all. However, this nightmare had been different in that he could remember it all vividly. Was there some significance to the dream, or was it just a jumble of random thoughts being misfiled by a troubled mind?

He was tired but his brain was still too hyperactive to allow sleep, so he tried to induce it by doing mental arithmetic.

'Two plus nineteen is twenty-one, plus thirteen is thirty-four, plus five is thirty-nine, plus twenty is fifty-nine, plus forty is ninety-nine, plus …'

Soon his eyes were heavy again and he fell asleep mumbling numbers to himself. This time he slept soundly, as though all his worries were suddenly non-existent.

Chapter Nine

By the time his Harry Potter clock began beeping the next morning, Reece was already in the shower. He wanted to make sure he was in plenty of time to catch the bus and get a seat next to Kara. He stepped out of the bathroom in a cloud of steam to hear the usual sounds of his dad making coffee, preparing breakfast and getting ready for his weekly trip to the warehouse in Truro. Reece threw on his dressing gown and joined him in the kitchen.

'Good morning son. How are you feeling today?' Concern was furrowed into his dad's forehead.

'I'm fine Dad. I had a really good sleep after my dream.'

'I don't mind telling you, you scared me half to death last night. You were screaming the house down. I actually thought someone was murdering you in your bed!'

Reece laughed. 'Was I really? Sorry Dad, I honestly didn't know.'

'I could see that from the way you nearly ripped my arm off when I tried to wake you. What were you dreaming about?'

'I can't remember now,' he lied, still not wanting to tell his dad that he'd nearly ripped his arm off because in his nightmare, he was dangling over a cliff. He decided to change the subject. 'Are you off to the cash and carry?'

'Yes, I need to get a few supplies. Although, the way trade's been this week, I hardly need to bother, but your aunt Debbie's arriving today and so I may not get time later in the week. Can you get yourself off to school?'

'Of course I can,' Reece replied, in an indignant tone. 'In fact I'm planning to get to the bus earlier today to...' he stopped short. He hadn't meant to divulge that he was desperate to see Kara. 'Well, I just want to make sure I'm on time, that's all.'

His dad threw him a knowing look and turned to put his coffee cup in the sink. 'Okay, I'll see you later then. Make sure you lock the door when you leave and I'll see you after school. Are you coming straight home today? Aunt Debbie will be dying to see you.'

'Actually, Mum's invited me to tea tonight. Do you mind?' He glanced at his dad just in time to see him wince.

'Of course I don't mind. Where's she staying?'

'She's renting a holiday caravan on Trevarnick Park for a while.' He wondered if Mum would mind him giving Dad her address, but she had insisted that he tell his dad where he would be, so he assumed it was all right.

'Okay Son, ring me and let me know what time you'll be home. Have a good day.'

'And you Dad. See you later.'

He left and Reece set about getting breakfast. He took a cereal bowl from the cupboard, filled it with cornflakes and poured the milk too quickly, splashing it onto the table. He cursed under his breath as he mopped up the mess with a tea towel before taking the bowl to his bedroom.

He wanted to see if Kara was online, so he switched on his laptop and shovelled cornflakes into his mouth while he waited for it to boot up. He eventually signed in to Facebook and Kara's icon flashed green in his chat box.

'*Ur bryt n early,*' he typed resorting to abbreviated text-chat because dyspraxia made his typing painfully slow.

'*So are you. Why are you online so early?*' Kara responded, but with her characteristic attention to detail.

'*Dunno,*' he replied, too shy to admit he was hoping to find her online.

Kara wasn't so shy though. '*I came on to see if you fancied walking to school today instead of taking the bus, but if you don't want to it's OK.*' Her honesty made him regret not telling her the truth.

'*Id luv 2. I wanna tell u about a dream I had last nyt,*' he typed.

'*Was I in it?* ☺' He sensed she was teasing him as usual.

'*Sort of, lol*' he replied.

'☺ *Bus stop in 10 minutes then!*' She logged out before he could reply.

He finished dressing, grabbed his school bag and was about to run downstairs when the phone rang. Thinking it would be his dad, he sped to the lounge and snatched up the receiver.

'Hello, The Smuggler's Watch,' he announced.

'Could I speak to Meester Veener please?' The voice sounded similar to the previous night's caller from the loan company and so he decided to do as his dad had said.

'Who's calling please?' he asked, with only a modicum of politeness. Kara was waiting for him and he was not in the mood to deal with the man at such an early hour. It was only just after seven thirty.

'My name is Ahmed Patel.'

Reece was certain his dad didn't know anyone of that name and he was suspicious that the man had not stated the nature of his call as most business callers did.

'Which company are you from?' Reece asked.

'Is Meester Veener there?' said the man, rudely ignoring Reece's question.

Reece was irritated. 'That depends on who's calling him. Tell me the name of your company and I'll tell you if he's available.' He was enjoying his momentary power trip.

The man stated he was from a company called DMS but Reece persisted and asked what the initials stood for.

'Debt Management Services,' was the reluctant response, confirming Reece's suspicions.

'I'm afraid Mr Winner's not here. You can leave him a message if you like.'

'No. But tell him I'll be calling back,' the caller threatened before abruptly hanging up.

'Yeah, good riddance to you too!' Reece muttered as he replaced the phone in the charger. He scribbled his dad a note about the call and left it next to the kettle in the kitchen, before hurrying down the stairs to leave.

He was about to lock the door behind him when he realised he had forgotten his bag and cursed the caller all over again for making him late. He ran upstairs, snatched up his bag and was back outside when he heard the phone ringing once more. He paused and thought about going back inside to answer it but decided that meeting Kara was more important than dealing with a persistent idiot. He locked the door and jogged along Seaview Rise towards the bus stop where Kara stood waiting for him.

He walked towards her, panting. 'Sorry. The phone was ringing.'

She checked her watch. 'Who rings you at seven thirty in the morning?'

'Oh, er... just the brewery,' he lied, hoping to avoid discussing his dad's money worries. He must have sounded unconvincing, because Kara gave him one of her looks. He averted his eyes, which made his dishonesty even more obvious.

'Is everything all right? Your dad's not in trouble is he?' she asked, with her usual incisiveness, which Reece, on this occasion didn't appreciate.

'No!' he asserted. 'What sort of trouble do you think he could be in?'

'Well, when my dad died, he left us with a lot of debts and I know my mum was hounded by loan and credit card companies for weeks until the life insurance came through, which took longer because it was a suicide case. They'd ring at all times of the day and night and sometimes reduce my mum to tears. You getting a call so early just reminded me about it, I suppose.'

Reece didn't want to admit to lying to her, but it seemed like she was the only person who understood what he was going through. 'It was a loan company,' he blurted. 'That rang just now. I'm sorry I lied, I just felt it was wrong to discuss my dad's problems behind his back.'

She took his hand. 'Reece it's fine. I lied to everyone at the time too. It's not something you want the world to know about, is it? I won't tell anyone, you know that, don't you?'

'Yes, of course,' he said, giving her a weak smile. 'Anyway, that's not what I want to talk to you about. I want to tell you about my weird dream last night.'

'Yes, I can't wait to hear about it. We'd better get a move on though; it's at least a forty-minute walk.'

They headed down the main coastal road towards Seagull Island Bay before taking the left turn that took them inland towards St Morgan, where their school was. On the way, Reece told Kara about the nightmare. She listened attentively and without comment, until he got to where he'd met the ghost of her father.

'My god, Reece, that's creepy!'

When he had finished his story, Kara let out a whistle.

'Wow, Reece. No wonder you nearly tore your dad's arm off. That was a pretty scary nightmare.'

'I've never had a dream like it,' Reece said. 'And I hope telling you about it didn't upset you.'

'No, of course not, Reece. I don't believed in ghosts or the afterlife, and even though it might be comforting to think of my dad looking for us to tell us he was sorry I'm not about to start believing such rubbish. Did you know though, that sometimes dreams can have hidden meanings?'

'Like what?' Reece asked.

'I'm not sure, but Mum had some awful dreams after Dad died and bought a book to help her interpret them. I read some of it but it was a bit heavy going. I do remember it saying that dreams weren't usually predictions or anything, but that they could be warnings about the effects of stress.'

'I suppose I have had a bit to deal with this week,' said Reece.

'Well don't worry about it too much. If I remember correctly, dreaming about death is usually symbolic. It simply represents the end of one part of your life and the start of the next or the change in your relationship with someone. The numbers could mean something though,' she added thoughtfully. 'I'm sure I read that they can represent good fortune. I'll get the book later if you like.'

Reece thanked her and then remembered he was going to his mum's after school and that his aunt Debbie was arriving.

'No problem,' she said. 'I'll bring it to school tomorrow and you can borrow it.'

Reece thought for a moment. 'Why don't you bring it round mine tonight and meet my dad and my aunt Debbie. My dad wants to meet you, and you'll love Debs, she's really cool.'

'I could do, I suppose. What time are you planning to get back from your mum's?'

'I was thinking about seven. That's not too late for you is it?'

'Well no, but don't forget we'll have maths homework to do tonight.'

'We can do that together round mine,' he suggested quickly, hoping he didn't sound too desperate to see her later.

'Okay, as long as you do your fair share,' she teased. 'Now come on, I can hear the bus coming.'

They walked through the school gates just before the bus pulled up outside. Reece wasn't in the mood to deal with **Fart Breath Boy** or **Brainless Dope,** who he was sure, would have something to say about his internet message the night before, so he was glad to get inside the building before the bus began spewing its passengers onto the pavement.

Chapter Ten

The day dragged. Even maths, one of Reece's favourite subjects had seemed dull. The only consolation was that the homework set by the teacher, Mr Moots, was straightforward and Reece was confident he and Kara wouldn't waste much of their evening getting it done.

There was some light relief during the lesson when Reece pointed out to the class that Duncan Moots was an anagram of '**Cannot do sum.**' This had even put a smile on the teacher's face who, until then, had appeared as bored as everyone else. Belinda Sopers and Robert Fathaby had remained strangely quiet all day and Reece got the impression that they'd had a tiff.

When the bell finally rang for the end of the last period, Reece was first out of the classroom. If he was going to get to his mum's in time to be home for seven, he needed to get there as soon as possible. He didn't want his mum to feel that he was in a hurry to leave her.

He decided to walk to Trevarnick Park as it was slightly off the bus route and he thought he could get there quicker if he didn't wait for the bus to arrive and load its unruly passengers before driving slowly round the narrow lanes towards Trevarnick. He was right to do so, because he reached the turning for the caravan park without the bus catching him up. The park entrance looked nothing like it had in his nightmare. There was a welcoming sign painted in bright colours and the hedge was neatly pruned. Inside, the lawns were manicured and every caravan had neat, brick pathways around them. He was surprised to find that number two was coincidentally in the same location as it had been in his dream, although it looked much less forbidding in real life. He resisted the urge to knock on the door of the first caravan to see if the ferocious dog in his nightmare actually existed. His mum's caravan door was open and he could see her sitting at the dining table inside.

'Hi Reece,' she greeted, as he climbed the steps. 'I see you found me. How was school?'

'Oh, same as ever,' sighed Reece, bending to kiss her on the cheek before sitting opposite her at the small dining table.

'Cup of tea?' she asked, getting up to fill the kettle in anticipation of his answer. 'How's your dad?'

He hadn't expected the question and replied with little thought for her feelings. 'What do you care?'

His sarcasm shocked her. She, like her husband, had failed to notice just how much her son had matured and had not anticipated his ability to be so witheringly judgemental. 'That's not entirely fair,' she retorted. 'No matter was has happened, I will always care for your dad.'

'So why can't you come home then?' His manner of interrogation appeared to annoy her. He hadn't intended to use his visit to cross-examine her, but he thought she deserved it by asking how his dad was, when it was obvious her leaving had upset him. His mother remained calm.

'Please let's not argue,' she sighed. 'I asked you over for a nice meal and to show you that no matter what happens between your dad and me, I'll always be here for you. There are a lot of things I can't expect you to understand, but just remember this, I love you more than anything in the world and hope that you never feel you have to choose between me or your dad.'

'So why can't you and Dad try to sort out your problems instead of splitting up?' he asked.

'Son, you know things haven't been good between your dad and me for some time. You've heard the arguments. I know he's under pressure with the pub not as busy as he hoped. I did try to warn him before we left London, but he was determined to make a new life for us all and I felt pressured into going along with it. I began to hate the pub trade and wanted to get out of it while we had the chance. I suppose I felt trapped doing what he wanted us to do and not what I wanted to do.'

'That sounds a bit selfish,' he muttered glumly.

'Yes, I suppose it is,' she conceded. 'But listen son, probably the most important piece of advice I could ever give you, is to live life to the full. If something is making you unhappy, deal with it. Life is too short to be doing things you don't want to be doing. There's a whole world out there and I hope you'll explore it fully before you fall into the same rut your dad and I fell into.'

He wanted to empathise with her but she wasn't offering him the comfort he was seeking. He sat miserably mulling over her words and coming to terms with the realisation that his parents' separation was looking more permanent than he was ready to accept. She finished making his tea and sat beside him as she placed it on the table. She put her arms around him and pulled him close and he returned the hug as the anger and rejection he had been feeling receded slightly. Maybe, if his parents could remain friends, life with them living apart wouldn't be so bad.

'I've made spaghetti bolognaise. Is that okay?'

One of the things Reece had worried about was missing his mother's cooking. She really was a good cook and spaghetti bolognaise was his favourite.

'Fantastic,' he replied. 'I'm starving.'

'Okay, get two plates out of that cupboard above your head,' his mother said, getting up to stir a saucepan on the stove. 'You'll find cutlery in the drawer next to the sink.'

Reece laid the table while his mother ladled generous portions of spaghetti on to two plates, which she then buried under a mound of minced beef in bolognaise sauce. She took a bowl of grated cheese from the fridge and sprinkled a handful over Reece's bolognaise, before putting the plate in front of him. He waited for the cheese to begin melting before winding a large mouthful of spaghetti around his fork, which he failed to get completely into his mouth. He sucked the dangling pasta fiercely, causing a whiplash effect, which splashed sauce up his nose. He glanced up expecting a disapproving look from his mum, but she laughed and wiped away the sauce with her tea towel. He felt unusually at ease and his mum seemed more relaxed than he could remember in a long time. He realised how much he was enjoying their time alone, probably because at the pub, they hardly ever had the chance to chill out together.

During the meal, they exchanged news. Reece told her briefly, about how he'd dealt with Robert Fathaby. He didn't mention what **Fart Breath Boy** had said about her and Elaine being in his pub because he didn't want to bring up something that might sour the mood. Instead, he skipped to the part where his fight had led to his new friendship with Kara. His mum listened, hopeful that a new friendship might divert his attention during a difficult period in their family life.

He avoided mentioning his nightmare because he didn't want her to think that the split-up was causing him to have sleepless nights. Instead, he asked her about her plans for the future. She told him that she had applied for a job as a warden in a local senior citizens' housing complex and that she hoped her pub management skills would stand her in good stead. It was a live-in position, which would also solve her accommodation problems and allow her to remain nearby. The news reassured him and so he wished her luck.

They cleared away the dishes and did the washing up together. The six o'clock news came on the television but neither of them paid too much attention to what the newsreaders were saying.

'Do you mind if I leave about six thirty, Mum? I promised Kara I would meet her later so we could do our homework together.'

'No, that's fine. I've got some washing to do and I was planning to go to the laundrette on the caravan site before it shuts. Let's have another cup of tea first though.'

Reece sat on the sofa while she made the tea, then they sat watching the television until the newsreader came to the final story of the day. There had been a record number of tickets sold in anticipation of the largest ever jackpot on the Global Lottery. The newsreader asked his female colleague to guess how many millions the prize money was expected to reach. She was pausing, pretending to think of a number when Reece announced, 'One hundred and fifteen.'

'The female newsreader responded with, 'Oh I don't know; ninety-five?'

'No it's even more than that,' her colleague declared. 'This week's Global lottery jackpot is expected to be a massive one hundred and fifteen million pounds!'

'How did you know that then?' his mum asked. 'Was it on the news earlier?'

'I haven't seen the news before now,' he replied, mystified that he could have predicted the correct number.

'Maybe you read it in the paper,' she suggested.

'I haven't seen a paper today.' He had a frown etched into his brow.

His mother shrugged off his guess as a coincidence and began wistfully talking about how one hundred and fifteen million pounds would solve all of life's problems, but Reece wasn't really listening. He was delving into his memory, searching for something he knew was buried there.

The music playing out The News, reminded Reece it was time to go. He thanked his mum for tea and asked when he could next come round.

'You can come anytime. There's a spare bedroom too if you want to stay over.'

'I know,' he replied, forgetting that his mother had not shown him any other rooms in the caravan and that he had only seen the bedrooms in his nightmare. She gave him a questioning look but didn't pursue it. He quickly gave her a kiss and said he would probably pop round with Kara later in the week. Then he threw his school bag over one shoulder and left, stumbling on the steps outside the door.

'Mind yourself,' she called, following him to the door, but he didn't respond. She watched him wander down the drive and out of the park gate. He didn't look back or wave, causing her to worry about what was going on inside his head.

Chapter Eleven

Reece walked past the windows of the pub and was happy to see that Kara was already inside and talking to his dad at the bar. He hurried inside, his pleasure at seeing her obvious.

'You've arrived just in time young man. Your dad was just about to get the baby photographs out.' He recognised the voice and turned to wish Mervin, who was sitting in his usual spot with Jake, a good evening.

'Whatever my dad's been telling you Kara, is all lies,' he joked.

'Actually, he's just been telling me how smart you are and how you're a wonderful son,' Kara retorted with a grin.

His dad laughed. 'Hey, don't tell him that Kara, he'll get too big for his own boots. How's your mum, Son? Did she feed you?'

'She's fine and yes, I've had spaghetti bolognaise.' He saw Kara was holding a glass of cola. 'Can I have one of those too, Dad?'

His dad reached for a glass from a shelf below the bar and filled it from the soda gun. 'If you want ice, you'll have to get some from the cellar. I haven't brought any up yet.'

'Okay, pass me the ice bucket and I'll get you some. Come on Kara, I'll show you around.'

Kara left her cola on the bar and followed Reece to the kitchen. They were about to open the door to the cellar when a voice called from behind the hot food servery. 'How's my favourite nephew?'

'Auntie Debbie!' Reece exclaimed. 'I'd forgotten all about you coming. Has my dad got you working already?'

'Of course he bloody has, although we haven't had a food order yet tonight. It's been so quiet.' She looked at Kara. 'Who's your friend then?'

'Oh, sorry, this is Kara. We're doing homework together.'

Auntie Debbie came bustling from behind the servery. She was the younger sister of David Winner by four years, but her face looked even younger. Her figure suggested to Reece that she probably enjoyed eating almost as much as she enjoyed cooking. She was wearing white kitchen overalls and a baseball cap and her cheeks were flushed from the heat of the kitchen. She hugged Reece with both arms and he almost went deaf from having his head buried in her ample bosom. Eventually she released him from his virtual suffocation and stuck out her hand in Kara's direction.

'Hello Kara, pleased to meet you.'

'Hello Mrs...' Kara paused, unsure how to address her.

'Just call me Debbie,' she insisted cheerfully. 'I've never married but I can't stand being called Miss Winner. It makes me sound like an unloved spinster when the truth is I just don't like men enough to want to live with one!'

Kara shook her hand warmly. 'Pleased to meet you, Debbie.'

'You must be hungry?' She fired the question like an accusation as she looked them both up and down, like they were Hansel and Gretel and she was the witch about to fatten them up.

'I ate at Mum's, thanks Debs,' Reece said.

'And I ate at home,' added Kara.

Debbie frowned, unconvinced. She folded her arms making her cleavage even more prominent than it already was. 'I've seen more meat on a butcher's pencil,' she said to Reece, before turning to Kara. 'And you don't get boobs like these from dieting.'

Kara glanced down at her own chest, the blood rushing to her cheeks.

Aunt Debbie laughed loudly. 'Take no notice of me. I'm only joking. You don't need 'em. You're gorgeous as you are!'

Kara smiled. Reece had been right; his aunt Debbie was cool and more than a little outrageous.

'How do you like Trevarnick?' Kara asked, hoping normal conversation would cool her face.

'Oh, it's a gorgeous place. If I didn't have a house in Nottingham mortgaged up to the hilt, I reckon I might sell up and move here too. Have you always lived here Kara?'

'Yes, born and bred, but it can get a bit boring here sometimes, especially in the winter.'

'I suppose that applies to most places,' Debbie said. 'But at least you always have your incredible coastline. I don't think I could ever get bored of seeing that.'

The printer that was connected directly to the tills in the pub, rattled into life to declare there was an order for food.

'Action stations!' announced Debbie, looking excited at the prospect of having something to do. She tore the paper from the machine and read it. 'One portion of bloody chips, is that all? It's hardly worth turning on the fryer.'

Reece opened the door to the cellar. 'We'll leave you to it Debs; we've got to get ice for my dad.'

Kara followed him through the door and down the steep cellar steps, heeding Reece's advice to use the hand rope and to watch her step. Reece filled the ice bucket with ice cubes from the machine while Kara explored the cellar. There were two, cave-like chambers hewn out of the rock. One contained aluminium barrels, some of which had clear, plastic pipes connected. Each individual pipe came from a bundle, encased in black insulation, which snaked round the walls and disappeared through a hole in the rock ceiling to the bars above. The second cave had a raised stone slab along the walls on which crates and boxes of bottles were stacked.

'Wow. I've never been down a pub cellar before. Don't you find it a bit spooky, Reece?'

'There's supposed to be a ghost down here,' Reece said, laughing.

She rolled her eyes. 'I've told you, there are no such things as ghosts.'

'Really, how can you be so sure?' It was his turn to tease and as Kara launched into her reasons for not believing in ghosts, Reece slipped his hand around the corner of the wall and flicked the light switch. The cellar was plunged into total blackness and Kara screamed in shock.

'Wooooooo...' he wailed loudly and then emitted a demonic laugh which reverberated off the cellar's stone walls.

'REECE, STOP MESSING ABOUT!' she shrieked.

Her uncharacteristic outburst shocked him, but he continued his ghostly wailing and moaning until a punch on the arm stopped him dead.

'TURN THE LIGHT BACK ON!'

He flipped the switch and the fluorescent tubes flickered on again. The glare from Kara told him she had not appreciated his joke. 'What's up Kara? I was only messing about.' It was the first time he had seen her lose her composure. She was clutching herself as though the cellar was suddenly freezing and Reece could tell that another few seconds in the dark would probably have reduced her to tears. He rubbed his arm where she'd punched him.

'I'm sorry, did I hurt you?' she asked, her sarcastic tone suggesting that she wasn't really sorry at all.

'Yes, you did actually!' He rolled up his sleeve and examined the glowing red blotch. 'I reckon I'm going to have a serious bruise there.'

'I'm sorry,' she repeated, her apology sounding more genuine this time. 'I'm actually terrified of the dark.'

Reece stopped examining his arm to look at her. Her arms remained clasped across her chest and she was staring at the floor. This was not a joke anymore. He really had frightened her.

'I'm sorry Kara. I wouldn't have done it if I'd known.' He put his arms around her and she leaned against him but still without unfolding hers.

Gradually, he felt her relax. Her arms unclenched and she briefly returned his hug. 'We'd better deliver that ice,' she said. They went back up the steps, slipping out of the kitchen and back into the Bar without Debbie noticing. Kara waited by the door to the flat for Reece to deliver the ice bucket to his dad.

'Are you all right now?' Reece asked when he returned.

'Yes, I'm fine. It was stupid of me and I'm sorry for punching you. Is it still painful?'

'Not at all,' he lied, with a grin, happy to see her displaying her usual good nature. 'Come on, let's go upstairs.'

He tapped the combination into the door and held it open for her to go first. At the top of the stairs, she surveyed the long landing that ran the length of the flat. 'Wow it's huge up here.'

He showed her to his room, anticipating her reaction to the view. He watched as she walked trance-like to the window overlooking the vastness of the Atlantic Ocean. The final hour of spring sunshine was casting a golden glow on the turquoise sea, promising to turn it the colour of blood as the sun succumbed to the massacre of nightfall. She stood at the window transfixed, as if seeing the scenery before her for very first time.

'Oh Reece,' she sighed. 'This is one spectacular view. I'd love to wake up to this every day.' She turned to the other window on her right and peered towards the marina and the harbour. 'You really can see the whole bay from here.'

He sat on his bed and enjoyed watching her absorb the panorama. He pressed the remote control to bring the television to life and when a news channel appeared, he remembered again the strange premonition he'd had at his mother's.

'Hey Kara, something pretty weird happened to me earlier.'

'What was that?' she asked, his question snapping her back into reality.

'I was listening to the news at my mum's and they said that this week's Global Lottery was going to be a new record. They were about to announce the jackpot when I got a strange feeling that I knew how much they were going to say. And I was right!'

'Really? Are you sure you just hadn't heard it earlier?'

'I couldn't have. I've been at school all day and I don't think the prize was announced yesterday.'

'How much is it?' she asked.

'A hundred and fifteen million. What I could do with that amount of cash.'

'Couldn't we all?' she sighed. 'I really want to travel. There's so much world to see and I want to visit as much of it as possible.'

'Me too,' Reece said. 'I've been to a few interesting places on holiday already, like The Caribbean, The Maldives and France, but I want to see a lot more.'

'You're lucky,' she said. 'The furthest I've been was a holiday in Spain five years ago and I've almost forgotten what that was like. Mum's always wanted to go to The Maldives. Is it really as nice as it looks?'

'It's gorgeous. I felt like Robinson Crusoe on a desert island. I bet you'd love swimming on the coral reefs.'

'I'm sure I would. Did you go snorkelling?'

'It was about 5 years ago when I went, and I wasn't a good enough swimmer then. But Dad's friend took me on his glass bottomed boat instead. It was brilliant. I can't wait to go back one day, now I can swim better.'

'Your dad has a friend there?'

'Yes. He's called Afeef. He's a manager in one of the resorts. Dad met him when he was on holiday there a few years ago and they stayed in touch on the internet. If your mum ever decides to go, tell her to have a word with my dad and he can ask Afeef for a discount.'

'Fat chance of that happening. Mum never seems to have any spare money, which is why we've not been on holiday since before Dad died.'

Reece was gazing into space. 'I can't see us going back in the near future either. Not the way things are looking round here.'

'One hundred and fifteen million is an odd figure to spring to mind. What do you suppose could have made you come up with that?' she asked.

'Well, it was actually just one hundred and fifteen, but it was as if I had heard the number somewhere else recently.'

'We had maths earlier. Could it have been in the lesson?' Kara suggested.

He pondered for a while. His memory was stirring, giving him a strange feeling that maths did have a tenuous connection to his puzzle, but he was sure it hadn't been in school. When else had he done any maths lately?

'I've brought the dream book, by the way,' she said, breaking his train of thought. 'Mum said you could borrow it for a while.'

'Hmm, thanks,' murmured Reece distractedly, as a jumble of thoughts jostled to put themselves in order.

Kara took the book from her bag and handed it to him. He opened it at the index. There were two pages of subjects listed alphabetically and he drew his finger down until he came to *'Death'*. He quickly thumbed to the given page and was relieved to read that dreams of death were not prophecies of the event happening in real life. Dreaming of the death of a parent could simply be the dreamer acknowledging a change in their relationship with that parent.

'There you go,' Kara said. 'I told you it was nothing to worry about. You said there were lots of numbers in your dream, what does it say about those in the book?'

Reece flicked to the index and looked up *'Numbers'*. The book said that dreaming about numbers symbolized material gains and possession. Numbers could also represent special dates, ages, addresses or lucky numbers that may be significant to the dreamer.

'You did dream about my address I suppose,' Kara said.

'Hmm, but I don't remember dreaming about the number one hundred and fifteen.'

He went over the nightmare in his mind once more, trying to piece it back together.

'Maybe it was just a coincidence or that you thought you'd heard the number before; you know, like déjà vu.'

'What's déjà vu?' he asked.

'I think it's when you feel as if you've seen something or been somewhere before but you know you haven't. It's a sort of trick your memory can sometimes play on you.'

'I don't think it can be that,' he said. 'If I remember, I said the number out loud before the newsreader announced it. I didn't just *think* I knew it, I actually *did* know it.'

Kara turned the book towards herself and continued reading, while Reece's mind was elsewhere, probing his memory for the answer he was sure was lurking there. Suddenly he leapt from the bed, making Kara jump.

'Kara! That's it!'

'That's what?' she asked, sitting up sharply from the shock.

'I think one hundred and fifteen was the total I got when I was adding up all the numbers in my dream.'

'I don't understand,' she said, clearly puzzled. 'Why on earth would you add up the numbers in your dream?'

'I was trying to get to sleep and I often find that doing mental arithmetic makes me tired. That's what I was doing last night and I'm sure the numbers I was adding together, were the ones in my nightmare.'

'Really?' Her brow was furrowed with scepticism. 'Well let's check. What were they?'

'Well, there was the number of Mum's caravan, number two.

'I'll write them down,' she declared, getting up to get a pen from Reece's desk. 'Do you have any paper?'

'There's some in the printer,' he said, pointing to the machine on a shelf above his desk. Kara took a sheet out of the tray and jotted down the number two. 'There was also your house number.'

Kara wrote down nineteen. 'Wasn't there the number on the bus?' she asked, prompting him. 'Number five, wasn't it?'

'Yes,' he said, getting more excited. 'Then your dad gave me forty pence because I only had a twenty pound note. How many's that so far?'

'I've got five numbers adding up to eighty-six.'

'I also remember mentioning the broken number on your gate, number sixteen.'

'Oh,' said Kara, sounding disappointed. 'That's already six numbers, totalling one hundred and two, yet we're still thirteen short of a hundred and fifteen. I was rather hoping that maybe the numbers were a winning lottery prediction,' she joked. 'But we've already got the six numbers you need to enter.'

'Thirteen was in the dream too,' Reece said. 'Your father's ghost said he had a thirteen year-old daughter.

'Well, that's certainly one hundred and fifteen. Wow, what a weird coincidence! Wouldn't it have been spooky if your dream had been a prediction and given you the winning lottery numbers as well?'

Reece's eyes widened with excitement. 'Who's to say it hasn't?'

'There are too many numbers,' she said. 'You only need to pick six numbers for the lottery.'

'That's the British lottery, Kara. This is the Global lottery and I'm sure you need seven numbers for that.'

'Are you sure? Go to the website and check,' she suggested.

Reece booted up his laptop and searched for the lottery website. It came up quickly and they clicked the button for the Global Lottery.

'It's asking for an account name,' Kara said, reading over his shoulder.

'I wonder if my dad's details still work. This used to be his laptop before he got a new one a few months ago and he used to run a lottery syndicate at our last pub. Maybe the account's still active.'

He typed 'davidwinner' into the username box and then what he knew was his dad's regular login password.

'How do you know that?' Kara asked.

Reece sniggered. 'I used to have to ask my dad for his password every time I wanted to borrow his computer. Then one day he was too busy to come and type it in and he told me what it was. I've remembered it ever since and I'm sure he uses the same password for everything.'

There was a pause of a few seconds before the lottery website greeted him as 'David Winner'.

'We're in!' he announced dramatically. 'See. I was right. The Global Lottery requires seven numbers to enter. And look at that, my dad still has £6.50 in his account. I bet he's forgotten all about it. I reckon it's months since he last entered.'

Kara looked at the screen and read the entry instructions. 'So you need to pick five numbers from one to fifty and then two lucky dip numbers from one to nine. Where are your dream numbers Reece?'

Reece handed her the paper where she had scribbled the seven numbers.

'Well you only have two numbers from one to nine, that's two and five, so they would have to be your lucky dips. The others would be your main numbers,' Kara said. 'You do know you have to be sixteen to enter the lottery, don't you?' she added.

'Well it's not me entering is it?' Reece said with a grin. 'If I enter on here, they'll think it's my dad, won't they?'

'You can't do that without asking your dad first, can you?'

'What if I ask him and he says no? How would it feel to have predicted the winning numbers and then not entered?'

'Reece, the chances of winning are millions to one. The chances of your dad finding out you hacked into his account and entered without telling him are pretty high. Is it worth the risk?' Her pious tone annoyed him slightly.

'If we don't win, I doubt my dad will ever find out. This money's probably been sitting in his account for months,' he argued. 'I doubt he'll miss two pounds and if we do win, I don't think he'll complain for too long, do you? I might even let him slap me all the way to the bank.'

'Well, it's up to you, I suppose. Just don't tell him I helped you.'

'Stop worrying Kara. It'll be fine.' He began typing in the numbers. 'Read them out to me, Kara.' He checked he had correctly entered the numbers she read out to him. 'Here we go!' His finger hovered over the enter key before he finally clicked it down. The screen flashed a confirmation of his entry and with a triumphant tone, he declared that there was no turning back now.

His exuberance was dampened, when Kara appeared to demonstrate her disapproval by reminding him that they still had maths homework to do. He felt a bit guilty for going against her and tried to make amends by working out most of the answers they needed on his calculator and reading them out to her. With the homework done, they were soon laughing and joking again.

'Do you fancy a cup of tea Kara?'

'Sounds good. Shall I give you a hand?' She followed him into the kitchen and helped by putting teabags into two mugs while Reece filled the kettle. 'What would you do if you won?' she asked.

'I suppose it depends how much. If it were a few thousand, I'd give it to my dad to pay off his debts I suppose. What about you, what would you do with it?'

'Same as you I guess. Give it to Mum to pay some bills and get some work done on the house. But, if I won that jackpot I'd really like to buy my mum a brand new house with a view like this one.'

Reece looked thoughtful as he poured boiling water into the two mugs. 'You know what I'd really like to do if I won millions?'

'Go on, tell me,' Kara said, expecting to be treated to a long shopping list of boys' toys.

'Did you see that short documentary that Jhesa Bellita posted on Facebook about her home town in The Philippines? It was called *Chicken a la Carte*.'

'I saw the link, but I haven't watched it yet. Why, what's it about?'

'It's a film about world hunger. It shows a man on a tricycle, with two bins attached, going to the back of a Fried Chicken restaurant in Manila and collecting all the scraps of food that people have left on their plates. When he's filled the bins, he pedals to a village where loads of kids come running from their houses, so happy to see him. He lets them help themselves to the food before he takes what they've left to feed his own family. These poor kids are so hungry they're grateful to be chewing on the meat someone else had left on a chicken leg or in a burger.'

'Urgh, that's gross! I know it's not their fault but it's awful to think that there are people so hungry they are forced to eat scraps like dogs. ' She visibly shuddered as though she couldn't imagine a worse ordeal.

'That's what I thought. No one should be so poor that they have to eat someone else's leftovers. So if I won the lottery, I'd go to that village and buy them what they needed to start their own farm so that they could produce their own food.'

Kara sat at the table watching him intently as he spooned sugar into their cups and continued to enthuse about how he'd spend a lottery win.

'There was another program on telly a few weeks ago about a boy in India who was about fourteen. He was so grateful that his family could afford to send him to school, that he spent his evenings and weekends teaching all the poorer kids in his village what he had learnt that week. He had no classroom, just a muddy yard, so when it rained he had to abandon his class. If I won millions, I'd go there and give him the money to build a school and pay for a proper teacher to teach there.' He was removing the teabags from the cups of tea, when he noticed that Kara had said nothing. He glanced up and saw she was staring at him. He frowned.

'What's up?'

'Nothing,' she said.

He carried the two cups of tea to the table and sat opposite her. She took his hands in hers, leant across the table and kissed him on the cheek.

He was shocked, but thrilled and the tingles running down his spine made him twitch. 'What was that for?'

'No reason,' she said. 'Except that you are probably one of the nicest boys I've ever met.'

He felt the blush radiating from his face and his shyness compelled him to find something to do with his hands. He picked up the two cups again and offered one to her. They sat blowing the steam from their tea, occasionally glancing into each other's eyes. She appeared to be enjoying being the cause of what he was going through. The heat slowly dissipated from his cheeks and his pulse returned to normal. He wanted to return her compliment but he knew it would sound forced and clumsy, so he simply thanked her.

'What for?' she asked.

'For being just what I need right now.'

Now it was she who blushed and his turn to enjoy being the reason.

The phone in the living room began to ring the single tone of an internal call coming from either the bar or kitchen downstairs. 'That'll be Dad,' he said and left the kitchen to answer it. His dad wanted him to bring a bottle of vodka down from the spirit cupboard in the office. He fetched the bottle and returned to Kara in the kitchen.

'I've got to take this to my dad. Do you want to come down for a game of pool, if there's no one on the table?'

'Only if you can stand being beaten by a girl,' she joked.

'Oh. Think you're good enough, eh? Well we'll see about that.'

They ran down the stairs and Reece delivered the vodka to his dad who was chatting to a customer in the Lounge. The Bar was empty, so Reece asked his dad if he could have the keys for the pool table so that he wouldn't need to put money in. He set the balls up and suggested to Kara that he should break off.

'No, I'll break,' she said, chalking a cue and checking it for straightness. She positioned the white ball with the cue then bent over the table to line up the shot. She addressed the cue ball several times, smoothly sliding the cue between the thumb and forefinger of her left hand. There was a loud crack as she drove the white ball into the pack of reds and yellows with so much power the balls flew in every direction. Reece stood open mouthed as two yellows disappeared down different holes. She potted two more yellows before missing. Reece took his shot and potted a red before missing the next. Kara finished the game at her next visit by clearing up the remaining yellows followed by the black.

'Where did you learn to play like that?' he asked.

'Down at the surf club. I often play the guys down there if there's no surf.'

'Well I'm never playing you for money,' he said, as he set the balls up for another game.

The phone rang and Reece went behind the bar. He checked in the Lounge to see if his dad was going to answer it but he was pulling a pint of ale, so he picked up the handset.

'Hello, The Smuggler's Watch,' he announced.

The caller asked for 'Meester Veener'.

'Who's calling please?' He listened to the response. 'Oh, it's you again. Hang on a minute. I'll see if he's in.'

He went through to the Lounge where his dad was handing the customer his change. He had heard the phone ring. 'Who is it?'

'It's DMS again. Do you want to speak to them, or shall I tell them you're out?'

His dad pondered his options for a second or two. 'Nah, I can't be bothered with them tonight. Tell them I'm out.'

Reece's chest swelled with pride that his dad should trust him to deal with the call. He returned to the Bar and picked up the phone. 'I'm sorry; he's not here at the moment. Can I take a message?'

The caller was as rude as the one who had called that morning and told Reece that he didn't believe him. Reece was angry that a total stranger should jump to that conclusion even if it were correct. The caller couldn't possibly know that he was lying and so Reece figured he had no right to accuse him of doing so.

'Are you calling me a liar?' he demanded. 'If you are, would you like to give me your name, so my dad can complain to your manager?'

The phone went dead as the caller abruptly ended the call. Reece turned to his dad who was standing behind him, listening. 'They've hung up.'

'Persistent little buggers aren't they?' his dad said with a wry smile.

'Did you see my note this morning, Dad?'

'I did. I can't believe they rang as early as seven-thirty.'

'Are they allowed to ring at that time?'

'I'm sure there are laws against it, but they probably think that anyone who owes them money will be too scared to complain and it was probably lunchtime in Mumbai when they rang. If they continue harassing us like this though I'll have to see if there's anything I can do to put a stop to their calls.' He glanced at the clock on the wall. 'It's eight-thirty, shouldn't Kara be going home?'

'Yes, I suppose,' he groaned. 'Is it okay if I walk her?'

'Of course it is, as long as you're not late back.' He called to Kara, who had decided to continue the game of pool alone. 'It was nice to meet you Kara.'

'Thanks for having me,' she replied politely. 'And thanks for my drink.'

'You're welcome. Hope to see you again soon.' He disappeared into the Lounge again.

'Come on,' Reece said. 'I'll walk you home.'

She put on her jacket and they stepped outside. They waved to his dad as they passed the Lounge windows and then she slipped her hand into his for the walk home. Reece glowed inside as their fingers intertwined like pieces of a puzzle that fitted perfectly together.

They walked silently, enjoying the fresh night air. Reece marvelled at the millions of stars piercing the twilight. He was somehow sure that Kara was thinking the same thing. They reached her gate and she turned to face him. He panicked, thinking that she was about to kiss him because he wasn't sure he was ready. What if he was useless at it? What if his breath smelled? What if he was such a bad kisser she never wanted to see him again?

A curtain moved behind her and a young boy's face appeared at the window of her house. Kara noticed Reece's eyes focused on something over her shoulder and turned sharply to see her brother grinning back at them. She self-consciously took a step back and tried to look anywhere except at Reece. His concerns about her potential kiss evaporated into disappointment.

'That's my brother, Ethan,' she explained, although Reece had already guessed it was. 'I'd better go in; we'll get no privacy now.'

The boy at the window was waving and smiling at him so Reece waved back. He looked a couple of years younger than Kara, with very similar features but darker hair. His gestures and facial expressions were innocently extravagant and Reece immediately identified with the young boy's openness. He thought he'd probably like Ethan when the time came for them to meet properly, but right now he wished he would bugger off and let him find out if Kara had planned to give him a goodnight kiss.

'Sorry about him,' she said, waving her hand, as if to shoo her brother back behind the curtain. He didn't move, and simply continued to stare at them, with wide eyes and an even wider smile.

'He seems happy to see you,' Reece said, with a hint of jealousy. He had often wondered what it would be like to have a brother or a sister. He thought that it would be great to have someone nearer his own age to come home to every day.

'He misses me quite a lot when I'm out for so long. Most of the time he's lovely but sometimes he can be a little too clingy and I have to tell him to give me some space. He wanted to come with me tonight and there was nearly a scene until my mum promised to let him stay up late to watch a movie.'

'You could've brought him along if you'd wanted to,' Reece said, even though he was secretly glad she hadn't.

'I wanted you all to myself,' she said coyly, sending the usual tingles up and down his spine. 'Shall we walk into school again tomorrow?' She sounded matter-of-fact again.

'Yeah, if the weather's okay. Meet you at the bus stop about seven forty-five?'

'That's a date!' she declared happily. She turned to walk up the path and immediately her brother disappeared from the window to meet her at the door. She seized the brief chance of privacy to turn and blow Reece a kiss. He snatched at the air as if to catch it and blew one back.

The door was suddenly yanked open and Ethan, wearing only pyjamas, threw his arms around Kara's neck and wrapped his legs around her waist, almost knocking her flying.

'Hi Reece,' he yelled, as if he had known him years.

'Hi Ethan,' he replied with similar familiarity. 'Pleased to meet you.'

Kara stumbled clumsily through the door, her brother still hanging from her neck. She managed to turn and waggle her fingers at Reece and splutter a final 'Goodnight,' before slamming the door shut with her foot.

He waited to see if she appeared at the window and was disappointed when she didn't. Nevertheless, he walked home on pavements of air.

Chapter Twelve

Wednesday morning Reece awoke at six-thirty. He leapt out of bed and threw open the curtains, pausing for just a few moments to drink in the view. He spotted the man walking his Red Setter and smiled as the dog gambolled about on the leash making it impossible for the man to read his newspaper. A boisterous sea beneath a dirty sky threatened rain and Reece made a mental note to put his cagoule in his bag.

By the time his alarm went off at seven o'clock, he had already showered and was eating his breakfast. The house was quiet and Reece assumed that his dad and Aunt Debbie were still asleep. There were no deliveries or cash and carry trips to do on Wednesdays so Reece knew there was no need to wake them. He finished his cereal and decided to check Facebook while drinking his tea.

His inbox showed a message from Kara that simply read, '*Good morning. See you soon. Kara, FTW! X*' He was amused by her use of the online gaming abbreviation for '*For The Win*' obviously to tease him for losing at pool the previous evening. He typed, '*Next time I'll live up to my name and it'll be Reece Winner FTW! X*'. She was no longer online and so didn't reply. He closed his laptop and was rinsing his mug at the sink when the telephone rang. It was exactly seven-thirty and he was sure it had to be the loan company again. He snatched up the receiver before the sound woke his dad and Debbie.

'Hello, The Smuggler's Watch,' he snapped, failing to disguise his temper.

'Meester Veener please,' came the terse reply in a voice different from the previous day's caller, but with a similar sounding accent. The answering machine in the base of the phone charger had a record facility and so Reece pressed the button, hoping that the caller wouldn't hear the bleep as it began to record their conversation.

'Mr Winner works until late at night and so doesn't take calls before ten o'clock. Who's calling please?' Reece replied.

'My name is Mohamed Iqbal and I need to speak to Meester Veener urgently please.'

'Which company are you from?' Reece demanded.

The caller clearly believed he was actually speaking to Reece's dad. 'Meester Veener, you know who ve are, stop vasting my time.'

Reece bristled. He didn't want to allow the caller to intimidate him, but neither did he wish to break his promise to his dad and be rude.

'Are you a colleague of Mr Patel's?' he asked, sarcastically. The caller seemed surprised by the question and stuttered that there were many Patels in their call centre.

'Well I told the Mr Ahmed Patel I spoke to yesterday, that Mr Winner would ring back at a time convenient to him, so why are ringing again at the same time?'

'Meester Veener, you owe us a lot of money and ve vill continue to ring at any time ve like until you pay,' snapped the caller.

Reece remembered his dad saying that for the caller to divulge personal information without doing a security check first, was illegal. 'I am not Mister Winner, I am Mister Winner's son, and I'm sure you're aware that you have broken the law by talking to me about my dad's account. My dad could sue you.'

'Vell, you vould have to prove it first, vouldn't you?' sneered the caller.

'I can Mr Iqbal. I've been recording every word of this conversation.' The line suddenly went dead and Reece glowed with pride at winning the battle of wills with the caller. He wrote his dad a note telling him to listen to the recording before grabbing his bag and heading for the door.

Outside, the gusts that had unsettled the ocean ripped through his clothing and covered him in goose bumps but the sight of Kara waiting for him at the bus stop momentarily chased away the rawness.

'Morning, Kara.'

'Good morning, boyfriend!'

Hearing her confirm their status as a couple energised him like he'd touched a live cable, but he was too embarrassed to respond except to look down and cough nervously. He shifted uncomfortably and opted to distract her from his shyness by rummaging in his bag for his cagoule.

He retrieved the jacket, which Kara helped him wriggle into by pulling it down at the back. As soon as he had thrown his bag back over his shoulder, she slipped her hand into his. He was glad she was happy to take the initiative, because he was certain that he would never be brave enough to. They set off in silence until Kara asked if he was all right because he seemed quiet.

'We got another call from the loan company this morning,' he sighed. 'I'm worried about Dad and what they'll do if he can't pay.'

'I'm sure it'll be fine,' she said, giving his hand a reassuring squeeze. 'I saw on the news that lots of businesses are finding things difficult in this recession and the banks can't bankrupt all of them or they'd lose a fortune.'

'I hope you're right. If we lost the pub we might have to leave Trevarnick and I'd hate that.'

'What would you miss most?' she asked.

'Well my mum, of course, if she decided to stay here. And I'd miss my bedroom with its fantastic views. There's Robert Fathaby; I'd miss him, like a broken leg. Then there's Tom's fish and chips.'

'Anything else?' she asked, pretending to look hurt.

Reece looked skywards, stroking his chin. 'Nothing else springs to mind', he said with a grin.

She released his hand before striding off ahead of him. He laughed and caught up with her, putting his arm around her shoulder. 'I'm sorry', he said. 'I'm only teasing. You know I'd miss you too.'

'Humph!' she said, rejecting his apology and continuing to stride ahead of him.

Reece began to think she was seriously upset. He ran in front of her, walking backwards trying to make eye contact. She attempted to dodge around him, her eyes fixed on the ground. Reece was worried; the last thing he wanted was for her to take his teasing seriously. He took her by the shoulders, forcing her to stop walking, but she maintained her downward stare, making it impossible for him to read her facial expression.

'Kara, don't be like this, I was only joking. You know I love you.' He blurted it out and instantly felt silly. They had only been friends for three days and already he was telling her he loved her. He wished he could retrieve the words but it was too late. Her shoulders began to shake and he was horrified that now he'd made her cry.

'I'm sorry Kara. Please don't cry, I didn't mean it.'

Kara slowly raised her head and Reece could see that she wasn't crying, she was laughing. 'I'm sorry, Reece,' she giggled. 'You didn't really think I was being serious did you? I knew you were joking.'

He was relieved he hadn't hurt her feelings, but then remembered what he had just said and felt stupid. He playfully pushed her away and called her a bitch for winding him up. Now it was his turn to look hurt and for her to apologise. He feigned a sulk until she linked her arm in his and told him that what he had said was very sweet. His mood was uplifted again, leaving him perplexed by the rollercoaster of emotions he experienced whenever he was with her. He decided to change the subject.

'When should we start looking for Coppinger's cave?' he asked.

'We could make a start tonight if you like. Then if we find anything promising we could have a proper search at the weekend.'

'That sounds like a plan,' he said. 'Shall we start on Seagull Island?'

'I suppose we could. Then if we don't find anything there, we can search further along the coast on Saturday or Sunday. There are quite a few caves along Jasmine Point.'

'Right then,' Reece said. 'Let's catch the bus home from school tonight, get changed and meet back at the bus stop at five-thirty. That'll give us a good couple of hours or more of daylight.'

'Okay,' she agreed enthusiastically. 'Shall I bring a torch?'

'Good idea. I'll bring my dad's camera as well. Then if we do come across anything interesting, we can take photos for our project folders.'

They continued the walk to school speculating about what they might find and chatting about how exciting it would be if they could really discover evidence of Cruel Coppinger's smuggling activities. The journey seemed to take no time at all and soon they arrived at the school gates.

They had discussed whether it was wise to publicly display their new status as boyfriend and girlfriend and had decided that it might be better not to. They didn't want to attract unwanted comments from the likes of Robert Fathaby or any other idiots, so they stopped holding hands before the school came into view. They arrived at the gates just as their usual bus overtook them and began chaotically ejecting its passengers onto the pavement. They were weaving their way through the sea of pupils, when Robert Fathaby jumped off the step of the bus and landed squarely onto Reece's foot. His leg immediately buckled and he sank to the ground clutching his right foot, his face grimacing from the pain. Fathaby grinned down at him.

'Sorry Loser, I didn't see you there,' he sneered.

Reece instinctively lashed out with his other foot and kicked Fathaby hard on the ankle. Fathaby screamed and was about to deliver a kick to Reece's ribs when Kara swung her bag at his head causing him to lose his balance and land in a heap next to Reece. Reece seized the opportunity to throw himself astride him, wincing from the pain in his foot as he did so. He used his weight to pin Fathaby to the ground and grabbed both his ears. He proceeded to use them as handles to bash his head repeatedly against the ground until Fathaby was screaming like a baby.

'GET HIM OFF ME! SOMEONE GET HIM OFF ME!'

Reece stopped banging his head, long enough to ask, 'Have you had enough yet, ***Fart Breath Boy?***'

'Get stuffed Loser!' Fathaby spat. Reece responded by twisting his ears hard and pulling his head sharply upwards ready to pound it once more into the ground. 'Okay, okay!' Fathaby panted and for the first time Reece saw very real fear in the bully's eyes.

'Are you going to apologise?' Reece demanded.

Fathaby glanced at the throng of people surrounding them. He knew he couldn't apologise without losing face so the words simply wouldn't come past his lips. His head hit the ground once more, as Reece drove home the advantage and Fathaby knew he had no other choice but to submit.

'Okay, sorry,' he muttered almost inaudibly.

'I WANNA HEAR IT!' screamed Reece, yanking Fathaby's ears once more to make it clear what would happen if he didn't.

Finally, the bully succumbed. 'Okay, I'm sorry.' This time his voice was subdued, but clear.

'Is this the end of it?' Reece demanded. 'If I let you up, are you going to shake hands?'

'Yes!' snapped Fathaby, sounding less submissive than Reece wanted to hear.

'Yes, what?' he demanded, tightening his grip on Fathaby's ears once more to remind him of the consequences of further belligerence.

'Yes Reece.' This time his response was calm and muted.

Reece let go of his ears and leaned back, removing most of his weight from his chest. Kara helped him to his feet and he leaned on her, bearing his weight on his good foot. He offered his right hand, which Fathaby cautiously took and pulled himself up with little difficulty, suggesting the kick to his ankle had not done much damage. The two of them dusted themselves down and Reece once again held out his hand to Fathaby in a gesture of reconciliation.

'Shake, Robert?'

Fathaby paused and Reece feared he was considering reneging on their truce; but he didn't. He returned Reece's handshake before walking away in silence.

The crowd that had gathered immediately began chattering about the bully's defeat. One or two slapped Reece on the back and told him 'Well done!' as they drifted off to their classes.

Reece attempted to walk, but putting weight on his right foot was painful. He tried to limp towards the school building using Kara as a crutch, but could feel his shoe tightening as the swelling increased. He groaned from the effort and was forced to ask Kara to let him sit once more. Mr Poutril appeared from where he had been talking to the driver on one of the other school buses. He had not actually seen the altercation between Reece and Fathaby, just the crowd swarming around them.

'What's wrong Winner?' he barked, in a tone that sounded accusatory. Rupert Poutril was an ex-army gym instructor and was one of the few teachers who still preferred to call pupils by their surname. He was an intimidating man who stood no nonsense during sports lessons. Reece thought **Pupil Torturer** was a very apt anagram of his name, but doubted he would ever have the nerve to tell him.

'He's hurt his foot, Sir,' Kara responded on his behalf. 'Someone stamped on it and it seems to be swelling up quite badly.'

The teacher stooped down in front of Reece and took hold of his foot. He undid the laces and slipped the shoe and sock off. Reece winced, but Mr Poutril was surprisingly gentle. He instructed Reece to wiggle his toes and to try bending them upwards and downwards as far as the pain would allow.

'Well I don't think it's broken, Winner, but it has swollen quite a bit. Come with me, I have some spray that will help.' He put Reece's sock back on and slipped his shoe onto his foot without tightening the laces. 'Leave it like that for now. Can you manage to walk to the gym?'

'I think so, Sir,' Reece replied, as he tried to get up once more.

Rupert Poutril took his arm and firmly, but again quite gently, helped him to his feet. He turned to Kara and instructed her to get to class and to tell their form master where Reece was and that he would be joining them shortly.

'Yes, Sir,' replied Kara. 'See you later Reece.' Kara hurried off to class, leaving Reece to hobble, with the help of Mr Poutril to his office next to the gymnasium.

'Sit down and take your shoe and sock off.' His words were not so much abrupt in their delivery, as efficient. Reece imagined that the gym teacher was a man of few words, not because he was unsociable, but because he was impatient and hated to waste time on unnecessary niceties. The teacher went to a cupboard and took out an aerosol can.

'This'll feel very cold,' he warned while simultaneously spraying Reece's foot. The words came too late to prepare Reece for the shock and his foot jerked alarmingly almost kicking the teacher.

'Try and hold still Winner,' Mr Poutril said. 'This will really help the swelling.' He continued spraying and the initial shock gave way to welcome relief as the spray numbed the pain in his foot. 'That should be feeling better already,' he suggested.

'Yes, it is thanks,' Reece replied.

'So I'm guessing it was Fathaby who jumped on your foot. On purpose too I bet.' He gave Reece a look that said no response was necessary.

Reece muttered a vague 'Hmm.'

'He's not always been a bully you know,' Mr Poutril declared. 'He's just insecure like many kids from broken families.'

'I didn't know he was,' Reece replied, a note of surprise in his voice.

'Of course,' said the teacher pensively. 'You weren't here then were you? It was a couple of years ago when they split up. Prior to that he was a nice lad; a lot like you actually.'

The sensitivity in the words shifted Reece's perception of the normally austere man who most pupils feared. It was not simply the compliment he had paid Reece, but his depth of understanding of why Robert Fathaby was the way he was that moved Reece to feel a new respect for him.

'Do all boys whose parents split up become bullies?'

Mr Poutril was at the cupboard returning the aerosol can. He turned to stare at Reece as if drawing on his years of experience as a teacher and military man to glean the reason for the question. His philosophy was that there were no stupid questions, only stupid answers.

'Not the stronger ones,' he eventually replied.

Reece considered his words for a moment as he put his sock and shoe back on, tying the laces as loosely as possible.

'My parents have just split up and I don't think I'm very strong. Does that mean I could become a bully?'

'We all have that potential Winner,' he declared. 'But you have dyspraxia don't you?'

'Yes,' he replied with a frown, not understanding the significance of the question.

'So you find PE quite difficult and therefore less enjoyable I suppose?'

'Well I'm not very good at sport no matter how hard I try,' admitted Reece.

'And that Winner is exactly my point. Strength is about determination and effort, not how good you are. Now do you think you'll manage to get around on that foot today?'

'I'll try,' he replied.

'I know you will. Now can you do me a favour Winner?' It was more of a demand than a request.

'What's that, Sir?'

'Drop the **Fart Breath Boy**, eh?' Mr Poutril gave him a wry grin. He could see from Reece's expression that he was wondering how he'd heard the nickname. 'It was the talk of the staff room yesterday, Winner and we could all see the funny side of it. But I doubt Fathaby can, so maybe it's time to drop it?'

'Okay Sir. I will. But do you think you could have a word with Fathaby as well and perhaps ask him to back off?'

'I already intend to, I just wanted to be sure I could rely on your cooperation first. And of course if he continues to provoke you I want you to come and see me, Reece.'

His use of his first name didn't go unnoticed and Reece smiled at him as he turned to leave. 'Thank you, Sir. I'm going to have to find a new anagram for *your* name now though.'

'Why, what is it at present, Winner?' His voice sounded stern again and Reece was afraid he had misjudged the teacher's sense of humour. He wished he could quickly think of something less insulting, but obviously couldn't.

'Come on Winner, I haven't got all day,' he prompted.

'**Pupil Torturer**,' Reece blurted, trying to look apologetic.

The teacher stared at him and Reece imagined he was calculating how many detentions the comment was worth. 'No Winner that one will do fine. Now get to your class. And Winner?'

'Yes sir?' Reece replied meekly.

'Don't you dare tell anyone I was nice. I've a reputation to uphold.' He was smirking and Reece heaved a sigh of relief.

'Okay Sir, I won't.'

Reece closed the door behind him and could hear the teacher laughing as he did so.

Chapter Thirteen

The day went quickly. Reece's injured foot meant that Mr Poutril had excused him from PE and Reece had used the time to complete all of his homework so that he would have the evening free. His foot was feeling better and he was hoping that he might still be able to explore Seagull Island later with Kara.

The homework had been Religious Instruction and had asked for a list of comparisons between Christianity and Islam. The teacher, Herbert Good, made no secret of being an evangelical Christian, whereas Reece had decided at quite a young age, that all religions were merely humankind's primitive attempts to understand the universe. He had reached his conclusions after following his dad's advice to read about all the main religions. The inconsistencies he'd discovered and the realisation that the main religions couldn't all be the perfect teachings of an all-powerful, all-knowing god, had brought him to the conclusion that such a deity simply couldn't exist. If he did, he would have to be either inept or cruel to sit back and watch while wars and atrocities killed millions of people over centuries, rather than produce clear proof of his existence.

The other compelling argument that had swayed him was the food chain. Reece loved animals and there could be no doubt that animals suffered distress and pain when hunted, torn to shreds and devoured by the creature on the next rung of the food ladder. Would a loving god create the Earth and everything on it and then subject his creations to the horror of being someone else's dinner? Reece had decided only a psychopath could devise such a system of survival and as an omnipotent god couldn't also be a lunatic, then it followed he couldn't be real.

He was, however, interested in learning about the influence of religions on people and cultures around the world and so even though he didn't believe in gods, Reece had learnt more about different religions than most people his age. As a result, he'd finished the homework, in less than half an hour, without having to do any research.

He had spent the remainder of the PE lesson discovering that an anagram of Herbert Good was ***God Botherer*** and wondering if he should test the teacher's willingness to 'turn the other cheek' by telling him during his next lesson.

The final lesson of the day was English and when the bell went at the end, Reece hobbled as quickly as he could, out of the classroom to where Kara was waiting for him in the corridor.

'I think we should cancel tonight,' she said.

'What for?' he groaned.

'Well, your foot of course. You can't go tramping across cliffs on that, can you?'

'I'll be fine,' he said. 'It's really much better and I think I'll be even more comfortable in training shoes.'

Kara looked unconvinced. 'If you trip over a rabbit hole or something, it's really going to hurt. Are you sure you want to risk it?'

'Of course I'm sure. The paths to Seagull Island are quite good so I should be fine.'

'Well I don't want you hurting yourself. If it starts to become painful I want you to promise you'll tell me so we can come straight home.'

Reece loved hearing her concern for him and wanted to kiss her right there, but he knew he couldn't with so many people around. He probably wouldn't be that brave even if they were alone. 'I promise,' he said. 'Now hurry up before we miss the bus.'

By the time Reece had hobbled to the bus stop, most of the pupils were already on board. He followed Kara up the steps and the door hissed shut immediately behind him. There were no double seats free and so Reece sat down next to a younger boy, a few seats before where Kara had sat next to a girl from their class.

'Hi Reece,' said the younger boy, with a respect that he wasn't used to hearing.

He didn't know the boy's name and so simply said, 'Hi.'

Reece spent the journey playing a game on his phone. When the bus was close to his stop, he wrote Kara a text saying he would call for her at her house as soon as he had been home and changed. He signed it with an 'X' for a kiss and then paused to pluck up the courage to send it. The bus was slowing down for his stop so he quickly hit the send button and then was too shy to look at her when he heard her phone play the 'text received' tone.

He stood up early to get off first. There were about six others getting off at his stop and Kara and the girl she had sat with, were the last of them. Reece headed straight for the pub but glanced back to see Kara and her friend crossing the road towards where they lived. Kara stole a smile and waved at him. He noticed the girl who was with her, giving him a knowing grin too. He presumed Kara had told her that they were going out together and knowing that she had been happy to tell another person, gave him a warm feeling inside.

He turned into Seaview Rise and limped as quickly as he could to the Smuggler's Watch. His dad and Aunt Debbie were sitting in the Bar eating shepherd's pie.

'Hello Reece. Sit down and I'll get you some,' Debbie said, wiping her hands on a napkin.

'I'm meeting Kara straight away,' Reece said, trying to make it to the flat before Debbie or his dad objected.

'Well you can eat first,' she said, getting up from her meal to go to the kitchen.

Reece knew he couldn't argue. 'Okay, I'll get changed first then.'

He hurried up the stairs, taking them one at a time because of the tenderness he was still feeling in his foot. He quickly changed into jeans, a long-sleeved shirt and a hoodie and with welcome relief, slipped his feet into a pair of comfortable trainers. He went down the stairs quicker than he had come up by using both handrails to take his weight and swinging past several stairs at once, landing each time on his good foot. In three swings, he was at the bottom and hurriedly limped his way back to the Bar, where his aunt had served him a large plate of shepherd's pie.

'Why are you limping?' his dad asked.

'Oh, someone accidentally stood on my foot,' Reece explained, trying to deflect his dad's question.

'So you haven't been fighting with anyone?'

Reece glanced at his dad and could tell from his expression that his explanation hadn't satisfied him. He looked down at his plate and complimented Debbie on her delicious pie.

'Fathaby again, was it?' There was no getting away from his dad's interrogation.

'Well, yes it was, Dad, but we've sorted it out now. He jumped on my foot as he was getting off the bus so I ended up roughing him up a bit. He finally apologised and I've promised one of the teachers that we'll try to get along better from now on.'

'And do you think Fathaby will follow your example?'

'I hope so,' Reece replied honestly. 'Mr Poutril said he'd have a word with him.'

'I thought you didn't get on so well with Mr Poutril? Isn't he the **Pupil Torturer?**'

'Actually, I've seen a whole new side to him today. He was kind and gave me first aid. He told me that Robert used to be quite a nice boy and only became a bully after his parents split up a couple of years ago.'

'I wasn't aware they had,' his dad muttered.

Reece thought his dad sounded uncomfortable talking about separation, so he changed the subject. 'Kara and I are off to look for Coppinger's cave now. Do you mind if I borrow a camera?'

'No I don't mind, but take the compact. It's waterproof and rugged enough to stand being dropped. It's in my bedside drawer.'

'Okay Dad,' Reece said, as he scooped the last spoonful of pie from the plate and shovelled it into his mouth. 'Thanks Debbie, that was gorgeous.' He left the table to take his plate to the kitchen.

'There's more if you want some,' she offered, clearly pleased at the speed with which her cooking had disappeared.

'No, that was plenty, thank you.' He limped upstairs to get the camera and reappeared a minute or two later. 'Right, I'll be off.'

'Don't be late. And ring me every hour.'

'I will Dad,' Reece replied, before disappearing out of the door.

Outside it was bright but cool and he was glad he had worn the hoodie. He walked as briskly as his foot would allow towards Kara's house and was pleasantly surprised to see her striding towards him.

'I thought I'd save your foot the trouble of walking round to mine,' she said. 'How is it?'

'It's not too bad at all. I'm sure it'll hold up.'

They decided to walk to Seagull Island by road rather than along the beach. Kara took his hand as usual and they strolled along happily, even though Reece continued to limp a little. They crossed the road when they reached the peninsula that stretched out into the Atlantic towards Seagull Island and went through the gate onto the footpath that ran down the long finger of land separating the two bays. The path was well trodden but quite narrow and so they walked in single file, Kara leading the way. She kept her left hand behind her back so that Reece could continue to hold it and from time to time, when the path became particularly uneven, she would turn to offer him support to keep the weight off his weakened foot.

At the end of the point, the footpath became natural steps in the rock leading down to the wooden bridge where Reece's dad had played his practical joke on him several weeks previously. He smiled to himself, remembering his dad's laughter as he took the photo of his drenching.

Beneath the bridge was the pass where he and Kara had crept along the ledge a couple of days earlier. The rock pool was full again and they could see small fish swimming in it.

'The tide's still quite low,' Reece said. 'Which means we'll see no active blowholes today.'

At the end of the island, they found themselves standing on a rocky lip protruding like a diving platform above the waves below. Reece imagined being able to dive from it when the tide was higher, but he could see that getting back to land would be impossible in the ferocious waves crashing relentlessly against the deadly sharp rocks. He had a lot respect for the sheer power of nature along this coastline.

'There's a cave right below us,' announced Kara. 'I've never been close enough to see how deep it is but it looks to go back a fair bit. It appeared to bend to the right if I remember, which means if it's got an entrance up here it'll be over there somewhere.'

She pointed to an area of land covered in small, dense shrubs, hiding uneven grass that was springy underfoot. The number of holes was evidence that it was also undermined with rabbit warrens. Walking across it looked a daunting prospect for Reece with his aching foot, but he didn't want to disappoint Kara who was already picking her way carefully through the scrub. He gingerly followed her, trying to avoid being scratched by the gorse, until suddenly she called to him.

'Look at this.'

He cautiously joined her and looked to where she was pointing at her feet. She was standing on an iron grid, hiding in the shrubs and the grass.

'What's that?' Reece asked, joining her to stand on the iron bars and to look down into the black hole beneath their feet.

'Probably an entrance into the cave that's been covered to prevent people falling down it,' she suggested.

'Can we see down it?' He knelt to clear away the encroaching vegetation. 'Damn. I forgot to bring a torch.'

'I've brought a wind-up one,' she said, producing from her pocket a small flashlight with a fold-out handle that charged the battery when wound. She turned it quickly a few times and knelt beside Reece to shine the faint beam between the bars. The light barely penetrated the blackness of the cave below them, but they could see that the grate did not cover a sheer drop like a well, but a tunnel, with a steeply sloping floor that led towards the cave entrance they had just been standing above at the end of the island.

'This could've been Coppinger's cave you know,' Reece said, disappointed that their exploration had come to an abrupt end. 'But we're never going to find out. There's no way past these bars.'

'Well take a picture anyway,' Kara said. 'We can always say this was *possibly* Coppinger's cave when we do our project.'

Reece took a photo of Kara standing on the grate and she took one of him. Then using the delayed timer, they dangled the camera through the bars in the hope of photographing the cave below. Unfortunately, the results were not good and so they decided to look on the other side of the island where Kara said she had seen another cave while she had been surfing.

Here, the ground was much more uneven and had no visible footpaths. They picked their way carefully between the rabbit holes, which would occasionally give way underfoot and the gorse, which would have scratched their legs, had they not been wearing jeans. Reece's foot ached from the constant jarring but he pressed on, keen to keep up with Kara. Occasionally, she would ask if he was okay and each time he replied that he was fine, but when they reached the cliff on the other side of the island, Reece was glad of the opportunity to sit on a rock and rest his foot.

'You should've said if it was hurting,' Kara said, seeing him massaging it.

'It was just beginning to ache a bit stumbling over those rabbit holes,' he said. 'I'll be fine in a minute. Where's the cave?'

'You're sitting on it. It's right underneath you.'

Reece turned towards the sea and strained his neck to look over the edge of the cliff. On this side of the island, the rocks sloped into the sea, rather than being precipitous and Reece could see the huge slabs of granite beneath him forming the entrance to the cave below.

'Do you think we could possibly climb down there and look into the cave?' he asked Kara, certain she would condemn the idea.

'Well the tide never goes out far enough to let you walk into it. But I suppose if we went down as far as possible we could get a good photo of the cave entrance and maybe see how far back it goes.'

'Shall we try then?'

'I don't think you should go down there with that foot.'

'Well I can hardly go without it, can I?' he replied with a grin.

Kara gave him a playful slap. 'You know what I mean. I don't want you falling. Let me go and have a look first.'

Reece looked over the edge of the cliff again and assessed the route down the rocks. He was sure under normal circumstances he would be able to manage it, but his foot was still hurting and so, reluctantly, he agreed to let Kara venture down the rocks alone.

She was extremely agile and gracefully picked her way down the natural steps formed in the granite, until she was just above where the waves were breaking.

'Don't go too far,' Reece shouted. 'Remember, the tide's coming in.'

'I can't see much, even from here,' she called back. 'But the cave looks quite deep and I think I can see daylight shining in at the back of it.'

'Really? That means I should be able to see the other end of it from up here. How far back do you think it is and in which direction?'

'It looks to be about twenty metres straight back,' she replied, pointing her arm in that direction.

Reece surveyed the ground lying straight back from the cliff edge. It was as uneven and overgrown as the ground they had already crossed, but he thought he could make his way over it.

'I'll have a look,' he called back to Kara. 'Wait there!'

He tested the weight on his painful foot and was pleased that the short rest had eased it a little. He clambered cautiously over the irregular ground, trampling down the nettles and the gorse with his feet to prevent them attacking his legs. When he estimated he had gone twenty metres from the cliff, he found himself up to his knees in thick vegetation. He scanned the area around him but could see nothing to suggest that the brush was camouflaging an entrance to the cave below. He tried to sweep the undergrowth away with his hand, but it was too coarse and springy, so he reverted to trying to trample it underfoot. Ahead lay a particularly dense row of gorse bushes, which he reckoned he'd be unable to wade through without tearing his jeans to shreds. It stretched several metres to his right and left and he could see no easy way to navigate round it. However, the natural barrier was not very high and as little as a metre across in places. The ground beyond was covered with more dense, springy grass, which seemed to end abruptly at a cleft in the ground. He wondered if he might be able to leap across the gorse onto it. Maybe he would have to try a sort of hop; taking off and landing on his good foot. The twinge in his right foot made him question whether he would be able to get any sort of a run-up to help him. He faltered and reassessed his options, conscious of the incoming tide threatening to sweep Kara off the rocks.

'It's only a metre,' he cajoled himself. 'Even I can jump that!'

He took a couple of steps back and mentally practiced coordinating his take-off and landing on his left foot. He rocked back and forth a couple of time to try to get the timing right and then propelled himself forwards as quickly as his limp would allow.

He took off successfully from his left foot, but didn't get the necessary height into the jump. As he tried to swing his left leg forwards, ready for his landing, it was snagged by the grasping barbs of the gorse. Instinct took over and his right foot immediately came to save him from landing on his face. It hammered into the ground and sank deeply into the spongy grass. His already weakened ankle turned and he stumbled forwards, tearing his skin as the momentum ripped his left leg from the grip of the gorse thorns. He screamed in agony and rolled into the crevice, bashing his head against the rocky wall opposite. His eyes were showered with sand and gravel and blindly he realised he was rolling backwards into what seemed to be a tunnel. He clawed panic-stricken at the walls as he slid and rolled down the steep floor of the passage.

The grit in his eyes was hurting, but he knew he must open them to try to see a way to save himself. He had already calculated from the direction he was tumbling, that he must be rolling into the back of the cave; probably down the source of the daylight Kara had seen. If he didn't stop himself falling, he knew he could end up crashing into the cave below. He splayed his arms and legs, despite the pain of them scraping against the rocky walls. It seemed to work as his tumbling ceased, leaving him sliding feet first on his belly. His hands scrabbled in the shale to slow himself further and just when his legs plummeted into nothingness, his left hand caught hold of a chink in the rock.

Then everything stopped and he yelled out with intense relief.

He hurriedly tried to assess his predicament. His legs were dangling in midair, his chest was barely resting on the floor of the tunnel and the only thing keeping him there was his tenuous grip on a small handle of rock that was already cutting into his left hand. He knew he could not hold on for long. Below him, the sound of waves was echoing around the cave but he was unable to twist his head to look down, for fear of losing his grip. He blinked his sore eyes to clear them of the grit that had blinded him and looked back up the tunnel into which he had fallen. It was steep and looked slippery from the loose shale covering the floor and he doubted he would be able climb back that way even if he could pull himself up onto the ledge from which he was hanging. Somewhere he could hear Kara screaming his name and asking if he was all right. He could not yet find the breath to reply.

He tried to find something to push against with his feet but he seemed to be hanging through a hole in the ceiling of the cave and his feet flailed about erratically without success. His right arm had gone numb from where he had landed on it, but when the feeling returned, he groped around for another handhold with which to pull himself back from the brink and into the immediate safety of the tunnel. His fingers dug into the shale seeking something to grasp in order to secure himself and give some relief to his weakening left hand.

He had a flashback of a newspaper story he had read years previously, about a solo climber who had suffered a fall high on a mountain and got his hand pinned in a crevice by a dislodged boulder. He had hung there for days, unable to move. Eventually, his survival instinct had forced him to accept the grim realisation that he would die unless he was able to free himself, and so he had; by cutting off his own hand with a penknife and then successfully climbing back down the mountain to safety

At the time, the story had both horrified and inspired him. Now it motivated him to do what the climber had done and put in one final effort to save himself. He gripped the rock handle tightly with his left hand and dug the fingers of his right deep into the loose dirt and shale until he could feel the solid rock beneath. Fighting the pain of muscle fibres being tautened to snapping point, he heaved his body upwards until his belly was securely resting on the rocky shelf. He rolled over onto his back and shuffled backwards until he was able to sit on the ledge and look down into the cave below. He estimated that the floor of the cave was about four metres below him. The sea was already over two metres high at its highest inward surge and at least a metre high on the ebb flow. He looked towards the mouth of the cave and could see the feet of Kara still standing on the rocks outside. He called her name and watched her legs turn her in each direction as she tried to discern where his voice was coming from. He called her again, louder this time, until she stooped her head to look deeper into the cave. He waved at her and shouted, 'I think I'm stuck.'

She looked horrified to see where he was perched. 'Oh my god Reece, how did you get there?'

'I fell into a hole and rolled down this tunnel. I nearly ended up falling into the sea, but managed to stop myself in time. I'm a bit bashed up, my foot hurts a lot more than it did and I don't think I can make it back up the tunnel.'

'I'll come up and have a look,' she said, turning to begin her climb back up the rocks to the cliff top.

'Be careful. The hole is hidden in a crevice just beyond a row of gorse bushes. Don't do what I did and jump over them or you could fall in too.'

'Okay Reece. Hang in there. I'll get you out somehow.'

Then she was gone, leaving Reece isolated and afraid. He thought about the rising tide and wondered how long he had before the sea reached where he was sitting. He checked his watch. It was already six-thirty. He recalled that low tide on Monday had been about three-thirty and so today, it would have been four-forty. Therefore, high tide would be about six hours later. Of course, he had no way of knowing how high the water would come, but he knew that if the tunnel was a blowhole, he would certainly be facing raging waves forcing their way up to the surface, an hour or two before high tide. He shuddered, realising that if the tunnel wasn't going to become his tomb, he might only have a couple of hours to get out.

He decided to examine the tunnel more closely and rolled over on to his knees to look up the shaft. Immediately in front of him, the tunnel sloped steeply upwards for about two or three metres. Beyond that, the slope was noticeably gentler; probably gentle enough for him to crawl up without too much risk of slipping back to where he was, or worse, into the frothing water below. If he could only find a way past the steeper section, he might be able to climb out. He was considering his options when Kara slid cautiously into the crevice that had hidden the opening from him. She appeared at the top of the tunnel, dislodging sand and stones which showered his face once more.

'Careful!' he shouted, the fear of his situation injecting aggression into his voice.

'Sorry. Are you okay?'

'I'm battered and bruised, I'm stuck down a bloody hole I can't climb out of, I'm probably going to drown in a couple of hours and you're kicking stones on my head. Yeah, I've never been better!'

'Shouting at me won't help will it. I can't help it if the ground is loose, and I've said sorry. Now stop being a drama queen and talking rubbish. You're not going to drown.'

Reece took a breath to deliver a retort, but realised she was right. This was not her fault and he had no right to attack her with his sarcasm.

'Okay, I'm sorry,' he eventually replied, his voice calmer. 'How am I going to get out though?'

'Just hang on. I'm going to see if I can reach you. The tunnel's not too steep up this end and if I can reach you I may be able to help you climb back up.'

'Kara, wait! Don't you think you should call someone before you try that? If you got stuck down here as well, no one would find us in time.'

She had already started to shuffle feet first down the tunnel but now she stopped. Reece was right, it was important to call for help before doing anything reckless.

Kara suddenly felt sick. Before leaving the house, she had agonised over which jeans to wear; the baggy ones with loads of pockets, or the tight ones, which showed off her figure. She had vainly decided on the tight ones. The decision she'd made after that was the one now making her want to throw up. Unable to squeeze both a torch and her mobile phone into her pockets, she had decided that the wind-up torch might be more useful. She had reasoned that Reece would almost certainly have his phone with him, so she had left hers charging in her bedroom.

'What's wrong?' Reece asked, seeing her rapt in thought.

'We have a problem,' she replied hesitantly.

'What?' Reece demanded, impatience again creeping into his voice.

'I don't have my phone with me.'

Reece sighed and almost involuntarily fired more unkind words at his friend, but she looked despondent and he didn't have the heart to hurt her more. Instead, he patted his pockets to search for his own phone and retrieved it from his jeans pocket. He turned it on and stared expectantly at the screen.

'No signal,' he announced, with a note of desperation. 'Now what are we going to do?'

'Do you think you can you throw it up to me? I might get a signal up here on the cliff top.'

Reece surveyed the distance between them and questioned his ability to throw the phone accurately enough for Kara to catch it. He hated his dyspraxia more just then than at any other time in his life.

'I don't think I can Kara,' he admitted, trying to disguise his embarrassment. 'There's hardly room to swing a cat down here.'

'Okay Reece, let's think a moment,' she said, gauging the distance between them. 'If you can just throw it past the steepest part of the slope, I might be able to come down and reach it.'

'What if I can't?'

'"Well then we've lost nothing have we? The phone's no good to us without a signal, so we might as well try.'

He was left-handed and the ceiling on his left was lower than on the right. This meant there was a real danger of catching the rock above his head when trying to throw the phone. He shuffled as far to the right as he could to give himself as much room as possible and practiced his technique a couple of times before finally releasing the phone. His first throw saw it hit the roof only a metre ahead of him and slide back down to where he was kneeling. He thought he heard Kara sigh and he muttered an apology, even though Kara had not actually said anything.

'That was unlucky Reece. If you can just keep it lower, a similar throw will get the phone pretty close to me. Try again.'

He appreciated her words of encouragement and was confident he could do better next time. He had another couple of practice swings before finally launching the phone towards her. This time the phone caught the floor of the tunnel much too early and skidded to a stop out of his reach but just above the steepest part of the slope.

'That was pathetic!' he rebuked himself. 'Sorry Kara. I'm bloody useless, aren't I?'

'Don't worry Reece, I might be able to reach it,' Kara said and began to edge feet first down the tunnel towards the phone.

Reece watched her picking her way carefully down the slope. A couple of times she slipped, sending a shower of stones and dirt into his face, but now he was too impressed with her bravery to complain. He remembered her reaction when he'd turned the lights off in the pub cellar and knew that she was summoning every ounce of courage within her, to overcome her fear of dark places and venture down that claustrophobic shaft.

She was tantalisingly close to the phone when she paused. The slope was already starting to get steeper and Reece hardly dared breathe as she stretched out her foot to try to reach the phone and drag it towards herself. Her left foot touched it, but the loose gravel suddenly shifted beneath her and she slipped, nudging the phone a few centimetres further away.

'I can't reach it,' she groaned through gritted teeth.

She pulled herself back to where the slope was less steep and sat to compose herself before trying again. This time she turned herself round so she was lying on her stomach and approached Reece headfirst. With her right arm outstretched and using her left to clutch the tunnel wall, she inched herself towards the phone. She was less than a metre away, but she could feel her weight shifting with each centimetre she crept. Occasionally she paused, to assure herself that she was still in control and able pull herself back up the tunnel if she wanted to. At half a metre away, she felt herself slip again. It was almost imperceptible, but she was so close to the point of no return, she panicked and froze, hardly daring to breathe.

'It's no good Reece, I can't quite reach it,' she cried. 'We can't risk me falling and getting trapped as well because we'd never be found in time.'

Reece couldn't answer. He didn't want her to leave him alone to fetch help, but he knew she was right. If she fell, there was absolutely no chance of anyone finding them before the high tide filled the cave. Once again, Kara inched her way back to where she felt secure, her mind racing for a solution.

'Wait, I have an idea,' she announced and before Reece could respond, she began pulling her hooded sweatshirt over her head. Reece immediately understood her intention and held his breath as she once again inched her way head first towards the phone, holding the garment in front of her. When she was as close as she had been previously, she secured a good grip with her left hand and used her right to swing the hoodie towards the phone. Her first throw missed completely and she swore before yanking the sweatshirt back. On her second throw, the garment covered the phone entirely and she cautiously drew it back. The lip of the hood hooked under the phone allowing her to coax it slowly towards herself.

Reece gawped, as if watching one of those fairground grabbers that always seemed to drop the toy seconds before reaching the prize chute. This time though, Kara was a winner. The phone was in her hands and he cheered as she held it triumphantly aloft. She took the wind-up torch out of her jeans pocket and replaced it with the phone.

'You'd better take this Reece,' she said, holding the torch ahead of her. 'Can you catch?'

She tossed it just far enough for it to slide down the steeper slope towards him and Reece grabbed it gratefully. It was already getting dark so the light would be reassuring and allow him to see how close the encroaching waves were.

'I won't be long,' Kara said. 'I'll call the coastguard and they'll soon be here.'

'Ring my dad too,' pleaded Reece. 'The number's in the phone's address book.'

Kara climbed back up the tunnel and disappeared from Reece's view. She decided it would be best to ring Reece's dad first and let him call the coastguard so she wasn't wasting the phone's battery. She scrolled through Reece's contacts list and pressed the number next to 'David Winner'.

'Hello son. I was getting worried. Where are you?' came David Winner's greeting.

'Hello, Mr Winner,' she replied. 'It's me, Kara. I don't mean to alarm you, but Reece has had an accident and...'

'Oh no! What's he done? Is he okay? Where is he?' David Winner fired the questions like a machine gun, causing Kara to stutter her reply.

'H...h...he's fine, but he's stuck in a cave and can't climb out!' Until then, she had forced herself to stay calm, but the relief of offloading her stress onto another person was overwhelming and she sobbed as she blurted out her shocking news.

David sensed that for this seemingly mature young lady to be so distressed, the problem must be serious. He took a deep breath, lowered his voice and tried to console Kara in order for her to tell him everything.

'We were looking for Coppinger's cave on Seagull Island and Reece fell down an open shaft from the cliff top.

'Has he fallen into the cave?' David asked, his voice breaking as he imagined his son lying injured in the cave below.

'No,' she sobbed, 'but he's stuck in the tunnel above the cave and the tunnel's too steep for him to climb out again.'

'Is he hurt?'

'A few scratches and bruises, but nothing too serious,' she reported.

He gave a relieved sigh. 'So he's not in any immediate danger?'

'Mr Winner, I think he's in a blow hole and he could drown if we don't get him out before high tide!'

David Winner reached for the yellow tide table booklet he kept next to the till and flicked through the pages to find the date.

'High tide is at 10.26 tonight,' he said, his voice now sounding scared. He glanced at his watch. It was just before 7pm. 'That doesn't give us very long. Kara, I'm going to hang up and call the coastguard. Are you okay? Can you stay with him?'

'Yes, I'm fine Mr Winner and of course I'll stay with him. Just hurry!'

'Okay Kara. Don't worry. I'll be there in a few minutes.' He pressed the 'end call' button and immediately stabbed 999 into the phone.

'DEBS!' he yelled for his sister to come from the kitchen.

She bustled out, wiping her hands on a kitchen towel. 'What's up with you? You terrified me half to death.'

'It's Reece. He's stuck in a cave and the tide's coming in. Is there anyone still eating in the Lounge?'

'No, the only diners we had have just left. There's just Bill and his mates drinking in—'

'Hello? Yes. Coastguard, please.' He interrupted her as the operator answered his call. While he waited for the operator to put him through, he returned to his conversation with Debbie.

'Can you look after the bar for a while and I'll ask Pete to come in immediately. Close the restaurant now because it'll be too much to try and look after the bar and be in the kitchen. If anyone complains, tell them I've had to leave on an emergency.'

Debbie wanted to ask her brother for more details about what had happened to Reece, but the operator had now put him through and he was relaying information to the coastguard. She took repeated sharp intakes of breath as she listened to David give the exact details of where Reece was trapped. She heard him give the operator Reece's mobile number before begging them to hurry. When he'd ended the call, he stabbed another number into the handset and thrust it at her.

'It's ringing Pete's mobile. Tell him what's happened and ask him to get here as soon as possible.' He ran to the cellar from where he emerged a minute or two later with a large torch and a coil of rope. 'Is Pete coming?'

'Yes, he'll be here in ten minutes. You go, we'll be fine!'

David hurriedly kissed his sister and ran through the side door of the pub that led to the car park. He threw the rope and the torch onto the passenger seat of his car and turned the ignition. Seconds later, he was accelerating out of the gate; his wheels spinning as they struggled to find traction under full throttle.

On the road, the engine of the people carrier screamed as he thrashed it unmercifully in his manic demand for speed. He planned to drive onto the peninsula through the gate that allowed delivery access to the small snack cabin that sold ice creams and teas to holidaymakers. He was hoping the gate was unlocked but briefly imagined crashing through it if it was not.

In a few minutes, he was turning right off the main road and into the gateway. The gate was closed, but he could see the chain hanging loosely from the gatepost. He leapt from the vehicle and swung the gate back as far as it would go before returning to the car and driving onto the peninsula.

The track leading to the snack cabin, although primitively laid with hard core, was relatively level and he sped across it, firing stones behind him as the rear wheels skidded and spun. Beyond the cabin, the track became a deceptive blanket of turf, which shrouded the potholes and bumps that lurked beneath and in his desperate bid to get as close as possible to the island where his son was trapped, David Winner ignored the jarring of his body as the people carrier skidded and bounced across it.

Ahead the ground rose sharply to a plateau where he knew he would have to abandon the car and descend the rocks on foot to reach the wooden bridge to Seagull Island. He was reminded of the trick he'd played on Reece a few weeks earlier and fought back tears as he remembered how he'd panicked when the waves had engulfed the bridge with much more ferocity than he'd expected and Reece had momentarily vanished from sight in the viewfinder of his camera. He recalled his split second of terror, when had he feared his son might have been swept away and the relief that had engulfed him when the avalanche of water had subsided to reveal Reece clinging to bridge, drenched but unharmed. He doubted Reece had had any idea of his panic as he had run to scoop him up in his arms and carry him off the bridge, or the nightmares he had suffered periodically since. Reece had simply taken it as a joke, in his usual, good-natured way.

As he blinked back his tears, he floored the accelerator to give the vehicle the momentum needed to propel it up the steep slope. It may have been the adrenalin, or the tears impairing his vision that made him misjudge his route. Whatever it was, the front bumper made contact with the rising ground and the rear wheels spun wildly as the impact lifted them into the air. The people carrier lurched violently and when the wheels next made contact with the slippery grass, the rear of the vehicle swung uncontrollably to the left where the ground dipped sharply towards the rocks and beach below.

He slammed the brake pedal into the floor in a last ditch attempt to stop the car's inexorable slide to tragedy. When the wheels refused to grip, he desperately tried to scramble out of the car. He released the door handle and pushed hard, but the steep angle of the car as it slid sluggishly backwards, made the door too heavy and it immediately slammed shut again. The vehicle's rate of descent increased and his terror compelled him to shove his entire weight against the door in a final, desperate attempt to escape. He fell out in a single motion and as he hit the ground, he felt the excruciating pain of the bottom of the door scraping over his body, threatening to slice him in half or drag him over the cliff edge.

The people carrier gained momentum and somersaulted onto its roof to the accompanying sound of breaking glass and bending metal. It hurtled to its destruction on the beach, leaving a deformed David Winner splayed precariously on the rocks above. He passed out, oblivious to the crashing sounds echoing round the bay.

Chapter Fourteen

On Seagull Island, Kara received a call on Reece's mobile from the coastguard who wanted detailed information about Reece's location and injuries. She explained that she'd been able to see him from the seaward facing entrance to the cave when she'd been down on the rocks, but that she believed dropping a harness down to him from the tunnel entrance on the cliff would be the most straightforward way of getting him out.

The coastguard was thanking her for her information and reassuring her that they would have someone there as soon as possible, when the sound of a crash reached her ears and distracted her. She swung round trying to ascertain where the noise had come from.

The coastguard was waiting for an answer. 'Is everything all right, Kara?'

'Yes...yes, I'm fine,' she stuttered, wondering what the noise could have been. 'I thought...I thought I heard something like a car crash, but I guess it can't have been because I'm too far from the road.'

'Can you see anything Kara?' The coastguard sounded concerned.

'No nothing. Perhaps it was just a wave on the rocks,' she suggested, though not really believing that to be the case.

'Well, I don't want to waste your phone battery, in case the officers I'm sending need to ring you. Stay calm, and we'll have your friend out of there in no time. If you're worried about anything, call me on this number. My name's Mark.'

'Okay Mark. Thank you.' She was about to hang up when she decided to ask the question that the eerie crashing noise had put into her mind. 'Do you think the crash could have been Mr Winner, Reece's dad?'

'Is he the one who called us?' asked Mark, who, having already considered the possibility that the crash might be a relative rushing to the scene, had scribbled a note for the cliff team to check it out on their way to the rescue site.

'Yes. I rang him first and he said he'd ring you. He only lives a few minutes away and I'm sure he would be here by now.'

'Okay Kara, don't worry. I'll get the cliff team to check it out, but I'm sure it's nothing. Like you said, it was probably just the sound of the sea playing tricks. Get Mr Winner to give me a call if he arrives though, okay?'

'Okay,' Kara said rather despondently, a cramp in the pit of her stomach telling her that this tragedy had just worsened.

She decided to give Reece the good news that the coastguard had despatched a rescue team. He was, of course, very relieved. He hadn't wanted to worry Kara, but his legs were already starting to feel cold and wet from the spray thrown up by the splashing waves less than two metres below him.

'Is my dad coming too?' he asked, wanting nothing more than to hear the reassurance of his dad's voice.

'I...I'm not sure,' stuttered Kara, not wanting to mention the crashing sound. 'They might have told him to stay by the telephone.'

'Hmm, maybe,' agreed Reece, unconvinced. He knew his dad, and waiting was not something he did well.

At that moment, a much larger wave crashed its way through the cave below him and threatened to wash the ceiling through which his legs were dangling as he sat on the ledge. He instinctively leapt to his feet which narrowly avoided the drenching they would have received had he not. He glanced at his watch and realised that the cave was now noticeably darker and he needed to press the button on his watch to light the face. It was almost 7.30pm and he feared he only had another hour or so before the sea would completely fill the cave and start forcing water up the tunnel.

'Any sign of anyone yet?' he shouted up to Kara.

'Not yet Reece, but I'm sure they'll be here soon.'

'Good, because I'm getting soaked down here and it's bloody freezing!' He tried to say it jokingly but his shivering made his voice tremor and he sounded scared.

After around half an hour more had passed, he heard a new humming noise, which seemed to come from inside the cave. He strained his ears to discern what the sound was. It grew steadily louder and was soon accompanied by a light flicking across the surface of the water from the cave entrance. As the lifeboat came into view the sound of the engine subsided.

'Kara! They're here!' he yelled excitedly up the tunnel.

Kara stood up from where she was sitting at the tunnel entrance. She too had heard the outboard engine of the lifeboat echoing up the tunnel but could not see it without returning to the cliff edge. She was about to go and look, when she spotted four people in blue overalls and helmets, carrying what looked like a stretcher and other equipment, walking towards her. She waved and called to them.

'The cliff rescue team are here as well,' she called down to Reece. 'You're going to be fine.'

The inshore lifeboat was a small RIB with three crew members on board. It had dropped anchor a few metres outside the cave entrance and was slowly approaching on the end of the line. As it entered the cave, a searchlight fell on Reece who waved and called to it. The helmsman asked Reece if he was okay, then he radioed to the cliff rescue team that he had 'visual with the casualty'.

At the other entrance to the tunnel, the cliff crew were now looking down the hole at Reece and reporting to the helmsman in the lifeboat that they should be able to effect an extraction from their end, but that the lifeboat should stand-by. Reece was relieved; he did not relish the idea of being dropped into a lifeboat, or worse, having to jump into the sea and then climb aboard a lifeboat, as waves tried to smash it into the cave walls.

The cliff rescue team started to set up a four-legged frame with a pulley at the apex. Ropes were unwound and one of the men stepped into a harness.

'I'm going to climb down to you Reece so make sure you're standing securely and holding on to the wall. Try to make a little room for me so that I can drop in alongside you.'

He was soon in position on all fours, ready to crawl backwards down the tunnel. He took one last look over his shoulder and called down to Reece not look up in case he kicked dirt in his eyes. Reece took up a position to the left of the tunnel, keeping a firm grip on the handle of rock that had saved him from falling earlier. As his rescuer descended, Reece forgot his advice not to look up and was immediately showered with grit and stones. He shielded his eyes, unable to resist the urge to watch, as the coastguard got nearer.

In no time at all, the coastguard was standing beside him on the narrow ledge. 'Hi Reece, I'm CWO Derrick Buscombe and I'll be your rescuer today,' he joked, trying to put Reece at ease.

The Coastguard Watch Officer was about his dad's age Reece thought and his accent suggested he was very much a born and bred Cornishman. He had a kind face and gave Reece every confidence he would soon bring his adventure to a safe conclusion.

Another line, with a harness attached, was lowered and the coastguard secured Reece into it. He called to the crewmember above to take up the slack and advised Reece simply to use his feet to walk up the tunnel as the winch pulled him. Reece felt the tightening of the belt that Derrick had wrapped around his back and under each of his arms and slowly he began to walk up the steep face of the tunnel, like he had seen Batman walk up buildings on the TV. On the gentler slope of the tunnel, Reece resorted to crawling on his hands and knees as the winch operator skilfully kept the line tense enough to prevent him slipping back, but not so taut as to drag him up too quickly. Within a minute or two, one of the other coastguards was helping Reece out of the hole and back on to the cliff top.

Kara immediately threw her arms around him and gave him a hug.

'Are you okay?' she asked, looking him up and down to satisfy herself that he was.

'I'm fine,' he said, enjoying the attention. 'Has my dad arrived yet?'

Before she could answer, two paramedics arrived with another stretcher they had carried from their ambulance. They got Reece to sit while they examined him. One of them asked him questions about how he had fallen, had he banged his head during the fall and if he felt any pain anywhere. Reece answered their questions cursorily, hurriedly even, wanting really to ring his dad and tell him he was okay.

The coastguard, who had rescued him, reappeared at the top of the tunnel and began hurriedly taking off his harness.

'How's the other team getting on?' he asked the man who had been operating the winch and was now, with the help of the other two coastguards, dismantling the equipment they had used, with an urgency which struck Reece as odd.

'They've found a casualty halfway down the cliff. It looks like he was able to jump out of the car before it slipped down the rocks, but he's badly injured. James thinks he might have gone under the car or something because he's pretty smashed up. They're hoping to lower him to the beach if they can stabilise him.'

While Reece wasn't looking, Derrick Buscombe tried to make a gesture to tell his colleague, not to say too much, but Reece spotted him and looked at him with a questioning frown.

'What's wrong?' he asked. 'Have you got another rescue to go to?'

'I'm afraid we have Reece.'

He turned back to the winch operator and asked him to radio the lifeboat. 'Tell them to go ashore and see if they can help them down on the beach. I'll be there in a few minutes. Is R193 coming?'

'Yes, they're on their way, ETA four minutes. Shall I tell them on the beach to set off smoke?'

'Yes. Obviously, we don't need the helicopter up here, but it sounds like we're going to need it to airlift the other casualty. Now let's pack up here and get down there.'

The other coastguards quickly finished packing away the kit they had used to rescue Reece and started to carry it back towards the Land Rover they had left the other side of Sea Gull Island's bridge.

Reece's head was spinning from all the activity happening around him and he wanted to ask the coastguard what was going on. Who else needed rescuing? Who would be driving a car along the cliffs at this time of night? Was it perhaps, a member of the rescue team who had driven off the cliff?

Derrick Buscombe's next question was like a punch between the eyes and brought him to a new level of consciousness. 'Reece, does your dad drive a blue people carrier?'

'Yes he does. Oh damn, it's my dad who's crashed, isn't it?'

Reece leapt up and attempted to run after the other coastguards in the direction of the bridge, but his damaged ankle buckled and the coastguard caught him and held him in a gentle but firm grip.

'Wait Reece, you don't want to go down there just now. Let my men do their job and I'm sure your dad will be fine. I need you to let these guys check you over and if necessary take you to the hospital. Can you promise me you'll do that?'

'I want to see my dad!' Reece cried.

'I know you do son. I know you do. But let's get you checked out first and I'll let you know what's happening as soon as I can. I promise.'

Reece resigned himself to taking the coastguard's advice and Derrick Buscombe lowered him onto the waiting stretcher.

'Everything'll be fine, I'm sure.' He tousled Reece's hair then hurried away towards the bridge.

The paramedics followed, carrying Reece between them on the stretcher across the uneven ground. Reece sat up on the stretcher, resting on his elbows, anxious to try to catch a glimpse of what was happening down on the beach. Kara held his hand as they walked, until the narrowness of the bridge forced them into single file. Ahead they could see the flashing blue and red lights of emergency vehicles. One was the ambulance waiting for Reece just beyond the bridge, but others were reflecting off the orange signal smoke from down on the beach to their right. As they crossed the bridge, the throbbing sound of a helicopter came from the distance and soon, its searchlight cut an intense beam of almost alien white light through the orange smoke rising above the cliff top. Gradually it descended to the beach and out of Reece's view. The whole scene had appeared surreal until the bright lights of the ambulance's interior brought harsh clarity to his eyes.

'Kara, go and see what's happening,' pleaded Reece, ignoring the paramedic's question about whether he felt any pain when he manipulated his ankle.

Kara dithered, torn between leaving Reece and obeying his request.

'GO!' He demanded impatiently. 'I need to know he's okay or else I'm not going anywhere.' He looked through tearful eyes at each of the paramedics for some sign of acknowledgement.

'Well you can try Kara, but they're not going to let you get close to the scene,' said the paramedic who was examining his foot. 'But we'll wait a few minutes while you see if you can find out anything.'

She left Reece biting his nails while the paramedics cleaned up his grazes and checked him for signs of concussion.

'We've no reason to be too concerned about you, but there's always a chance of concussion when you've suffered a fall so we're going to take you to hospital to let them check you over, Reece. Is that okay?' The paramedic was trying to sound normal but Reece was sure that his eyes were glistening with sympathy.

Kara returned, sounding breathless. 'They won't let me near I'm afraid Reece, but I'm sure it's your dad's car. One of the coastguards told me they were going to airlift him to Truro hospital.'

Reece turned to the two paramedics. 'Can't I go with him?'

Adrian Degnan had been a paramedic long enough to have witnessed some gruesome accident scenes. He had heard the cliff rescue men describe the casualty's injuries as 'life-threatening' and he knew he couldn't allow Reece to witness his dad fighting for his life. His mind raced to find an answer that would appease him.

'I'm sorry Reece, you won't be allowed in the helicopter. There's very little room in them and if they need to give your dad first aid you wouldn't want to be in the way, would you?' He was pleased to see that Reece appeared to succumb to his reasoning. 'I'll tell you what,' he continued, his voice sounding as perky as the situation allowed. 'We'll take you to Truro hospital as well and I'm sure you'll be allowed to see him there as soon as you've both been looked at. How does that sound?'

'Can Kara come with me then?'

'Of course she can, Reece. If we get off now, we might even get there before the helicopter.'

Reece half-heartedly nodded his agreement and Adrian Degnan gave his colleague the signal that they were ready to go. He stepped out, closed the rear doors of the ambulance and walked round to the driver's door. He climbed into his seat, fired the ignition and carefully trundled the ambulance across the cliff top.

* * *

David Winner slipped in and out of consciousness according to the amount of pain wracking his body at the time. He was unaware that the warm, sticky wetness he was lying in was his own blood, oozing from the laceration the door had inflicted when he he'd leapt from the car. The pain bothered him less than the absence of feeling in his legs, one of which was twisted at an unnatural angle. He was certainly unable to move them and when the urgent desire to reach Reece forced him to try, the agony from his dislocated hip became unbearable and he blacked out.

When he next came to, he was surrounded by faces. One appeared to be shouting silently and grimacing as if angry with him. In his confused mental state, he believed he was under attack, the excruciating pain offering tangible support for his hysteria. He instinctively lashed out with his arm, unaware, that his attempt at self-defence amounted to not much more than a twitch, because his muscles were unable to respond.

After seconds, minutes or hours, he didn't know which, the agony of having his wound put under pressure to stem the escape of his lifeblood, made him scream and with what he was sure was his dying breath, he mumbled the name 'Reece'.

The cacophony of sounds assaulting his senses were deafening, but the voice of someone repeating 'Reece is fine,' penetrated the acoustic fog and seduced David Winner to accept, with renewed calm, the insidious creeping of death. His eyes closed to the rhythmic lullaby of helicopter rotors beating the air.

Chapter Fifteen

The ambulance pulled up at the Emergency entrance and the driver walked round to open the rear doors. Kara stepped out as the paramedics installed Reece into a wheelchair and wheeled him onto the tarmac. While Adrian Degnan closed the ambulance doors, Reece's eyes darted around like those of a rabbit trying to decide which way to run to escape headlights. He had never been to this hospital before and being in unfamiliar surroundings unnerved him.

To his left, he noticed a large circle of tarmac surrounded by a safety net of cables held with metal rods set into the surrounding stone wall. In the centre of the circle was a white-painted cross, enclosing a large red 'H'. 'What's that?' he asked the paramedic, pointing to it.

Adrian Degnan replied in a voice like the one a parent uses when trying to make something sound exciting to a small child. 'That's the helipad for the air ambulance.'

'Can I wait for my dad to arrive? I really want to see him.'

Adrian saw the anguish in Reece's young face and wanted to say anything to make him feel better, but his years of experience told him that in some situations, words were impotent and only time could bring consolation or devastation. 'Your dad won't be landing here Reece. He's arriving in a naval Sea King helicopter which is too big to land on this pad, so he'll come in over yonder.' He gestured to indicate somewhere on the other side of the building they were about to enter. 'Let's get you triaged and then before you know it you'll be free to visit your dad when he's been treated.'

He didn't wait for Reece to respond. He pushed his wheelchair through the automated glass doors, into the fluorescent-lit, antiseptic atmosphere

123

of the hospital. Reece thought he heard, in the distance, the whapping of helicopter rotors but the sound melted away as the doors slid shut behind them. He turned to ask Adrian if it was his dad arriving, but the paramedic had stepped away and was already talking to a receptionist.

'Kara, did you hear a helicopter just then?'

'Yes, I think so,' she replied, craning her neck to look through the window. Reece got out of the wheelchair and walked towards the entrance doors, which swished open again. He stepped outside as the descending Sea King helicopter flew overhead, seemingly inches above the hospital roof, before disappearing from view. He wanted to run to the other side of the building to where the helicopter was landing, but the paramedic was now behind again him with the wheelchair, coaxing him to sit back down. He fumbled and almost missed the arm rests as he collapsed into the seat, before Adrian Degnan wheeled him back into the Emergency Unit.

A nurse began talking to him, bombarding him with questions. Kara was stroking his hand. Adrian was pushing him slowly towards a treatment room. The smell of antiseptic made him want to vomit and his head throbbed with the effort of preventing it rising up within him. Sounds began to echo in his skull and he closed his eyes to stop the room spinning. Then his world went black. His nervous system went into meltdown, as his mind threw a trip switch to shut down all but his vital functions in order to prevent any further emotional or psychological damage.

When he came to, he was in a cubical, being looked at by a young woman in a white coat leaning over him. 'You left us for a while there, Reece. How are you feeling?'

He grunted incoherently, trying to remember where he was and how he'd got there.

'I think you're suffering from delayed shock so we're going to keep you in overnight as a precaution. A good night's sleep is probably all you need so I'm giving you a sedative to help.' She turned to a nurse who confirmed that she had arranged for him to go to a ward and that a porter was waiting to take him. She said goodbye to Reece before he'd had chance to gather his thoughts and when he next opened his eyes he was looking at a much older man, pushing him on a trolley out of the cubical and through the emergency department.

He wanted to ask a hundred questions but the hustle and bustle made him feel like an insignificant cog in the giant hospital machinery. Soon they were in a lift and the porter turned his back to select a button. He whistled to himself, seemingly oblivious to Reece's presence. The lift doors opened onto a quieter corridor and the porter pushed his trolley into the first ward they came to. He briefly chatted to a nurse who helped him push Reece to one of the beds in the room. They helped Reece shuffle from the trolley onto the bed and the nurse helped him out of his clothes and into hospital-issue pyjamas before covering him with the bedclothes. He felt woozy from the sedative and was grateful to sink into the surprisingly comfortable bed and simply close his eyes.

It was still dark when he awoke. He sat up, and once he realised where he was, his brain cruelly treated him to a flashback of the previous day's events. He saw he was in a small ward with five other beds whose occupants appeared to be sleeping. He wondered if one of them could be his dad. He was about to slip out of bed when he noticed that the bottoms of the badly-fitting pyjamas he was wearing, were clinging to him, soaking wet.

He groaned with annoyance and embarrassment and flopped back onto the mattress, angry that he was effectively a prisoner in the bed. The clock on the wall said five-forty and Reece could see a couple of nurses chatting and drinking tea at their station. One of them glanced in his direction and he raised a hand to summon her to him. He considered what would be the least embarrassing way to tell her about his accident; simply saying he'd wet the bed, sounded pathetic.

'Good morning, Reece. How are you feeling?' she whispered, so as not to wake the other patients.

'How's my dad?' he asked. 'Is he going to be okay?'

The nurse's smile was momentarily replaced with a frown, as if he'd caught her off guard. Quickly, she forced the smile to return but it looked faked and Reece feared the news was going to be bad.

'Well,' she started. 'As far as I know, the good news is he's stable. He's been to theatre and is now in intensive care, which is where he will get the best treatment. They'll know more when the doctor has examined him later this morning.'

Reece sighed with relief. At least his dad was alive. 'When will I be able to see him?' he asked, straining to read the name badge on Nurse Debbie Panton's uniform.

She glanced up from the clipboard she had taken from the foot of his bed. 'As soon as the doctor's given you the all clear, I'm sure you'll be allowed to see him. In the meantime, have you been to the toilet yet?'

Reece looked down and muttered that unfortunately, he had and nurse Panton surveyed him, with hands on hips.

'I see,' she said, clearly teasing him. 'So I guess you'll be needing some new pyjamas then?'

'I'm sorry,' he mumbled.

She told him not to worry about it and disappeared to get the pyjamas and fresh bedding. When she returned, she helped him out of bed and asked him how his foot was feeling, before escorting him to a bathroom at the end of the ward.

'You pop in there and take a shower,' she said brightly. 'I'll get your bed changed. Don't lock the door and if you feel ill or faint just pull this cord here.'

'Thanks Debbie,' Reece said, glad that he was to be allowed to shower in private. 'I've got an aunt called Debbie.'

'I know. She's around here somewhere. I sent her to the canteen to get some coffee and then she was going to ITU to ask about your dad. She's been here all night.'

Reece cheered up. Knowing that his aunt was somewhere in the hospital, made him feel less lonely. 'Do you know what happened to Kara?' he asked.

'I presume she's your girlfriend, who came in the ambulance with you?' she said with a wink. 'Her mum came to collect her last night. Now do you want me to help you with this shower or are you going to let me get on with changing your bed?'

'No, I'll be fine, thanks.'

The nurse stepped out of the bathroom and closed the door.

During the hot shower, Reece went over in his mind the events of the previous day. He blamed himself that his dad was now laying in hospital because he had stupidly fallen down a hole. He tried to console himself that his dad was at least alive but then wondered how they would be able to keep the pub running with his mum gone. Pete certainly couldn't run the place single-handed and Aunt Debbie would need to go home eventually because of her own job. He remembered his dad saying that a new chef was starting next week, but she would need someone to train her. Everything was a mess and Reece couldn't help thinking it was entirely his fault. He tried to think of things he could do to make things better. Maybe he could stay off school and help at home. At least he would be there to look after his dad, do some cleaning in the pub and maybe help in the kitchen. He thought about the calls he would be getting from the loan company and rehearsed in his head how he might deal with them.

When he emerged from the bathroom, Aunt Debbie was sitting in the armchair next to his bed. His heart leapt and he threw his arms around her when she stood up to greet him.

'Have you seen Dad?' he asked eagerly. 'Is he going to be okay?'

'Yes, I went over there just now,' she replied. 'They say he's critical but stable, whatever that means, but at least he's alive and I'm sure he wouldn't want you worrying.'

'But this is my fault,' muttered Reece into his aunt's sweatshirt as she hugged him to her. 'If I hadn't gone off exploring, none of this would have happened.'

She pulled him away from her and turned his face to hers. 'Now you listen here young man. One of the reasons your dad moved to Cornwall was so that you could grow up somewhere out of the city; somewhere you could be free to roam. You must not go blaming yourself for what has happened. Falling into that hole was an accident, as was his car skidding off that cliff, so stop thinking it was your fault. It was simply a series of unfortunate events.'

Yes, that would explain everything. Lemony Snicket had magically become the author of his real life.

'Here, I've brought you something to read.' She handed him a puzzle magazine and a pen and he spent the next hour trying to solve Sudoku puzzles while she read the newspaper. He struggled to concentrate and soon became bored of number puzzles, so he tried to amuse himself instead by doodling and finding anagrams of his nurse's name.

When eventually, a doctor arrived at his bedside, Reece was hungrily tucking into the breakfast that a friendly orderly had delivered on a large, stainless steel trolley. It was 9am and sixteen hours since his last meal. The doctor was a young, Asian man, only a few inches taller than Reece, so Aunt Debbie seemed to dwarf him. He asked Reece lots of questions about how he felt, had he slept well, had he felt faint and was his foot bothering him.

'I obviously don't need to ask if you have an appetite, do I?' he remarked, watching Reece continue to devour bacon and scrambled eggs while he spoke.

'I'm fine,' Reece said, hoping the doctor would discharge him so that he could go and see his dad. 'The ankle's still a bit sore but I can walk on it okay, can't I Debbie?'

Both his aunt and the nurse responded at the same time and the doctor looked over his spectacles at them as he wrote on Reece's notes.

'Are you his guardian?' he asked.

'I suppose I am at the moment,' Aunt Debbie replied. 'His dad was brought here too last night. He's in the Intensive Therapy Unit. His mother doesn't even know he's here yet. They've recently separated you see.'

Reece grimaced. He was not yet ready to hear his parents' marital status become a matter of public record.

'Are you a relative?' the doctor asked.

'Yes. I'm his aunt. I'm staying with them for a while.'

'Okay...' drawled the doctor. 'I think we can let you go Master Winner. Perhaps nurse, if you could put a Tubigrip on that ankle for support and if you, Aunt Debbie, can just keep an eye on him and contact us if he suffers any dizzy spells or any other sort of faintness, then he should be fine to go home.'

Both Debbies nodded in agreement and the doctor brusquely said goodbye before striding to the other end of the ward to see another patient.

Aunt Debbie began gathering his things. 'I brought you some clean clothes. They're in your bedside cabinet.'

'You be getting dressed then Reece and I'll get the surgical support for your ankle,' Nurse Debbie said. 'I know you can't wait to go and see your dad.' She pulled the curtain round the bed before she left, so that Reece could dress in private.

Aunt Debbie had packed a rather colourful outfit of brown and khaki camouflage trousers, a yellow polo shirt with a lime green hoodie. He threw them on quickly and emerged from behind the curtain. 'Are you colour blind, Debbie?' he asked, holding his arms outstretched to emphasise his point.

Debbie sniffed and said something about it being all she could find and Reece decided that in the circumstances his complaint was trivial. Nurse Debbie returned with a short length of support bandage. She sat Reece down, measured the stretchy tube against his ankle, cut a slit for his heel to fit through and eased it over his foot. 'There, that should give it some extra support and you should still get a shoe on. Where are your socks?'

Reece pulled a pair of bright red socks out of his bag.

'You look like a rainbow!' exclaimed the nurse brightly, as she put the socks on his feet and Reece fired an *I-told-you-so*, look at his aunt, who pretended not to notice.

Reece eased his feet into his training shoes and loosely tied the laces. He stood, tried walking and noted that the bandage really helped.

'Thanks Debbie,' he said to the nurse, as he gathered his phone and bag of dirty clothes.

'Yes, thanks for taking such good care of him Debbie,' his aunt said. 'You've been lovely.'

'It's been a pleasure,' she replied, which made Reece wonder what she did for fun, if changing urine-soaked sheets was a pleasure. 'I hope your dad's okay, Reece,' she added. 'I'm sure he will be.'

'I hope so,' he sighed.

They were about to leave when the nurse stopped them again. 'Do you want to keep this?' She was reading the sheet of paper he'd been doodling on and was smiling at the cartoon drawing of a nurse holding out a bowl to a patient, with a speech bubble above her saying, ***Bed pan! Be on it!***

'You can keep it if you like,' Reece offered. ***Bed pan, be on it***, is an anagram of your name.'

She looked again at the drawing and then laughed as she saw that it really was. 'I'll put it up above my desk, but if I get the nickname Nurse Bedpan, I'll be blaming you!'

He returned her smile, before turning to follow his aunt out of the ward.

They walked down the bright corridor, impervious to the gaiety of the artwork, painted by previously incarcerated children. Reece was wallowing in pessimism despite his aunt's best endeavours to sound positive. They walked around a corner to the lift where a porter held the doors open with his hand and invited them to share it with him and the corpse lying on his trolley. At least he looked like a corpse to Reece, until he noticed the almost imperceptible rise of the blanket from a shallow breath.

'Second floor?' asked the porter exuberantly, as if the fact that his charge looked minutes from death was irrelevant.

Debbie, who looked even less enthusiastic than Reece about sharing the lift with the Grim Reaper's next appointment, squeezed in beside the trolley.

When the lift doors opened, they followed the signs marked ITU, which Debbie explained stood for Intensive Therapy Unit. Reece thought 'therapy' sounded reassuring. After all, people underwent therapy for trivial reasons, such as trying to lose weight or to stop smoking and this suggested that his dad might be less seriously injured, than he feared.

A sign told them to sanitise their hands before entering the ward. There was a bottle containing a pungent hand-lotion in a dispenser by the door, which they both used. At the desk, a nurse recognising Debbie from her earlier visit, asked them to wait a few minutes because the consultant was presently attending Reece's dad.

The plastic seats were hard and Reece squirmed from both impatience and discomfort. Aunt Debbie produced two boiled sweets from her handbag and they sat silently sucking them until, a little way down the corridor, a door opened and a man's voice rattled out instructions to his female colleague. Both wore white coats and carried clipboards and Debbie stood up as they approached.

'Hello doctor, how is he?' asked Debbie.

'To whom are you referring?' Reece thought his tone sounded condescending.

'David Winner. I'm his sister, Debbie Winner and this is his son, Reece.'

The doctor looked over his spectacles; first at Debbie and then at Reece. He stared as if trying to assess his ability to stomach bad news.

'Let's sit,' he commanded, waving his hand in the direction of the seats behind them while he dragged two more from nearby so that he and his colleague could face them. He turned his seat the wrong way round and sat astride it resting his arms on the back. This simple act of informality brought his head down to Reece's eye level and the next time he spoke his voice was no longer condescending, but reminded Reece of Professor Dumbledore, imparting wisdom to Harry Potter.

'Your dad nearly died last night Reece.' He paused, as if waiting for Reece to absorb the seriousness of what he had just said. 'In fact, I think I would be right in saying that at one point he did die, didn't he Dr Baker?' He turned to his colleague, who nodded. 'But thanks to some excellent work by Dr Baker and her team I think your dad is *physically* out of the woods. By that, I mean we have stopped the bleeding and stabilised him.'

Reece couldn't be sure, but it sounded like the doctor was giving them good news and so he flashed an uncertain smile. However, he sensed the word *'physically'* lay lurking in the shadows, waiting for light. 'So he's going to be okay?'

'Well the truth is Reece we can't be sure. Your dad lost a lot of blood and one of the things blood does is carry oxygen to the brain. If the brain is deprived of oxygen it can suffer damage and we won't know if this has happened to your dad until he regains consciousness.'

Reece didn't want to know how the symptoms of brain damage might manifest themselves. He preferred to take comfort from knowing that his dad was probably not going to die. 'Can I see him?'

The doctor turned to ask Debbie if she approved and she nodded her consent.

'Well before I take you in there, let me just explain that intensive care can look a little scary, but don't worry, the equipment is all there to help your dad's recovery. You'll see a lot of tubes and wires attached to him. Some are feeding him and keeping him hydrated. Others are giving him pain relief and drugs to help him recover. They look uncomfortable but I can assure you your dad is not suffering any pain.' He stood and gestured Reece and Debbie to follow.

At the door, the doctor paused, hand on door handle. 'Don't be afraid to talk to him. He may look completely out of it, but there's every chance that he can hear you, and sometimes hearing a familiar voice can work wonders.'

He stood aside and Reece looked past him at a scene he had only ever seen in hospital dramas on television. In most of those though, the image of the patient looked sanitised and airbrushed in order to safeguard the viewers' sensitivities. What he witnessed now was raw in comparison. He felt his aunt's hand on his shoulder and he cautiously, reluctantly almost, shuffled into the room, the urgency to see his dad vanishing under a shroud of fear.

There were two plastic chairs against the far wall, which Debbie fetched and set as close to the bed as the equipment, which resembled a NASA workstation, would allow. Reece sat on the chair nearest his dad's bruised and swollen face. He stood to hold his hand, but the tube, attached to a large needle buried in the back of it, stopped him and his hand hovered in midair, unsure of what to do. He decided to put his hands in his pockets to prevent himself from accidentally touching something he shouldn't.

'Hi, Dad, can you hear me? How are you feeling?'

His voice broke as he spoke, forcing him to cough the words out from where emotion had taken them prisoner in his throat. If his dad could hear him, there were certainly no visible signs. His breathing remained regular, which Reece probably wouldn't have noticed, had it not been for the reassuring beep from the monitor.

He sat. Found he was too low to see his dad's eyes and so stood again. When they opened, he wanted to be the first thing they saw, *if* they opened. Surely they would. He felt a tear forming in the corner of his eye and wiped it away urgently. He could not let his dad see him thinking the worst.

Debbie stood to moisten her brother's lips with a small sponge. She combed his hair with her fingers and stroked his cheek. Reece imagined a flicker of his eyelids but they stayed stubbornly shut. Both stood, looking down solemnly on the shell of a person they loved dearly. Debbie put her arm on Reece's shoulder and he leant into her, allowing her sweater to soak up another wayward tear.

Eventually they sat again, silent and meditative, while time ticked slowly by. Reece remembered the doctor had suggested that his dad might be able to hear him and that a familiar voice might even help to bring him round. He stood again and stared into his dad's face willing his eyes to open. He didn't know what to say, and even if he did he felt awkward speaking with someone else in the room.

As though sensing his dilemma, Debbie got up. 'I'm going to get a drink, would you like one, Reece?'

'No thanks Debbie. I'll stay here with Dad.' He watched her until she disappeared from the room.

'Dad,' he whispered, as soon as they were alone. 'Wake up! I need you.' He slid his hand under his dad's palm, careful not to disturb the tube. 'Dad, let me know you're going to be okay. Please!' He gently squeezed his dad's hand and felt the tears returning once more. He tried to reach the tissue in his pocket but realised he couldn't release his hand from his dad's. Was it his imagination, or was it being held? Was his dad consciously communicating with him or was it just a muscle spasm? He spoke again, his tears forgotten as he explored the possibility that his dad was showing a response. 'Dad, can you hear me?' He paused silently, focusing hard on his hand, willing to feel his dad's fingers squeezing a reply. He held his breath. There was nothing.

He exhaled a sigh of disappointment but proceeded to tell his dad about the previous day's events. How he had fallen into the tunnel. How Kara had had to crawl down the tunnel to get his phone. How he wished she had just called the coastguard so that he wouldn't have come racing to find them. How he had watched the helicopter land on the beach. How he had later watched it fly over the hospital. How he had blacked out and been kept in hospital overnight. All the while, he scanned his dad's face for some acknowledgement, but still there was nothing.

The silence enveloped them again, except for the beep of the machinery. Yet, it was a taunting silence. It chastised him, as though pointing an accusatory finger until eventually he cracked. He broke the silence with a sobbing, guilt-ridden apology. He stammered how sorry he was for getting trapped and how it was his stupid fault his dad was lying there, in pain, unable to move, unable hold him and tell him everything was going to be okay.

Then he felt it.

It was almost imperceptible but still very real. It didn't feel like an involuntary twitch, but a purposeful application of pressure. The gentle squeeze of his hand, ceased a second later, so Reece whispered directly into his dad's ear.

'Dad, can you hear me?'

Again, he felt a squeeze and this time he returned it. Now he needed to be sure it wasn't his imagination.

'Dad, squeeze twice if you can hear me.'

He held his breath as he felt another squeeze, the same as before, except this time when it faded, another immediately followed.

He wanted to shout someone into the room but didn't think anyone would hear. He couldn't leave Dad when he believed he was trying to communicate with him, so he stayed where he was, daring to feel for the first time that maybe things were going to be all right. He continued to speak to his dad, but got no further responses from him. Perhaps in his dad's fragile state, those few squeezes had taken a monumental effort and now he was resting.

The door opened and Debbie crept in like someone entering a church service late.

'Auntie Debbie! He heard me! He heard me!'

'Really? What do you mean he heard you? How do you know?'

'He squeezed my hand!'

Debbie looked disappointed. The momentary hope drained from her face as quickly as it had appeared. 'That can sometimes happen I'm afraid, Reece. Don't get your hopes up yet, love.'

Reece's voice was no longer subdued. 'No, really Debbie, I mean it. He squeezed my hand! I asked him if he could hear me to squeeze it again, and he did. Then I said if he could really hear me, squeeze it twice, and he did that too. It's not a coincidence. He heard me, I'm sure he did!'

Debbie now looked more convinced and took her brother's hand herself.

'David. It's Debbie. Can you hear me?' She waited, hardly daring to breathe. Sure enough, she too felt the tiniest movement of her brother's fingers as they rested in hers. Was it an involuntary movement or was it deliberate communication? She couldn't be sure.

'David!' She spoke decisively in a tone that sounded to Reece like nagging. 'If you can hear me, squeeze my hand twice.' She pulled away from where she had spoken into his ear, to watch his hand in hers. This time nothing happened. Reece saw her shoulders slump as her optimism did the same. He was willing her not to give up.

'Try again!'

She leaned forward once more and put her mouth close to her brother's ear. 'David! If you can hear me, let me know. Please!'

This time there was an instant response. David Winner's fingers slowly flexed and relaxed. Debbie was about to dismiss the negligible motion when it came again. This time it lingered, a second longer than the first, before flopping lifelessly again.

'Oh David,' she sobbed. 'Welcome back, dear. Welcome back.' She released his hand. 'Stay here with him, Reece. I'm going to tell the nurse.'

She was smiling. Her voice was brighter and seemed to give Reece permission to be happy. He jumped up from where he was sitting and took his dad's hand from Debbie who scurried from the room much more purposefully than she had entered it.

Reece sensed his dad was exhausted from the effort and so didn't try to make him respond again. He was content simply to stand there, willing him to get better. The door opened and Debbie bustled back in with the nurse, still explaining what they had just witnessed. The nurse looked matter-of-fact and Reece hoped she was not going to dismiss what they had experienced as insignificant. She looked at the charts and readings on the equipment and made notes on the clipboard she was holding.

'Well it may be nothing,' she explained. 'But you say you felt it too Reece?'

'Yes. Two single squeezes followed by a double squeeze when I asked him to.'

'Okay,' she replied, 'I'll give the consultant a call and let him know. We'll keep monitoring him. If you're right, it could be a sign that he's gaining some cognitive thinking.'

Reece didn't know what 'cognitive thinking' was, but it sounded positive and something to celebrate.

'Can I make a suggestion to you two, why don't you go home while we run a few tests? We have to give him more medication and change his dressings and you, young man, ought to get some rest yourself. Go home, get some decent food and maybe some sleep and we'll call if there's anything to report.'

Reece looked at his aunt. It was obvious that neither wanted to leave, but they both knew that hanging around a hospital corridor was pointless. Reece also wanted to ring his mum, because she still knew nothing of what had happened to Dad. Secretly he hoped that knowing his dad had almost died would make her realise that life without him was unthinkable and she would come home, look after him until Dad was better and then they could all live happily ever after. He also wanted to see Kara and find out more about what had happened after he'd passed out.

Debbie was having her own thoughts. She had to find out what she needed to do to keep the pub open, so she too wanted to ring Reece's mother and tell her to come back and show her what to do. Debbie hadn't always got on well with Naomi. They maintained a veneer of civility but Debbie thought Naomi was selfish, particularly when it came to putting herself out for her family. Well this time she had better put herself out, or else *she'd* have something to say about it.

'I think that sounds like a good idea Reece,' she said, taking the initiative. 'We'll go home, ring your mum, see what extra hours Pete can work and decide how to keep the pub running. I also need to ring your school and tell them why you're absent.'

The nurse looked relieved and reinforced her advice for Reece to do as his aunt was suggesting. 'I promise I'll ring you personally if there's any change, Reece. Okay?'

'Okay,' he agreed, his voice droning reluctance. 'So when can we come back?'

'My advice would be this afternoon. That'll give you and your aunt time to rest, and your dad too for that matter, and we can do what we need to make sure he's comfortable.'

'That sounds sensible Reece,' Debbie said. 'And if I'm too busy at the pub, maybe your mum can bring you back later.'

Reece cheered up a little at this suggestion. If he could get his mother here, to see the result of Dad's close encounter with death, maybe she would realise what she was throwing away. As soon as this thought came to him though, he wondered if the opposite might be true. What if seeing Dad in such a critical condition had the effect of scaring her away for good? If she had been prepared to leave him when things were normal, would she change her mind and cancel all her plans for the future now that Dad might be disabled?

'Reece?' Aunt Debbie's voice snapped him out of his trance.

'Sorry...erm...yes, we'll come back later...if that's okay with you, Dad.'

His dad didn't reply of course, leaving Reece to assume his agreement. He kissed his forehead and said goodbye. Debbie did the same, before they shuffled quietly towards the door. Reece paused to look back once more, prompting the nurse to assure him that she would take good care of him while they were gone.

Chapter Sixteen

Outside, the weather made no effort to console them. Heavy, grey skies delivered saturating drizzle and by the time they had reached Debbie's car, both had wet hair and rivulets of water ran icily down their faces and necks. The clock on the dashboard said 11.45am.

'It's a good job I asked Pete to open up for lunch,' Debbie said. 'We'll never be home for noon.'

She steered with her knee as she slowly drove the car towards the car park's exit while scrolling through her mobile phone's menu to find the number for The Smuggler's Watch. She pressed a button on the hands-free speaker on her visor and the sound of a ringing tone filled the car.

'Hello, The Smuggler's Watch, Peter speaking.'

'Hi Pete, it's Debbie. Just checking you're there. Is everything okay?'

'Yes, in fact I've already opened up because old Will was waiting outside. Are we serving food today?'

'I'm still about half an hour away, but if you do get anyone in asking for food, see if they mind hanging on until I get there. I doubt it'll be that busy.'

'All right Debs. How's Dave, any news yet?'

'Well he's still unconscious but he's shown signs that he might be able to hear us, so we're keeping our fingers crossed. I'll tell you more when I get back. Reece has been discharged. He's with me now.'

'Hi Pete,' Reece chimed in, loud enough for the speakerphone to pick up his voice.

'Ring me if you need me,' Debbie said, abruptly ending the conversation as she pulled out onto the main road.

They drove in silence for most of the way home. Reece was mulling over what his mother's reaction might be to the news.

'Debbie?' he ventured cautiously. 'Do we need to tell my mum yet?'

'Why shouldn't we? I need her help to keep the pub open. I can't do it on my own.'

'Well I can help. I know a lot about running the pub and so does Pete. Between us, we can manage, can't we? At least until we know how long my dad's going to be off.'

Debbie glanced at him, one eyebrow raised. She chewed her bottom lip as though working out if there was a hidden reason lurking in what he'd just said. Reece looked down hoping she wouldn't press him.

'Come on Reece. Tell me why you don't want her to know.'

'No reason. Just that she said she was hoping to get a new job and so she'll probably be too busy to come back to work at the pub.'

Debbie didn't speak until she'd finished negotiating a roundabout. 'And what are you going to do when I have to go back home? I've got a job too you know.'

'But if the new cook turns out to be good and if Dad gets well enough to deal with the admin and paperwork and stuff, we won't need Mum, will we?'

Debbie frowned. She couldn't understand her nephew's reluctance to have his mother return to help run the business. 'Are you afraid they might get back together, or something?'

'Of course not!' Reece snapped. 'I *want* them to get back together!'

'So what *are* you afraid of Reece?'

'I'm not afraid of anything. I just don't want her coming back to us out of sympathy.'

Debbie sighed. She was not equipped to deal with adolescent angst. She had no experience of it, other than her own and that was a distant memory. 'Reece listen,' she ignored his contemptuous sigh. 'From what your dad's told me, I don't think there's any chance of your mum and him getting back together. I know you don't want to hear that and I'm sorry, but that's the way life is sometimes.'

'Well I don't believe it! I think they can love each other again as long as Dad isn't...'

'Isn't *what* Reece?' She sounded angry. '*A cripple*? Don't you even *begin* to think like that! Your dad's a fighter and he'd expect you to be as well, so don't you *dare* write him off as a cabbage yet!'

Her apparent anger provoked him and he retaliated in a similar tone. 'I'm *not* writing him off! I'm just worried my mum might!'

Debbie was pulling the car into the Smuggler's Watch car park. She drove, almost without slowing, into the space his dad's people carrier used to occupy, for which he felt a twinge of resentment. The car jolted to a stop and she graunched the handbrake, took off her seat belt and twisted her large frame in the seat to look at him squarely in the face. She felt so sorry for him at that moment. She knew he was a sensitive boy, he always had been and she would give anything right now to take his crumpled life and iron out all the creases. Damn his mother! She was supposed to be the one supplying the reassuring words, wiping away the tears and telling him that their family was invincible. Instead, she was off on her own quest for 'self-fulfilment', leaving her son afraid to tell her what he was going through in case she ran from her vow to love and cherish 'in sickness and in health' faster than she had already run from 'for better or worse.'

'I'm sorry Reece. That was wrong of me and I shouldn't have said it. I know you're worried sick at the moment and I didn't mean to shout. Forgive me?'

He looked at her through dark brown eyes he had clearly inherited from their side of the family. 'It's okay Debbie. It's not your fault they split up, is it?'

She sighed. 'Maybe it's nobody's fault, Reece. I suppose people change and then want different things. But even though your mum's not here anymore, you can't keep this from her. She has to know. Now do you want to tell her, or would you rather I did it?'

'I think *I* should. I don't want to do it over the phone though so I'll go to the caravan park later. I want to ring Kara first and see if she went to school today.'

'But you're supposed to be resting.'

'I feel fine Debs. I had a pretty good sleep in hospital and I know I couldn't sleep now even if I tried.'

'Well I suppose no one can force you. Come on, are you hungry? How about a cheeseburger before you go?'

'I'm not hungry thanks. Maybe I'll get something at Mum's.'

They went inside to find only two customers in the Lounge. Peter was sat behind the bar reading a newspaper which he folded away guiltily as Debbie greeted him.

'Any problems?' she asked.

'No, it's been dead.'

'Well I know I shouldn't say it, but I'd be pleased if it stayed that way today. I'm knackered and I'm going upstairs for a cuppa. Ring me if you need me Pete. Come on Reece, let's get the kettle on.'

Reece keyed the code into the door to the flat and held it open for her. They trudged upstairs as though the effort was draining.

'Do you want tea Reece?'

'Please Debbie. I'll just ring Kara first.'

Reece wanted privacy, so he went to use the phone on his dad's desk in the office. He rang her home number first; conscious that calling her mobile would be more expensive. She answered on the first ring.

'Oh Reece, I was just about to call you. How are you?'

'Not bad. I've just got home.'

'Well I'm glad you're out the hospital. You gave me a real scare last night. One minute you were walking around wanting to see the helicopter and then when the paramedic finally got you to sit back in the wheelchair, you suddenly passed out and slid straight onto the floor.'

'Did I really? I've never done anything like that before.'

'The nurse said it was probably just delayed shock but they were worried it could be concussion and that's why they insisted you stayed overnight.'

'I really don't remember any of that Kara. How did you get home?'

'I rang my mum and she and Ethan came to collect me. It was quite late, which is why Mum said I could stay off school today. She told student services you wouldn't be in either because you were in hospital.'

'That's good. I'll tell Debbie she doesn't have to bother ringing them.'

'How's your dad?' her voice wavered as though afraid to ask.

'He's in a very bad way Kara, still unconscious in Intensive Care, but I'm sure he heard me talking to him and tried to answer by squeezing my hand. They're doing more tests today.'

'Oh Reece, I'm so sorry. You must be worried sick. Does your mum know yet?'

'No. I'm going to see her next. I don't want to tell her over the phone.'

'Would you like me to come with you?'

He wanted nothing more than to be with Kara and to hold her hand. She seemed to understand whatever was happening in his head and if she told him everything was going to be all right, he would probably believe it. 'I'd love you to,' he murmured.

'I'll be there in ten minutes.'

The phone clicked and she was gone, but at that moment, Reece thought he knew what being in love was like. He drifted into the kitchen and silently took the tea Debbie offered to him.

'Are you okay?' she asked.

'Yes, I'm fine. Kara's on her way and her mum's already told school why I'm not there today, so there's no need to ring them.'

He noticed the message light flashing on the answering machine and was about to press play. Then it occurred to him that his dad might not want Debbie to hear messages from loan companies, so he left it, hoping she would not notice the flashing light. He cooled his tea with extra milk and gulped it down.

'I'll be off now then Debbie. Will you be okay?'

'Of course, Reece, just tell your mum to ring me so that we can sort a few things out.'

'I will, and if you hear from the hospital you'll ring me won't you?'

'Yes, of course I will.'

She kissed him on his forehead before taking her cup of tea down the corridor to the living room. She closed the door so Reece decided to check the answer machine while he had the chance. There were three calls. One from the brewery offering some beer they had on promotion and two similar-sounding, foreign voices asking to speak to 'Meester Veener' about his account. He deleted all of them before going downstairs.

He said goodbye to Pete, who was now sitting alone in the Bar. It looked like there might be no customers to disturb Debbie this lunchtime. Their previous pub in London would have been wall-to-wall at this time with workers grabbing a pub lunch, but in Trevarnick, certainly at this time of year, it was almost not worth opening at lunchtime.

Outside the weather had done what it seemed to do best in Cornwall. The grey skies had gone, taking the drizzle with them and now fluffy, cumulous clouds radiated pure white as they basked in the sunshine and cast shimmering shadows on the aquamarine ocean. Reece crossed the road and walked to the cliff-edge. He leant on one of the wooden fence posts and drank in the air and the view. He wondered how people, who didn't live in such an uplifting location, coped with life's tragedies. If he were living in London now, he knew the gloom would be unendurable.

'Penny for them?'

Startled, he spun round. 'Oh, Kara, you made me jump!'

'Sorry. You looked miles away. How are you?'

'Better now.' He really wanted to throw his arms around her, but instead looked down at his feet, cursing his shyness.

She took his face in her hands and pulled it upwards. She searched for his eyes and he feared he would die from timidity if she found them, but she was too close to avoid. Her eyes bore onto his and held his gaze. He trembled as though energised by an invisible force. Her hair had the perfume of strawberries and her soft breath left mint lingering in the air. He wanted to kiss her but did not know if he should, or even how to. She would be his first proper kiss. What if she rejected him? He closed his eyes, frozen in indecision and as usual, Kara took the initiative. Her lips brushed his for a mere second. It was not the lustful, wet snog he had anticipated, but something more tender and sensitive. When she stepped away, he opened his eyes to her smile, the therapeutic effect of which was sublime.

'I thought you might need that,' she whispered.

'I...I...did,' he stammered, aware of the heat still radiating from his crimson face.

She took his hand in hers and they began to walk the couple of miles to Trevarnick Caravan Park.

* * *

'Hello Reece, to what do I owe this pleasure?' His mum was beaming with delight at his unexpected visit. 'And this must be Kara?'

Kara stepped forward, hand outstretched. 'Hello Mrs Winner, I'm pleased to meet you.'

'Oh please, Kara, call me Naomi. Cup of tea, you two?'

'Please Mum. Kara has it sweet like I do.'

'Well it doesn't seem to do you any harm, Kara. She's gorgeous Reece.'

Reece cringed and Kara looked coyly down at her feet. He was relieved that she was smiling, but he threw his mother a warning glare, which she returned with a playful wink.

'Mum. I'm afraid I've got some really bad news to tell you.' The smile fell off her face like a landslide. 'Dad's in hospital.'

She looked as though someone had driven a knife between her shoulder blades. 'Oh my god, what's he done?'

'He had a car accident on the cliff going to Seagull Island last night. They airlifted him by helicopter to Truro and he's in intensive care.'

She looked at him as if he was speaking a foreign language. 'He crashed his car on the cliffs going to Seagull Island? What was he doing driving along there at night?' She was almost shrieking now and Reece stumbled over his words as he panicked to tell her everything as urgently as her tone demanded. Kara came to his rescue.

'Why don't you take a seat Mrs Winner and we'll explain everything?' She ushered her over to the fitted sofa under the front window of the caravan. 'Reece, can you make the tea?'

Reece was happy to oblige, grateful for Kara's calm intervention. He began filling the kettle as Kara explained about their misfortune on Seagull Island. He was pouring boiling water into the teapot as she got to the part where she had called his dad and he'd summoned the coastguard before driving to find them.

Reece handed her a cup and saucer, the tension and his dyspraxia causing them to rattle and the tea to spill. His mother didn't notice, rapt in the story Kara was relating. Reece took over to explain how he and his aunt Debbie had believed his dad had responded by squeezing their hands in answer to their questions. Naomi Winner dabbed at her eyes with a tissue, renewing Reece's hope that her feelings for his dad might still be strong enough to make a future reconciliation possible.

'So he's still in the Intensive Therapy Unit?' she asked.

'Yes, he is Mum. He'll obviously be unable to work for a long while and Debbie has to go back home next week because she only has a week off work, so we need you to come home to keep the pub running.' He spoke as though any objection to his simple plan would be unthinkable, so his mother's response came as a shock.

'I can't do that Reece,' she replied, her eyes darting to his, to catch a snapshot of his reaction. She didn't like what she saw. 'Please don't look at me like that Reece; you know I've got an interview this week and if I get the job they may want me to start soon.'

'And what happens to the pub if there's no one to open it and Dad can't pay the bills?'

'Reece, that's not my fault, is it? I have to make sure I can support myself too you know. I'm sure your dad's insured or something.'

'But what about this week and next? Aunt Debbie doesn't know how to run the place, nor does Pete. There's a new cook, who'll need training, starting on Monday. Who's going to deal with that?'

Naomi Winner shifted uncomfortably under her son's verbal assault. 'I'll ring Debbie later and get her to check the insurance papers. I'm sure we were covered for the costs of employing a relief manager in this situation.'

'So that's it? You're just going to make a phone call to Debbie? I'll remember that when the bailiffs kick us out on the street!' He stood to leave. Kara hovered uneasily, half sitting, half standing, ready to make a quick exit.

'Reece, what is wrong with you? I can't simply put my life on hold to bail out your dad's business.'

'IT'S NOT HIS FAULT, IS IT?' he yelled. 'I'm sure he'd rather be behind the bar than unconscious in a hospital.'

'Well god knows what he was thinking of, driving his car along the cliffs at night. He should have walked. And then none of this would have happened.'

Reece's mouth gaped as he struggled to voice his contempt for his mother's comment. He could tell from her expression that she knew she had said the wrong thing, but it was not in her nature to apologise. When he found his voice, it was quiet but vitriolic.

'He was driving along the cliffs at night because he thought I might drown. What would you have done? Stayed home? Gone out getting drunk with Elaine?'

'Reece, don't be ridiculous! You know I wouldn't do such a thing. I just don't think I'd have gone driving across the cliffs.'

'Well we'll never know what you would've done will we? Because you weren't there last night and don't care about Dad or me.'

'Reece, you know that's not—'

'Mum, don't bother denying it. You've already made it clear you don't love Dad anymore and now you can't be bothered to put yourself out to keep the business running. If we lose the pub we lose our home, and I'll never forgive you. Come on Kara. This was a mistake.'

'Reece, stop being so melodramatically, of course I'll do what I can to help, I'm just not going to come back home. Your dad and I aren't ever going to get back together and I need to get myself a job and somewhere for you and I to live.'

'Don't worry about me,' he spat, 'I've already got somewhere to live.'

Kara was already by the door when Reece stormed past her. She glanced at his mother, unsure how to say goodbye in such awkward circumstances.

Naomi looked embarrassed and helpless. 'Sorry we had to meet like this Kara. Would you tell him I'll go to the hospital soon and call at the pub afterwards to see what Debbie and I can work out? I know he's angry right now; he's got every right to be, so can you keep an eye on him for me? He's all I have in the world.'

A tear ran down her cheek and Kara felt her pain. She wanted to give her a hug but it felt inappropriate having only met her a few minutes ago, so instead she whispered she would talk to Reece before saying goodbye.

Kara couldn't see Reece outside the caravan. She walked to the gate glancing around for him before spotting him waiting for her outside the park entrance. He was kicking stones into the road, hands thrust deep into his pockets, his shoulders hunched. She said nothing as she linked her arm in his and they began their walk back to Trevarnick.

'Do you think you were a bit hard on her?' she eventually ventured.

'No I don't. How could she go from loving my dad one minute, to calling him stupid for having an accident trying to rescue me, the next? Does she not realise he could have died?'

'To be fair Reece, she didn't actually say that did she?'

'As good as,' he sneered. 'I thought you were my friend. Why are you taking her side?'

'I'm not taking sides, Reece. I'm just asking you to try to see her point of view.'

'Kara, she's dumped my dad and now by not caring what happens to the business while he's lying in a coma, she's saying she doesn't care if we lose our home.'

'She could lose her chance of a home too if she doesn't get a job Reece.'

'Her home should be with us!' He was aware he sounded petulant but didn't care.

'Reece, if she's made up her mind not to be with your dad anymore, you can't expect her to change it just because he's in hospital. He wouldn't want her to either.'

'What makes you think *you* know what my dad wants?' His words dripped sarcasm.

'Don't be such a jerk, Reece! Do you think your dad would want your mum to go back to him out of pity?'

He stayed silent. He knew he was wallowing in self-pity, but felt entitled. They walked on; her arm still linked in his, even though his sulk kept him detached from her.

'Did we just have our first row?' she teased eventually, squeezing his arm with her hand.

'Humph!' he snorted, a flicker of a smirk revealing his lightening mood. 'Well, you did just call me a jerk.' He cocked his nose in mock contempt.

She pulled him towards her. 'Only because you were being one.'

Her eyes laughed playfully and her therapeutic effect on him was complete. He could not be miserable for long around her and he loved her for it. She was looking at him, glad that his usual mood was returning, which he confirmed with a rather clumsy kiss on her forehead.

'Would you like to come home for something to eat and then go with me back to the hospital?'

'Will Debbie mind?' she asked.

'No, I'm sure she won't. I can make us a sandwich or something if she's busy.'

It was just after four o'clock when they reached the pub. There were no customers and Debbie was sat on one of the sofas in the bar, reading a recipe book.

'Hi, you two, how are you? Hungry I suppose.'

'We are a bit,' Reece replied. 'Has it been busy?'

'No. It's been like a graveyard all lunchtime. I don't see how your dad makes this place pay.'

Reece didn't want to divulge to his aunt that his dad probably wasn't making it pay, which reminded him about the loan company calling. 'Any telephone calls?' he asked, trying to sound indifferent.

'The brewery rang to say they would be late delivering tomorrow, which is good, because it means Pete doesn't have to come in so early to help them load it into the cellar. Somebody rang to book a table of eight for Sunday lunch and some foreign-sounding bloke waffling on about needing to speak to your dad about a financial matter. Probably flogging insurance, so I told him your dad wasn't here.'

Reece knew exactly who it would have been. 'Yeah, we get a lot of those. Best just to say stop ringing us and hang up.'

'They're a pain in the backside those telesales people. The double glazing ones used to ring me every week until I started telling them that I rent my house and it's in a conservation area. That seems to have stopped them bothering me so much. Now, what would you two like to eat? I made a lovely steak and kidney pie yesterday to advertise on the 'Daily Specials' board, but we haven't had a diner all lunchtime. I guess it's possible people have heard about your dad and assumed we'd be shut.'

'Have you heard from the hospital?' asked Reece.

'I rang them about half an hour ago but there's been no change. He's still unconscious but stable.'

'Kara and I were going to go back in a bit. Is that okay with you Debs?'

'Of course it is. You'll no doubt see your mum then. She was on her way there when she rang me a while ago.'

'Really?' Reece sounded more surprised than he intended.

'Yes, we had a bit of a chat and she's calling in later to discuss a few things and to go through the ordering with Peter.'

'Huh, she's changed her tune then.'

'Why, what did she say to you?' Debbie asked.

'Oh, just that she wouldn't come and help because she had her own life to sort out.'

Kara threw him a disapproving look, which Debbie spotted.

'Well maybe she's had a little time for the shock to wear off and has done some thinking.'

'Hmm, maybe. Could you manage some steak and kidney pie Kara?' he asked, changing the subject. He was still too angry with his mother to discuss her.

Kara and Debbie seemed keen to drop the subject too and went off to the kitchen to prepare food. Debbie asked Reece to stay in the Bar and to call her if anyone came in, because Pete had gone home on his break and wouldn't be back until five.

Reece sat at the bar and picked up the day's local newspaper. The North Cornish Times carried a front-page picture of a car lying upside down on a beach. It took a few seconds for Reece to realise that it was his dad's car in the picture; it was so mangled he didn't immediately recognise it. The photograph had been taken in daylight, probably early this morning, after the rescue crews had cleared away the evidence of their attendance at the scene. Seeing the wreckage depicted in stark, black and white print, made him shiver. His dad had certainly been lucky to get out alive.

The telephone rang and Reece picked up the handset from behind the bar. 'Hello, Smuggler's Watch, how can I help you?'

'Ah, Meester Veener.'

'I'm afraid Mr Winner is not here. Who's calling please?'

'Still hiding from us eh, Meester Veener?' A sarcastic laugh came down the line and flipped a switch in Reece's head.

'Listen here you idiot, I'm sick of talking to you people. Mr Winner is in hospital, SO STOP RINGING!'

He stabbed the call cut off button and decided to get a coffee. He placed a cup under the spout of the machine and pressed the cappuccino button. The machine hissed and spat steaming milk into the cup followed by strong, dark coffee. He was sprinkling chocolate powder onto the foam when the phone rang again.

'Hello, Smuggler's Watch,' his lack of intonation was deliberately impolite.

'Ah young man, perhaps you vould be so kind as to tell me vhich hospital your father is in so that I may confirm it for our records?'

Reece was incredulous. For a second or two, his mouth gaped open, unable to create a sound that would adequately convey his anger. The caller, undeterred, repeated his request for the name of the hospital.

'Are you Mr Iqbal?' Reece asked.

'Oh, you remembered my name Master Veener.' He sniggered like before.

'Yes, Mr Iqbal, unlike you I have a very good memory.'

'I'm not sure I understand your point Master Veener.'

'The point is Mr Iqbal, that you seem to have forgotten that I am Mr Winner's 12 year-old son and you should not be discussing my dad's business with me.'

'Ah yes. I remember you now. My colleague also commented on you. Well if you vould just tell me the name of the hospital your father is supposedly in, I'll disturb you no longer.'

'Okay Mr Iqbal, you win. He's in St Bart's Asylum for the Mentally Ill. Do you know where that is? Oh of course not, you're in a cubicle in a call centre thousands of miles away aren't you?'

'Yes, I'm in Mumbai in India so I'm not familiar vith St Bart's Asylum for the Mentally Ill? Ven is your father being admitted there?'

'Some men in white coats came and took him away yesterday. He's been under a lot of stress you see and when a customer asked him if he could top his beer up for him, he went crazy. He poured the beer over the customer's head before stripping to the waist and screaming, 'Here, have the shirt off my back as well!' Unfortunately, my dad didn't realise the customer was actually a Trading Standards Officer and the police were called when my dad locked him in the cellar.'

The phone went quiet for a few seconds, which fortunately gave Reece the opportunity to mute the call while he tried to stifle a laugh.

'Could I have St Bart's address please?'

'Yes. It's Simpsons Street in Springfield,' replied Reece, hoping that Mr

Iqbal was not a fan of The Simpsons cartoon series. 'You'll need to ask for Dr Jass. He's looking after my dad. His first name's Hugh.'

'Dr Hugh Jass?'

'That's him,' snorted Reece, desperately trying to suppress his giggling fit. 'Goodbye Mr Iqbal.' He pressed the end call button and immediately burst into laughter.

'What's so funny?' Aunt Debbie had come in from the kitchen holding two plates heaped with golden, crusty pie with potatoes, vegetables and gravy.

'Oh I was just having a joke with some telesales person on the phone. That looks delicious Debbie. Thank you.'

Kara carried knives and forks and a cruet set and placed them on a nearby table. Reece jumped down from the bar stool and carried his coffee over.

'Would you two like coffee?' Reece asked.

'I'd love one,' Kara replied.

'Not for me,' Debbie said. 'I'll be in the kitchen portioning the rest of that pie. Shout me if anyone comes in.'

Kara sat and started tucking into her meal while Reece made her a cappuccino. He stirred in three sachets of sugar and carried it to the table. He told her about the call from Mr Iqbal and they both laughed when Reece got to the bit where he had told him to ask for Dr Hugh Jass.

'He won't be very happy when he finds out you've been pulling his leg though Reece. He'll probably be ringing more often now. Perhaps you should apologise if he calls again and tell him the truth.'

'They never listen though Kara, so they deserve everything they get.'

'Well I think you should give them another chance Reece. And your mum too, for that matter.'

'Hmm, you may be right. This pie's gorgeous. Debbie's such a good cook.'

Kara took his hint to drop the subject and they continued eating in silence. When they had finished, Reece took the plates through to the kitchen to wash them up. As he was doing so, Peter returned to work.

'There a bus into Truro in ten minutes Debbie. Is it okay if we go now?'

'Of course it is Reece. Pete, will you be okay to look after the place for half an hour, if I go and pick them up later? I won't be going until I shut the kitchen at eight.'

'I'll be fine Debbie,' Peter replied. 'How is Dave, have you heard anything?'

'Still unconscious, but stable is all they've said. Hopefully, we'll get some more information tonight.'

Peter went back into the Bar giving Reece an opportunity to follow and have a quiet word with him. 'Pete, you've probably heard my dad getting calls from a loan company?'

'Sort of,' Peter said. 'But I don't pay much attention to what isn't my business. Why?'

'Well, I don't think my dad wants anyone to know about it, that's all. So, if you do get any calls, could you tell them that he's in hospital and he'll contact them as soon as he's well enough? Please don't tell my aunt though; I'm sure my dad wouldn't want her worrying about it.'

Pete had worked with David long enough to learn a little about his character. He was a proud man, probably too proud to have his financial difficulties discussed openly, even among his family members.

'Okay Reece, if you're sure. What if she answers the phone to them though?'

'I don't think she likes answering the phone so hopefully she'll be happy for us to do it if we're around.'

Peter winked his agreement and then pointed at the clock to remind Reece that he had a bus to catch.

Chapter Seventeen

The following day was Friday. Reece stayed home from school and helped his aunt to get the pub ready. It didn't take long. The news of his dad's accident seemed to have kept customers away and so there was very little cleaning to do. Reece worried that there would be no customers left when his dad eventually came home.

By the time he and Kara had arrived at the hospital the night before, his mother had already left and was on her way to The Smuggler's Watch, where she and Debbie had drawn up a plan to get the pub through the crisis. His mum had shown Peter and Debbie how to cash up at the end of the day and told them what supplies to order and from where. She had negotiated with Peter to work longer hours, which had pleased him because he was saving for his first car. She had also telephoned the new cook and asked her to start work on Sunday to allow Debbie time to train her more thoroughly, before leaving to go back home on Wednesday. They had then arranged to place an ad with the job centre to recruit a new part-time barperson, to help Pete when he was busy and to cover his time off and similarly, a new kitchen assistant.

'Can we afford that?' Reece had asked Debbie earlier.

'We have no choice,' she had replied. 'If we don't have staff, we can't keep the pub open. At least this way, they'll be trained and ready for the tourist season when hopefully your dad will be back at work. Anyway, that's not my problem; your mum's going to deal with all the financial matters. She's checked your dad's insurance policy too and there is cover for the cost of relief managers if your dad looks like being off for longer than two months, so things aren't looking as bad as we first thought.'

Reece was pleased his mother had made the effort to help keep the pub running, even though she had stopped short of moving back in and working there herself. He didn't like to think people had a reason to criticise her, even though he had done so himself.

Debbie had decided to go to the warehouse for a few catering supplies, so she left Reece sat in the bar watching television and eating toast. He was bored. Kara had gone back to school, but had agreed to go with him later to visit his dad.

He decided to call the hospital to ask how Dad was. He was desperate to hear that he had come round and was going to make a full recovery. Lying in a coma made him look helpless and weak, and Reece didn't recognise him in those terms. He was usually strong and fit and could still run from Trevarnick Bay to Jasmine Cove. He was about to reach for the telephone when it rang. He answered it cautiously, hoping it was the hospital with good news.

'Hello The Smuggler's Watch, how may I help you?'

The response came in a thick Asian accent, 'To whom am I speaking please?'

Reece was tempted to hang up, but he knew the caller would simply call back. 'This is Reece Winner,' he replied. 'Who's calling please?'

'Ah, Master Veener, my colleague told me all about you. How are you today?'

'Would your colleague be Mr Iqbal, by any chance?' Reece asked sarcastically.

'Yes, that is correct, Master Veener. He described you as being a very intelligent boy. I hope he is correct.' The compliment sounded like a threat. 'You caused my colleague to vaste a great deal of time yesterday Master Veener. Vhy did you lie to him?'

'Because you people keep ringing and there is nothing I can do or say to make you stop.'

'But Master Veener, you must know that ve can't stop ringing if your dad refuses to make his regular payments. Now may I speak to him please?'

'I've told you, my dad is in hospital and he's in a coma, so you're wasting your time.'

'Please Master Veener, drop this silliness. We know you vere joking yesterday; Dr Hugh Jass I found particularly funny, but this is a serious matter and I must speak vith your father.'

'Okay, I know I shouldn't have lied to you yesterday, but I'm not lying now. My dad really is in hospital. He was in a car crash.'

'Then perhaps you can give us the details of the hospital so that ve can ring and confirm that. And please, no jokes this time.'

Reece was scared but determined not to back down. 'I'm sorry, but if you think I'm giving you confidential information like that, you've got another thing coming.'

'Then ve vill continue to ring you.'

Reece's temper erupted. 'Do what you like! I'll just continue to do this!' He blew a large raspberry down the phone and hung up. Seconds later, the phone rang again. He snatched it up, blew an even bigger raspberry into the receiver and hung up. He imagined the caller's face and chuckled to himself. He was about to call the hospital when the phone rang again. This time he pressed the answer button and waited silently.

'Reece...can you hear me?'

He recognised his aunt's voice. 'Sorry Debs. I couldn't hear you.'

'Well I don't know what happened when I rang a few seconds ago, I got a noise like someone farting into the receiver. It must have been interference on the line.'

'Yeah, must have been,' Reece said, grinning to himself.

'Anyway, have you rung the hospital yet?' She sounded excited.

'I was just about to. Why, what's happened?'

'He's woken up this morning!'

The words failed to register immediately. When they did, Reece was too scared to believe what they meant because the disappointment of being wrong would be unendurable.

'Did you hear me Reece? I said your dad woke up this morning. Isn't that fantastic?' The laughter and relief in her voice brought tears to Reece's eyes.

'Woo-hoo!' he screamed into the phone and did a lap of honour around the room before collapsing on one of the sofas near the fireplace.

'What did he say? When is he coming home? Can I go and see him straight away?'

'Whoa, whoa, calm down Reece. He's not out of the woods yet. But it is a very good sign.'

'He's going be okay though isn't he? I just know he is.'

'Well, let's hope so. If you want to go and see him, the hospital have suggested letting him rest again now for a few hours. He was in a bit of pain so they've given him more painkillers and they think he'll probably sleep now until this afternoon. Why don't you wait until Kara gets out of school and go with her as you planned?'

'I'm not sure I can wait that long,' whined Reece. 'I want to see him right now.'

'I know you do but let him get some rest now and who knows, he might wake up again later while you're there. Anyway, I'll be home in an hour and we'll chat about it then, okay?'

'All right then Debs. See you later.'

As soon as Debbie had hung up, Reece checked the clock. It was 10.30am and break time at school. He decided to text Kara the news. She replied simply with a smiley face and an X and 'See you soon.' Reece could not remember a time when he felt more excited and happy. At last, things were looking up.

He turned on the jukebox and selected some of his favourite songs to which he sang, loudly, while setting beer coasters on all the tables. At eleven o'clock, Peter arrived but Reece didn't notice him until he turned the music down.

'Are we celebrating something?' Pete asked, his face showing his amusement at hearing Reece's sing-a-long.

'Yes we are!' Reece shrieked. 'Dad woke up today!'

'Oh wow. That's awesome news Reece. Is he going to be okay then?'

'Well the doctors say it's still too early to be certain, but I know my dad. Now he's conscious he'll soon get better.'

'You know, I think you're right there Reece. Your dad isn't the sort to give up without a fight. That's bloody excellent news.'

Peter was grinning and his obvious delight cheered Reece even more. He knew his dad liked Pete and it meant a lot to him to know that Pete felt the same way about his dad. He offered to help Pete restock the fridges with bottles from the cellar and they shared jokes as they did so. He told Pete about his telling the loan company that his dad's doctor was Dr Hugh Jass, which made Pete laugh so hard he dropped a bottle onto his foot. The bottle didn't break and that made them laugh even more.

When Debbie returned, they unloaded the car then Reece unlocked the main doors and put the blackboards outside. Debbie made a plate of bacon sandwiches, which they ate while waiting for the first customers of the day. The smoked bacon was deliciously salty and crispy and the thick cut bread was slathered in real Cornish butter. It could have been his better mood and heightened senses, but Reece couldn't remember bacon butties ever tasting so delicious.

Lunchtime was comparatively busy. It was mostly locals, who had finally plucked up the courage to get first-hand information about David

Winner's condition. Their good wishes cheered Reece even more and he enjoyed being able to tell them that his dad had regained consciousness that morning. He spent the lunchtime clearing tables and helping his aunt to do the washing up. It helped pass the time before Kara would get out of school and they could return to see his dad in the hospital. When the last had customer gone, Reece grew impatient and asked Aunt Debbie if he could go to Kara's house to wait for her there. His aunt happily agreed and thanked him for all his help.

The air outside was crisp and exhilarating. Each breath imbued him with optimism and even the peninsula stretching out to Seagull Island, where his dad had almost died, appeared to crave his forgiveness with a spectacle of emerald radiance in the afternoon sun.

He strolled down Sunnyside Crescent towards Kara's house, where he sat on the front wall and texted her that he was already there waiting for her. A few seconds later, he got a return message that she was on the bus and would be home soon. The 'X' at the end of her message made him smile. A car pulled up at the house and Reece recognised the boy sitting in the back. It was Kara's brother Ethan. He bounced out of the car and ran towards him shouting, 'Mum, look! It's Reece.'

'Hi Ethan, how are you?' Reece offered the boy his hand which he shook exaggeratedly. He glanced at the woman for a clue that his turning up was not inconvenient while Ethan danced round him like an excited Labrador. Mrs Steigers retrieved a carrier bag of groceries from the boot of the small car before approaching Reece with her free hand outstretched.

'So you're Reece are you?' She smiled warmly and surveyed him up and down. 'I've heard so much about you. I'm Margaret Steigers, but call me Mags; everyone else does. Here, take this bag for me Reece and come in for a drink.'

Reece took the carrier bag from her and followed her up the garden path with Ethan virtually hanging from his arm.

'Leave Reece alone Ethan,' joked Mags. 'I'm sorry Reece, he gets rather overexcited.'

'He's fine,' Reece said. 'He's just being friendly.'

Mags opened the door and Reece followed her to the kitchen and set the shopping bag down on the worktop.

'Do you drink tea or coffee Reece, or would you prefer a cold drink?'

'I drink most things so whatever's easiest, thanks.'

'I'll make a nice pot of tea then. Take a seat Reece.' She gestured to the small dining table and Reece pulled out a chair to sit. Ethan took the seat next to him and sat smiling at him as though having a visitor was very much a rarity.

'Are you going to marry my sister?' Ethan asked, his face beaming with mischief. Reece spluttered a nervous laugh.

'Ignore him Reece,' Mags said, as Ethan giggled. 'Ethan, stop embarrassing our guest. Why don't you go and watch TV in the lounge? The cartoons are on now.'

'Yay!' Ethan yelled as he slid from the chair and ran from the room. A minute or two later the sound of the television on full volume boomed from the neighbouring room.

'TURN IT DOWN!' shouted Mags. 'There's never a moment's peace round here,' she sighed, feigning exasperation, while her face said she wouldn't have things any other way. She set a china teapot, a milk jug, sugar bowl and three matching cups and saucers on the table and sat opposite him. Her face softened to display the same genuine concern he had often seen in Kara.

'I was so sorry to hear about your dad, Reece. How is he?'

'He woke up today!' He exclaimed. 'So I'm hoping he'll be awake when we visit later. Will it be okay for Kara to come with me to the hospital?'

'Oh Reece, that's fantastic news, you must be very relieved. Yes, of course Kara can go with you. Would you like me to give you a lift, or do you kids want to be on your own?'

'That's very kind of you Mags but we can go on the bus. It's no trouble and I'll walk Kara home afterwards.'

'Well I can't pick you up later because Ethan will be in bed, so I'll be relying on you to take care of her and get her home safely.' Her tone implied a threat of dire consequences if he didn't, but the sparkle in her eyes and the smile playing on her lips said she was teasing him.

'Of course I'll look after her,' he assured her. 'Although it's usually Kara who looks after me, you know.'

'Well as long as you look after each other I'm sure you'll be fine. She's a sensible girl and—' the sound of the front door slamming and Kara bustling into the kitchen stopped Mrs Steigers in mid-sentence.

'Hi Reece, hi Mum. My ears are burning, what are you telling him? All good, I hope!'

'I was actually telling Reece that most of the time you're very sensible.'

'*Most* of the time? Humph! Any tea in the pot?'

'Yes, I've just made it.'

'Good. I'll have one in a minute. I'll just go and change.'

Mags tutted and rolled her eyes at the rapid thumping of her feet, as she ran up the stairs. 'See what I mean, Reece? Never any peace!'

He smiled and sipped his tea. It occurred to him that Mags and his dad bore certain similarities. The light-hearted ribbing, the subtle sarcasm and the jovial smile were all traits he recognised. Thinking about his dad, he fidgeted and glanced at his watch, anxious to get to the hospital to see him.

'She won't be long Reece. What time's the next bus?' Mags asked, reading his thoughts.

'There's one at half-past four, so we're okay for time.'

'Well Kara isn't one of those girls who spend hours in front of the mirror, so she'll be down in—' the rapid fire of footsteps coming back down the stairs stopped her in mid-sentence again.

'Okay Reece, a quick cup of tea and I'll be ready,' Kara panted.

'Slow down, we're still okay for time,' he said, amused by her urgency.

'What are you going to do about eating young lady?' her mother asked.

'I'm not that hungry so I'll be fine.'

'There a Cornish pasty in the fridge. Would you like me to warm it up for you?'

'Oh, all right Mum, if it'll stop you fussing. I'll take it with me,' Kara replied, good-naturedly.

She poured herself a cup of tea from the pot while her mother warmed the pasty. After a few gulps there was a ping from the microwave. Kara grabbed the pasty said goodbye to her mum and pulled Reece towards the door.

'Bye Mags. Thanks for the tea,' Reece said over his shoulder. 'We should be home on the nine o'clock bus.'

'Okay Reece. Kara, ring me if you're going to be late for any reason.'

'Will do, Mum. See you later.'

Once outside, Kara took his hand and they walked briskly towards the bus stop while Reece told her about his dad regaining consciousness. She sounded just as pleased as Reece had been and gripped his hand tightly, swinging both their arms in her excitement. At the bus stop, they shared the Cornish pasty and afterwards she held his arm in a bear hug, resting her head on his shoulder. It was a mature display of affection and Reece enjoyed the sensations flowing through him of his childhood passing the baton to adolescence.

Chapter Eighteen

When Reece and Kara arrived at the Intensive Therapy Unit, the two nurses who had been on duty the previous day greeted them at the nurses' station. Their cheerful manner boosted Reece's morale even more.

'Hello. We've been looking forward to you arriving,' one said, brightly.

'Your dad's doing really well,' said the other. 'He was cracking jokes earlier.'

Reece laughed. 'Oh that's brilliant! Is he still awake?'

'He was a few minutes ago when I went in,' the first nurse said. 'Go in and see for yourself.'

'Thanks,' Reece replied and led the way to his dad's room with Kara close behind. He opened the door quietly, with trepidation. There was no movement from the bed. Kara closed the door behind them as Reece walked tentatively towards where his dad was lying.

'Dad, are you asleep?' he whispered, as though afraid of waking him if he was.

'Hi Reece, what are you whispering for? I'm not dead!'

The voice was hoarse and strained, like an amateur ventriloquist trying not to move his lips, yet it still managed to sound jocular.

'Oh Dad,' he gasped, hurrying the last few steps. 'You're awake!'

'Of course I'm awake. You get no peace and quiet in these places you know.' He laughed weakly and immediately grimaced from the pain. 'Ouch! I won't be doing that again in a hurry, it bloody hurts!'

Reece wanted to laugh, and cry and celebrate and commiserate all at the same time. He was so happy to have his dad back, even though his physical injuries were still appalling and clearly it would be some time before he was back to normal. He hugged him, leaning across the bed and allowing their faces to touch side by side, while being careful not put any weight on his chest.

'I was so scared, Dad,' he sobbed.

'I know, Son. I was too, but we'll be fine. I'll be out of here in no time, I promise.'

Reece felt an almost imperceptible movement of his head against his. It had been an attempt by his dad to display physical affection, but instead it emphasised the very limited mobility he'd regained. He couldn't raise his arms to hold him; they remained pinned by his sides, as if held by invisible clamps and Reece considered the awful possibility that his dad could be paralysed.

'Did you come alone Reece?'

'No, Kara's here, look.' He stood aside so that his dad could see Kara behind him.

His dad's eyes strained to look in Kara's direction and he groaned from the effort.

'Hello Kara. Forgive my appearance, I'd have made more of an effort if I'd known you were coming,' he joked.

'I think under the circumstances, you look great, Mr Winner.'

'You're a charming young lady, Kara. Now stop calling me Mr Winner; it makes me sound as old as I feel. Come and sit this side of the bed and then I'll be able to see both of you.'

Kara walked round the bed and pulled up a chair from against the wall. They sat recounting the accident and answering David's questions about the pub. Reece gave him the sanitised version of how they were coping to avoid causing him any further worry. He would need to focus all of his attention on getting well. After an hour, his dad drifted off to sleep, leaving Kara and Reece to make small talk across him.

One of the nurses came in and checked the monitors and the charts hanging on a metal clipboard at the end of the bed. 'I see you've tired him out,' she said with a smile. 'He'll probably stay like that for a while now. He's had a very busy day.'

'Is he going to be all right?' Reece asked, carefully watching the nurse to ensure her body language didn't contradict what she said.

'He's doing very well under the circumstances,' she replied airily.

'He can't seem to move at all, could he be paralysed?' He studied her hard and spotted that she faltered.

She stopped writing on the clipboard and lowered it to regard Reece with a studious stare. She chewed the inside of her cheek while deciding how much she should tell him. 'It's still early days,' she said softly. 'But the doctors can find little physical evidence to suggest any permanent paralysis.'

'But he *could* be paralysed?' persisted Reece.

'Well I suppose anything is possible, but all the indications are good, so I think it's okay for us to think positively.'

Reece nodded, but the stoop of his shoulders and his downturned mouth displayed little positivity.

'Come on Reece, give us a smile,' she coaxed. 'He's doing well, don't give up now. He certainly hasn't.'

'I'm sorry,' he said. 'I'd just feel so much better if I could see him up and about.'

'Give him time Reece. He's clearly a fighter to have come this far.' Kara came round to his side of the bed and put an arm around his shoulder. 'You two look tired,' the nurse said. 'I think it's safe to say your dad's done for today, so why don't you go home and get some rest?'

Reece was about to protest, but a glance at Kara told him that she agreed with the nurse, so he kissed his dad on the cheek, whispered a good bye and a promise to return the next day.

Outside the drizzling rain offered no relief to Reece's sombre mood. By the time the bus arrived, they were both damp and cold. They sat quietly on the back seat of the empty bus, Kara resting her head on his shoulder.

'I'm sure he's going to be okay, you know,' Kara said. 'He seemed really alert and had his sense of humour back. Try not to worry Reece.' He squeezed her hand in response and they continued the journey in silence.

They had caught an earlier bus and so had arrived in Trevarnick an hour sooner than planned. Reece was drained and simply wanted to go home to bed. He walked Kara home and politely refused her offer to go inside for a drink. She kissed him good night on the cheek and asked if she should visit him tomorrow. Reece had forgotten the next day was Saturday and perked up at the thought of spending a day with her.

'Sure, would you like to come for breakfast; say about ten thirty, after I've helped Debbie get the pub ready?'

'Okay,' she replied. 'I'll see you then.' She pushed open her door and turned to blow him a kiss, but Reece didn't see her. He was already shuffling down the path, his hands in his pockets and his mind deep in thought.

Approaching the pub, he sighed at the sight of regulars standing outside smoking. He wasn't in the mood for idle chatter or to answer questions about his dad, so he slipped into the car park and through the kitchen delivery door. Debbie was mopping the floor and without looking up, snapped at him to wipe his feet. Reece methodically complied with her request, his silence causing her stop what she was doing.

'Are you okay?' she asked. 'Is your dad okay?'

'Well the nurses *said* he was doing fine, but he wasn't tap dancing, or even moving for that matter.'

'Was he awake? Did you speak to him?'

'Yes, for a little while.'

'And how did he seem? Was he lucid – you know, making sense?'

'Yeah, he was all there. The nurses even said he'd been cracking jokes before we arrived.'

'Well that's fantastic news Reece, so why so miserable?'

'He still can't move, so I asked the nurse if there was a chance he could be paralysed.'

'And what did she say?'

'She said it was possible.' He knew he was guilty of giving her the wrong impression without really understanding why. Maybe he was subconsciously over-dramatizing, in the hope of getting sympathy for the miserable mood he was in. The nurse had said that permanent paralysis was the worst possible outcome and certainly not the most likely, so he was not surprised at his aunt's reaction.

'Who told you that? How dare they put an idea like that into your mind? I've a good mind to ring them this minute!' She put away the mop and bucket and removed her kitchen overall with a determination that suggested she was about to do just that.

'Sorry Debbie, calm down a minute. The nurse didn't say he *would* be paralysed, but when I asked her if it were possible she did say it was too early to rule it out. I'm sorry, I didn't mean to alarm you, I suppose I'm just being pessimistic.'

'Come here you,' she said, gesturing with her finger. He edged forwards cautiously and when he was within range, she put her arms around him and pulled him tightly to her, almost knocking the breath out of him.

'Your dad will beat this,' she said. 'I've known him a lot longer than you have and he's as tough as old boots. When have you ever known him to let an illness get the better of him? For god's sake, his local doctor probably doesn't even know he exists and this is the first time he's ever been in a hospital in his life. Have some faith Reece. If anyone can pull through this, your dad can.'

The phone rang and Reece looked at his watch. It was quarter to nine and he wondered if it might be the loan company. 'I'll get it. It's probably Kara making sure I'm home safe. I'll take it upstairs and probably go straight to bed.'

'Okay. Good night then,' she replied, as he snatched up the handset and headed towards the stairs door.

'Hello, The Smuggler's Watch, how may I help you?'

'Ah, Meester Veener, how nice to get to speak to you —'

'Oh you can just get stuffed!' snapped Reece before pressing the end call button.

He assumed they might ring back and decided to call Kara so that the phone would be engaged if they did. It was almost nine o'clock and he didn't think they would call after then. He keyed in the number while switching on the kettle in the kitchen. Kara answered.

'Hi Kara, it's me.'

'I thought it might be. Are you okay?'

'Yeah, I just wanted to say sorry for being a bit quiet earlier.'

'Reece, it's fine. I understand you're worried.'

'Well I shouldn't take it out on you.'

'That's what friends are for, Silly. And girlfriends are supposed to nag as well, so get off the phone and go to bed. I'll see you tomorrow.'

'He could hear the laughter in her voice and felt better for it. 'Okay Kara. Good night.'

'Good night Reece.' She made a kissing sound with her lips, which gave him a warm glow and then she was gone.

He made a cup of tea and took it to his room, where he flicked through the channels on his television. It seemed to be all chat shows and documentaries so he switched on the Nine O'Clock News. He lay on the bed, trying to blot out imaginary images of his dad in a wheelchair, while half-listening to a news story about government plans to increase tax on alcohol. That would be another problem facing his dad when he got better, *if* he got better. He watched the program through heavy eyes that ached from the effort. Soon they were closed and only his subconscious heard the news reporter sign off with the day's customary happy story.

Chapter Nineteen

Reece awoke cold and uncomfortable. He was still in his clothes and his belt was cutting into him from lying on it. The clock said almost 6am and he arose stiffly, a headache throbbing at his temple. He undressed and put on his bathrobe. He thought about going back to bed but knew he was already too awake to get any meaningful sleep, so he decided to make coffee instead. The TV was still on and showing the Breakfast News. Politics seemed to be the story of the day, so he reached for the remote control to switch it off before padding down the corridor to the kitchen. After coffee and a breakfast of cereal, Reece hauled himself back to his room to shower and dress. He decided to go down to the bar early and get started on his chores, so that he could have the rest of the day free with Kara.

It must have been a busier Friday night than usual because the bottle fridges were quite empty. This cheered him up; being busy meant fewer money worries for his dad. He wrote a list of the different bottles and the numbers he needed to refill the shelves, before heading to the cellar to fetch them. He placed the crates of new stock in front of the fridges and paused to get his breath back. He made himself comfortable on the floor and began removing the old stock and putting the new bottles to the back of the shelves, before returning the old ones to the front. One of his dad's pet hates was poor stock rotation.

When he'd finished, he poured himself a cola from the dispenser and sat down to decide what to do next. He was sure he'd heard his aunt moving about upstairs and thought she'd appreciate having all the tables polished before she came down. He was getting what he needed from the cleaning cupboard when the phone rang. It was just after eight and his pulse raced in anticipation of it being the loan company again.

'Hello, The Smuggler's Watch, how can I help you.

'Could I speak to Mister Vinner please?'

The accent was less strong than the previous calls but still sounded Asian in origin.

'Look I'm tired of saying this, he's in Truro Hospital. Now leave us alone!'

'Oh, I'm sorry to hear that. Who am I speaking to please?'

The caller was more polite than usual and Reece assumed the loan company had passed his dad's account to a new person, to try a different approach. Perhaps they thought he was stupid and would let his guard down if they were nicer to him.

'This is Reece Winner, Mr Winner's son, and because I'm only twelve years old you're not allowed to discuss my dad's affairs with me.'

'You're... er, absolutely right Reece...er, you're a smart boy.' The voice sounded puzzled and Reece took satisfaction from knocking his opponent off balance.

'Don't patronize me Mr... I'm sorry I don't know your name.'

'My apologies, my name is Ajay Shah. My friends call me Jay.'

'Well Mr Shah, as I've already told you, my dad's in hospital so you'll have to wait until he comes out if you want to speak to him.'

'Reece, I know having your dad in hospital must be very worrying for you, but I have something very important to say to him. Could I reach him on his mobile perhaps?'

'No you can't! He can hardly move and I'm certainly not giving you his number. Mr Shah, I have lots to do, please don't call again until my dad is well.'

'Look Reece I don't think you understand—'

'Mr Shah, I'm not stupid. I know what you're trying to do, now good bye.'

He could still hear the caller protesting as he pressed the end call button.

He had to admit, the calls were getting to him, yet he couldn't think of a way to stop them. Heaving a sigh, he went back to polishing the tables. He had only done three when the phone rang again.

'Oh, for heaven's sake!' he slammed the polish can down on the table, strode behind the bar and snatched the phone out of the charger. 'Hello!'

'Could I speak to Meester Veener please?'

'Oh for—'

'Now please don't be rude young man, I just vant to speak to Meester Veener.'

'You people are really doing my head in. I've told you, my dad is seriously ill in hospital. NOW STOP RINGING!'

'But ve have been unable to confirm that because you von't give us the correct information young man, so vat choice do we have?'

'You can stop ringing until he's well. I'm not giving you any personal information over the phone so you'll either have to put it in writing or wait until he's home.'

'Ve can't vait and ve are forced to keep calling until ve come to some arrangement vith—'

'Oh change the record!' snapped Reece before once again, closing the call.

'He decided to keep the handset in his pocket in case they rang back, although he was sure that two calls in an hour was probably their limit for the day.

He had barely finished polishing the tables when the phone rang once more. He took the handset out of his pocket and took a deep breath.

'Hello the Smuggler's Watch, how can I help you?'

'Hi, is that Reece? It's Ajay Shah again. You seemed a little upset earlier so I thought I'd give it a while before calling back.'

'Reece was stunned into momentary silence. He had hoped the call was from Kara, as he really hadn't expected the loan company to be this persistent.

'Mr Shah as I've already told you, I'm giving you no information over the phone, so please stop ringing.'

'No, no, you're quite right Reece, I'm not asking you to do that. Can you just confirm that you said your dad was in Truro Hospital?'

'I didn't say that!' snapped Reece defensively.

'Well actually, you did Reece, when I rang earlier.'

Reece flustered. Had he said that? He must have done, how else could he know? 'So what if I did? If you ring the hospital you won't be able to speak to him unless you're a relative, so save yourself the call!'

'Yes Reece, I know that. I was thinking of visiting him.'

Reece's jaw dropped. It hadn't occurred to him that these people might heartlessly harass his dad in hospital. His anger welled up with tears that stung his eyes. 'Listen to me! You'll have to go through me to get to him. You go anywhere near him and I'll—'

'Reece, Reece, calm down, I'm simply trying to —'

'Don't tell me to calm down. You're not my dad. Just leave us alone!'

He stabbed the end call button and raised his arm, about to hurl the phone across the room, but there were other handsets around the building and they would still ring, even if he broke this one. He wanted to hit something, but instead decided to disconnect the main phone cable upstairs in the flat. He didn't think any important calls would be coming in on a Saturday morning and he would reconnect it after an hour or two. By then they should have given up ringing, for today at least. He ran upstairs and looked around for Debbie before unplugging the main phone. His aunt heard him and called through her bedroom door.

'Is that you Reece? You're up early. What are you up to?'

'I've been getting the pub ready. I've bottled up the fridges and polished all the tables. I was going to vacuum next.'

'Really? Oh you are good. I'm a bit behind schedule today, so that will really help. Thank you.' She bustled out of the bedroom and headed for the kitchen. 'Have you had breakfast?'

'Yes, I had some cereal.'

'Well, when everything's done, I'll make us some nice bacon butties.'

The thought of his aunt's bacon sandwiches put a smile on his face. 'Kara should be here soon, can she join us?'

'Of course she can. You know, she seems a very nice girl. I really like her.'

Reece blushed. 'Yeah, so do I.'

Chapter Twenty

Ajay Shah sat in his office, bemused by the two telephone conversations he'd just had. Why had the boy been so defensive and scared to talk to him? He turned on his computer and searched for hospitals in Truro. There was only one, so he noted down the address and telephone number and checked its location on an internet map. He entered the details into his mobile phone and then called the number.

'Truro Hospital, how can I help you?'

'Hello, I'm planning to visit a relative but I'm not sure which department they're in. Could you tell me please?'

'What's his name?' The voice was efficiently brusque.

'David Vinner.'

'What's your name please?'

'I'm Jason Vinner.'

'So you're a relative?'

'Yes, er, I'm his cousin.'

'Do you know when he was admitted?'

He wasn't prepared for the question but lied that he had been out of the country and had very few details.

'He's still in the Trelawny Wing, in our ITU. Would you like me to put you through to the ward? They'll be able to give you more information.'

'Yes, thank you.'

The phone switched to a ringing tone for a minute or so before eventually being answered. 'Hello, ITU.'

'Oh hello,' he said in his most charming voice. 'I'm told you can give me some information about my cousin David Vinner.'

'What's your name please?'

'My name's Jason Vinner. I've been away and so I've only just heard the news. How is he doing?'

'Well he is waking up regularly now and last night he began to get some movement back so things are looking a lot better than when he first arrived. It was a nasty car accident he was in, as you probably know.'

'Yes, so I heard. Can he take telephone calls yet?'

'No, I'm afraid not. But I'd be happy to tell him you called.'

'Is he allowed visitors?'

'Yes, of course. He hasn't had many so far, just his sister and his son.'

'Ah, so Reece has seen him, has he?' he said, reinforcing his lie that he was related.

'Yes he's been every day, but I'm sure David would be pleased to see a new face. Shall I tell him you're coming?'

'No don't do that. I live overseas you see and I'd love to surprise him. What time are visiting hours?'

'We don't have fixed times in ITU. Let us know when you'll be arriving and we'll try to accommodate you, as long as the patient's up to it.'

'Well I'm driving from Watford, so I'll give you a call when I get to Truro, if that's all right?'

'Yes, that'll be fine. And don't worry; I won't spoil your surprise.'

'Thank you nurse..?'

'I'm Jane; I'll be on duty until five.'

He hung up and dialled his secretary's extension. 'Hi Carol, I'm going to see our Mr Vinner in Cornwall. Can you find me a hotel for tonight in Truro and text me the details?' He doodled while listening to her. 'Yes, that's right. I doubt I'll get his agreement because he's in intensive care, but if do, I'll come back tomorrow. If not, I'll be back on Monday.'

He hung up the phone looking at David Winner's details scribbled on his notepad.

'Okay, Mr Vinner. I'm coming to find you. And I'm *really* looking forward to it.'

Chapter Twenty One

Kara arrived at ten thirty, just as Aunt Debbie was making bacon sandwiches. The gorgeous aroma filled the bar and Kara gratefully accepted Debbie's offer to join them. After breakfast, Debbie rang the hospital on her mobile, to see how her brother was doing. She came bustling in from the kitchen.

'Fantastic news! He's sitting up in bed and he's regained some movement in his lower limbs. The doctors say he's looking good for full recovery.'

'Reece almost choked on his sandwich as he jumped up and down in his excitement. Kara thumped him on his back and then gave him a hug that threatened to break his ribs. Debbie joined in and Pete found the three of them in a scrum when he arrived for work. He knew it must be good news, but waited for their celebrations to stop so they could tell him.

'Dad's sitting up and moving!' shrieked Reece.

'Oh, that's epic!' said Pete. 'Is he still in the ITU?'

'Yes,' Debbie replied. 'But they're hoping if he continues to progress as well as he is doing, he could be moved to a ward in a day or two.'

'Shall we go to see him Kara?' Reece suggested.

'They said they had physiotherapists working on him this morning so they expect him to be tired. They suggested waiting until later this afternoon. It would be good for you kids to get some fresh air too. It's gorgeous out, so go and have a walk and a nice lunch somewhere. I'll pay.'

'Ah, thanks Debs. You're the best. Where do you fancy going, Kara?'

'Tom's fish and chips?' she suggested with a grin.

'That's just what I was thinking,' Reece said enthusiastically. 'Except,

I'm so full of bacon butties right now, I don't know where I'll find room for fish and chips.'

'Then go for a walk on the cliffs and come back to Tom's along the beach,' Debbie suggested. 'I'm sure you'll be hungry again after a couple of hours in the sea air.'

They didn't need any more persuading. They helped Debbie tidy up their dishes before stepping out into the warm April sunshine. Reece was exhilarated. He didn't think the day could get any better.

They walked to Jasmine Cove and skimmed flat stones across the waves. The cloudless blue sky allowed the sun to turn the sand the colour of pure gold. They sat for a while on the rocks watching the tide go out to its lowest point. Then they walked back on to the cliff top and took the steps down to Seagull Island Bay.

They raced across the vast expanse of sand, left pristine by the outgoing tide. They hopped over rocks and explored the marine life in the crystal rock pools left stranded until the ocean returned. They climbed to the shelf that took them underneath the footbridge to Seagull Island and shuffled along it before jumping down onto Trevarnick Beach. Reece was glad that the recent horrific events had not tainted his love of his favourite locations. He and Kara held hands and laughed, enjoying the simplicity of being alive. He saw her light-hearted side, rather than the precocious seriousness that years of sorrow had instilled in her. For the first time, it felt to Reece like they were the same age.

Eventually they decided that they were getting peckish enough to head to Tom's for lunch. They played tag as they ran across the beach towards the café. When they arrived, they almost fell through the door together, out of breath and laughing uncontrollably.

'Whoa, whoa!' shouted Tom, as the door crashed open. 'You'll do yourselves an injury,' he said, in his usual affable voice.

'Sorry Tom,' panted Reece as Kara collapsed against him. 'She almost beat me that time.'

'Well it's nice to see you both looking happy. How's your dad, Reece?'

'We had some brilliant news today Tom. Dad's sitting up and getting some movement back.'

Tom's face beamed. 'Well I'm really happy to hear that Reece. I like your dad a lot.'

'Thanks Tom. I'll tell him you said that. We're going to see him later.'

'Well give him my best. Now then, fish and chips each?

'Yes please Tom, but I think one portion between us will be enough. We had bacon sandwiches a couple of hours ago.'

They sat in the window and ten minutes later Tom brought their meals over. 'Is it two milky coffees?'

'Yes please Tom,' replied Kara, glancing at Reece who nodded his approval.

They tucked into their food and argued about who had run across the beach the fastest. Tom brought the drinks to their table as two more customers came in, so he went back behind the counter to serve them. They fell silent while they ate and Kara glanced occasionally at the TV on the wall behind Reece.

'That was great as always,' Reece commented as he finished the last of his chips.

'Hmm,' replied Kara distractedly, as she stared at the TV behind him.

Reece sipped his coffee and looked up to see her frowning at whatever it was she was looking at.

'What's up?' he asked, twisting in his seat to follow her gaze.

The news was on, but the sound was turned down. Below the female newsreader was a row of lottery balls. Reece scanned the numbers quickly and recognised most if not all of them. He spun in his seat to see Kara with her mouth open.

'Are you thinking what I'm thinking?' she asked.

'YES!' shouted Reece and she immediately shushed him to keep his voice down.

He spun round again but a graphic showing £115 million had replaced the numbers.

'Kara, were those my numbers?' he hissed in a loud whisper.

'Well, I was asking myself that, but I didn't have time to see them all,' she replied excitedly. Come on, let's get out of here. We need to check.'

Reece went to the counter to pay Tom.

'Give your dad my best wishes,' he said, as he gave Reece his change.

'Yes, yes I will,' stuttered Reece, trying to disguise his impatience to get out of the café. 'Thanks Tom, we'll see you soon.' He bustled Kara out of the door and grabbed her hand. 'Come on. Let's get back to mine quickly.' They ran up the hill but Reece got stitch from the effort on a full stomach. They slowed to a walk and Reece breathlessly speculated what winning the lottery would mean.

'Don't get your hopes up Reece, we might be wrong. Let's check before we jump to conclusions.'

'Yes, you're right of course, but what if?'

'Reece, stop it! Let's check the facts first. Come on.' She pulled him up the hill and into Seaview Rise. They arrived at the pub and looked through the windows as they passed.

'We'll go through the Bar and sneak straight upstairs. There are diners in the pub, so my aunt will be in the kitchen.'

They ran upstairs and went straight to Reece's room. He closed the door and lifted the lid on his laptop. It seemed to take ages to boot, but eventually he was tapping in the address for the lottery website. He entered his dad's password and almost passed out from what was waiting on his account page.

'Kara, look!'

'I can see it. I just don't believe it,' she whispered, as if her vocal cords had frozen.

Where the figures £4.50 had been in his dad's account balance, there was now a line of digits. £115,299,904.50

Neither could speak. Reece was physically shaking while Kara seemed to be in a trance.

Eventually, Reece spluttered that he had to tell Debbie and was hurtling for his bedroom door. Kara grabbed his arm and stopped him.

'Reece, listen to me. You dad doesn't know he entered, does he?'

'Well, no, but so what?'

'So what? Think about it Reece, if they find out it was a twelve year old who entered they won't pay out.'

'Of course they will,' reasoned Reece. 'Look the money's already showing on his account.'

'But what if they have to verify it or if he has to submit a claim somehow? How can he do that if he doesn't know he entered?'

'Well let's go and tell him now.'

'Reece do you think he's ready for a shock like this in his condition?'

Reece thought for a few seconds. 'Nah, are you kidding? This is the best news anyone could ever get. I wouldn't be surprised if it made him leap out of bed and dance around his hospital bed. It could be just the boost he needs.'

'Reece, there's something else. If they know your dad's name and address from his online account, don't you think it's odd they haven't been in touch? The draw was last night and it's making the national news. Surely they would have telephoned or something by now.'

Reece tried to focus, but his pulse was racing and his heart was going so fast he was out of breath. Kara was right, he needed to calm down and think this through before doing something to jeopardise their good fortune. He thought about the phone calls that morning and then remembered he had unplugged the phone and forgotten to plug it back in before going out. He ran down the corridor with Kara following, asking where he was going.

'I'm going to check the phone line.'

'Why?'

'I unplugged it earlier because the loan company called three times this morning and got me really annoyed.' He reached behind the cabinet on which the telephone sat and pulled out the disconnected cable. 'They couldn't have got an answer, even if they have been calling. But now I've got a horrible feeling that they've already called.'

'What do you mean Reece? Called when?'

'I got three calls this morning. I'm sure one was from the loan company, but the other two were from a new guy called Ajay Shah.'

'What did he say?' Kara sounded impatient.

'Well he wanted to speak to my dad, but I assumed he was from the loan company so I told him Dad was in hospital and to stop ringing until he was better. Then he rang back and asked if he could reach him in hospital. I told him he couldn't take any calls and so he suggested visiting him.'

'Damn Reece, do you think he meant it?'

'Well I didn't. The loan company callers are usually in a call centre in India so I didn't take him seriously.'

'What time did he ring Reece?'

'About eight o'clock.'

'That's nearly seven hours ago. Does your phone have a call log?'

'The loan company always withhold their number Kara.'

'Yes Reece, but the lottery company might not. Plug that phone in and let's see.'

He fumbled several times with the plug until Kara eventually snatched it from him and plugged it in. She flicked through the phone's menu to the call log and saw that the last three entries were a withheld number with two identical numbers either side of it.

'Did the loan company call in between Mr Shah's calls?'

'Yes, why?'

'Because I think this is his number.'

She pressed the dial button and ushered Reece back towards his bedroom.

'What are you doing?' he asked incredulously.

'I'm ringing them of course.'

Reece stared back wide-eyed.

'Hello, Global Lotteries, Mr Shah's office.' Kara was stunned into brief silence. 'Hello, Mr Shah's phone,' repeated the voice on the other end.

'Hello,' Kara said, clearing her throat. 'Could I speak to Mr Shah, please?'

'I'm afraid he's out. Can I take a message?'

'Do you know when he'll be back?' asked Kara, in a grown up voice.

'If you could just hold the line a moment, I'll try to find out for you.'

Kara heard the phone go down on the desk and the woman call to someone else in the office to ask when Mr Shah would be back.

'He went to Cornwall first thing this morning,' said a distant voice. 'I booked him a hotel in Truro for tonight so he definitely won't be back until tomorrow, or possibly even Monday.'

Kara heard the phone being picked up again.

'I'm sorry. Mr Shah is away for a day or two. Would you like me to take a message?'

'No that's fine. I'll call him on Monday. Goodbye.' She hung up quickly before the woman could ask her any more questions.

'Reece, I've just heard them say that Mr Shah left for Cornwall this morning and has a hotel booked in Truro tonight.'

'Oh Kara, what if we're too late? What if Mr Shah has arrived and my dad has said he never entered the lottery this week? What will they do?'

'Reece I don't know. I don't even want to think about it. Where is Global Lotteries based?

'Why?' asked Reece.

'Maybe Mr Shah is still on the way. Maybe he'll go to his hotel tonight and visit your dad tomorrow.'

'Let's see where he's coming from,' he said, clicking the 'Contact Us' link on the lottery website. 'Their office is in Watford. That's north of London and it takes us about five or six hours to get from London to here.'

He glanced at his watch. 'He could be there already.'

'Could you try ringing the hospital and asking to speak to your dad urgently?'

'It's worth a try. But even if they give him the phone, do you think for one minute he'll believe me if I tell him he's won the lottery?'

'Reece you've got to try. There's a hundred and fifteen million at stake.'

Reece picked up the phone and pressed the auto-dial button for the hospital. He asked to be put through to ITU, where the nurse he knew as Jane answered his call.

'Hi Jane,' said Reece. 'I'm just ringing to ask how my dad is today.'

'Hello Reece. He's been doing really well. He had a good session with the physiotherapist and he's now fast asleep. Were you thinking of visiting him?'

'Yes, I was Jane. I was going to come on the next bus.'

'That'll be fine Reece. I'm sure he'll be awake by the time you get here because I've got to change one of his dressings soon and I doubt he'll sleep through that. He's got his other visitor waiting too.'

Reece's throat tightened and he croaked, 'What other visitor?'

'His cousin I think. The one who's just arrived from overseas?'

'I didn't know he had a cousin overseas,' Reece said. 'What's his name?'

'Er, Jason I think he said. Jason Winner. He's in the canteen at the moment getting a drink.'

Reece knew they didn't have anyone in the family called Jason. Was it possible that Ajay Shah was using the name Jason Winner as an alias in order to get to see his dad? Hadn't he said that his friends called him Jay and couldn't Jay easily become Jason?

'Oh,' Reece said, struggling to find the right words. 'I don't think I know him. Listen, do you think you could keep Jason out of the room until I get there? I have something I want to tell my dad first.'

'Huh, okay Reece. Is everything all right? You sound upset.'

'No it's fine, but I have something very important to tell my dad and I don't want anyone else in the room.'

'Okay Reece, just for you. I'll stall him for as long as possible.'

'Thanks Jane, I'll be as quick as I can.'

Kara was looking horrified when he finished the call.

'He's already there.' Reece exclaimed. 'We've got to get to my dad before he does.'

Kara looked at her watch. 'There's a bus due about now. If it's late, we might still catch it.'

Reece ran to the office and took twenty pounds from the petty cash tin that his dad kept in the top drawer of his desk, before chasing Kara down the stairs. They slipped out through the bar, too quickly for anyone to notice them and ran to the end of Seaview Rise. As they turned the corner, they both slowed. The bus was already driving away into the distance.

'BLOODY HELL!' screamed Reece. 'Now what are we going to do?'

'We could always ask your aunt to drive us,' Kara suggested.

Reece thought for a moment. His dad had once told him that if he ever won the lottery he wouldn't tell a soul. He had said that big winners often lost all their old friends and gained lots of new ones who were only interested in the money. Families argued and fell apart, leaving the winner abandoned and alone - ostracised was the word he'd used. He couldn't imagine his aunt ever abandoning them but he wasn't ready to involve anyone else in his deception yet.

'We could get a taxi. I've got two or three numbers in my phone.' He searched his phone's address book and called the first number. There was no answer after several rings so he stabbed the end call button and tried the next.

'ABC taxis.' The woman's voice droned and Reece imagined her filing her nails.

'I need a taxi to Truro Hospital urgently, please'

'Where from?' Reece could almost see her rolling her eyes, as though customers had no right to disturb her.

'From the corner of Seaview Rise, Trevarnick.'

'I've nothing for at least half an hour.'

'No, it's urgent. I'll have to try another, thanks.' He had struggled to stay polite.

'Please yourself!' was the apathetic response.

He hung up and scrolled to the next number.

'Kernow Kabs, how may I help you?' This sounded more promising.

'I need a taxi urgently from Trevarnick to Truro Hospital, please.' He was aware he sounded like he was begging.

'Whereabouts are you?' she asked.

'We're at Seaview Rise and it's very urgent.'

'I've got a car on its way past there about now; just hang on while I radio him.' She muted the phone and Reece wondered if the silence meant she had cut him off. He waited impatiently, wondering if he should hang up and call again. After the longest minute of his life, she came back on the line.

'He'll be with you in a couple of minutes.'

'Oh thank you,' Reece said. 'You're a life saver.' He put his phone in his pocket.

'They've got one coming in two minutes,' he told Kara.

She took his hand while they waited. Two minutes passed; then four; then ten.

'Where the hell is he?' spat Reece. Kara didn't answer.

He took his phone out and recalled the number. The same voice answered.

'I ordered a cab ten minutes ago and it's not here yet.' He intoned the statement like a sarcastic question.

'From Seaview?' she asked. 'He went there and couldn't find you. Hang on I'll radio him.' She muted the call again, for what seemed like forever. 'He's sat in the car park,' she eventually reported.

'Which car park?' He realised he was almost yelling.

At Seaview Caravan Park, of course. Where are you?'

'We're at Seaview *Rise*, not the caravan park!'

'Oh I'm sorry. I must have misheard you. I'll send him straight away.'

He told Kara about the mix up and complained about the operator's stupidity. She took his hand again and told him to calm down. He paced back and forth, shivering as though with fever as the turmoil boiled inside him. The difference one hundred and fifteen million pounds would make to his family was beyond his comprehension. It had such colossal consequences he didn't feel he would ever recover if it was snatched away from them now. His dad could buy the best medical care in the world. He wouldn't have to worry about the pub anymore. In fact, he could sell it. Hell, he could afford to give it away, like loose change. Maybe his mum and dad could get back together without the pub and all its problems stressing them out.

The thoughts were hammering inside his brain, like a hundred woodpeckers and he thought he might be sick. He gripped Kara's hand and wondered how he could ever have dealt with the past week without her.

They heard a car approaching and he sighed with relief upon seeing the taxi sign on its roof. It slowed to a stop and they both got in the back seat.

'Sorry about the cock up,' the driver said amiably. 'Truro Hospital isn't it?'

'Yes please. How much will it cost?'

'It's about twelve pounds on the meter I reckon,' said the driver.

'Get us there as fast as possible and I'll pay you twenty,' Reece said.

With that, the driver swung the car round in the road and accelerated hard. Soon they were doing sixty miles per hour down the narrow roads. Reece wasn't worried; he seemed to be a good driver, but he and Kara both put their seatbelts on and hung on to the grab handles. They turned onto the main A30 and Reece noticed with a sense of satisfaction, the needle on the speedo nudging eighty miles per hour.

Soon they were turning off towards Truro and the driver was forced to slow down as he drove into the city. The traffic was heavy with people making their way home after a leisurely Saturday spent browsing the shops. Reece could feel the tension rising within him again and his grip on Kara's hand grew tighter. Eventually, they escaped the city centre and sped towards Treliske. Soon, the taxi pulled into the hospital car park and Reece thanked the driver for doing the journey in record time. He gave him the twenty-pound note he had taken from the petty cash tin, before he and Kara ran towards the main entrance. They took the stairs to the Intensive Therapy Unit and paused to compose themselves before entering.

Reece didn't recognise the nurse at the nurses' station so he asked her where Jane was.

'She's on her break. Who have you come to see?'

'My dad, David Winner.'

'He already has a visitor, so one of you will have to wait outside,' said the nurse.

Reece felt sick. The blood rose to his head as the enormity of what she had said, hit him like a sledgehammer.

'Who...who is it?' he stammered.

'I think he said he was a cousin.'

She spoke so matter-of-factly that Reece wanted to scream at her and tell her how she had destroyed his life, by allowing the man in against his wishes. But she couldn't be blamed. If Jane hadn't told her, how could she possibly know?

He backed away from the counter and felt the tears coming.

'That's it Kara. We've lost it.'

'You don't know that Reece. Go in there and see what's happening.'

'I can't. I don't know what to say. What if I'm in trouble? I've broken the law and maybe Mr Shah will see to it that I'm charged with fraud or something.'

'Well you've nothing to lose now Reece. Just stay calm and get in there.'

He leaned on the wall, taking deep breaths. He was shaking from head to foot. It felt like the stage fright he experienced when he'd entered his previous school's public speaking competition and had stammered his way into last place. Only this was worse - one hundred and fifteen million times worse!

Kara kissed him on the cheek and rubbed his back.

'Go,' she said. 'You'll be fine.'

He edged towards the door. He counted the floor tiles between him and the rest of his life. He peered through the circular window and saw a man sitting by his dad's bed with his back to the door. He had black hair and wore a light tan suit. His dad was sitting up in bed looking better than he'd seen him on any previous visit and this spurred him to push the door open, but still with the trepidation of someone entering a gas chamber.

The two men didn't hear him enter, so he closed the door silently behind himself. He was scared to advance to the bed and stood there trying to listen to what they were saying. It was his dad who was speaking, his tone flat and without emotion.

'So you still have to conduct some security checks?'

Reece stopped breathing. The security checks would somehow prove that his dad had not been the one who had entered. He regretted his deceit and his stupidity. Why hadn't he told his dad about his dream? Why hadn't he asked him to complete the entry on his behalf? How would his dad feel, knowing they had come within sniffing distance of one of the biggest lottery wins in history, only to face prosecution for entering illegally?

He wanted to run away. He couldn't face his dad. He couldn't look him in the eye and see the pain he had put him through. First their separation, then the accident and now this, how could they endure such a catalogue of terrible events and go back to the way things were? When Mr Shah spoke, Reece felt his knees buckle. He wanted to run and hurl himself upon him, but he couldn't move.

'That's right Mr Winner, but that's just routine. Once I've confirmed your identity, the money will be paid into your account. Congratulations. You're now one of the richest men in Britain.' He shook his dad's hand and stood as if to leave. 'And of course we'll respect your wishes for no publicity. Shame really. It would have made a great story, so if you change your mind…'

'I'm sorry Mr Shah, but that's not going to happen.'

Both men laughed. Mr Shah looked towards the door and spotted Reece.

'Now let me guess, you must be Reece, right?'

Reece paid less attention to the question, than he did to seeing his dad turn his head in his direction.

'Dad, you're moving!'

'Yes son. I told you I would. It's time you had more faith in your old dad. I suppose you've had a very worrying time.'

'You wouldn't know the half of it, Dad.'

'Oh, I think I would. I believe you've spoken to Mr Shah on the telephone. I think you owe him an apology.'

'Mr Winner, he owes me nothing of the sort. He was simply looking after your interests. He sounds like a very sensible boy.' He held out his hand, smiling from ear to ear. 'Hi Reece, I'm very pleased to meet you. It seems your dad's a very lucky man.'

Reece nervously shook his hand. His mind was racing. How had they got away with it? Had his dad simply had the presence of mind to say that he had entered the numbers, even though he hadn't? If he had, he deserved a medal for such quick thinking, especially while lying seriously injured in an Intensive Therapy Unit.

'Why don't you sit down Reece? Your dad has something to tell you and you really aren't going to believe it.' He turned back to his dad. 'Mr Winner, I'll leave you to chat to your son. I'm sure you've a lot to discuss and I'll have my team working on your preliminary instructions immediately. I'll visit again tomorrow, when everything has been cleared.'

'Okay Mr Shah and thanks again. I still can't believe it.'

Mr Shah said goodbye to Reece and left the room.

His dad waited a few seconds until he was sure Mr Shah had gone, before turning to Reece. 'Come here you! What do you think you've been up to?'

Reece sat on the edge of the bed and hugged his dad. 'Have we really won a hundred and fifteen million pounds, Dad?'

'We?' replied his dad. '*We?*' He dropped his voice to a whisper. 'I never entered the lottery, so it can't have been me can it?'

'Dad, I came here at almost a hundred miles an hour to try to stop you saying just that to Mr Shah. How did you know to say the right things?'

His dad laughed and winced from the pain. 'Reece, didn't it occur to you when you thoughtfully entered the lottery on my behalf, that I might get an email confirmation?'

'No it didn't,' he said, realisation planting a broad grin on his face.

His dad laughed again. 'Well I did. I meant to have a go at you for it and find out how you hacked my online account, but I never got the chance.'

'So you knew all along?'

'I certainly did, so I was able to tell Mr Shah, that you had selected the numbers, which was true, and the fact that it was on my secure, online account was all the evidence he needed that the entry was mine and therefore entirely legal. But I'm curious to know what made you do it?'

'Reece quickly explained about his dream and his premonition about the lottery amount, while his dad listened in amazement. They laughed and chatted nineteen to the dozen about what they could do with one hundred and fifteen million pounds, until his dad turned serious again.

'Reece, this has to be our secret. You must promise not to tell another living soul about this.'

Reece remembered Kara, still sitting out in the corridor. 'I can't do that I'm afraid, Dad. Kara already knows. In fact, if it weren't for her help in deciphering the dream, we would never have won. And now I feel awful, because she's sitting outside and must be wondering what on earth's going on.'

His dad sat thoughtfully for a few seconds. 'So you're saying that she deserves as much credit for this win as you?'

'Of course, although she didn't want me to enter behind your back.'

'And she was quite right; it could have cost us everything. But anyway, we'll forget about that now. So, do you think she deserves a share of our good fortune?'

'Well, yes Dad. I suppose she does.'

'And what do you propose would be fair?'

'I don't know. It's your money really isn't it?'

'Yes, I suppose it is. It'll be my bank account it goes into at any rate. But this is an awful lot of money Reece and it needs to be handled sensibly.'

He closed his eyes, deep in thought and for a moment, Reece wondered if the excitement had been too much for him and he'd fallen asleep, but after a minute or two he spoke. 'Okay, this is what I think ought to happen. How do you feel about a five-way split?'

'A five-way split?'

'Yes five. Your mother and I are still married and so this win could form part of any divorce settlement. We had many good years together and you're going to be spending quite a lot time with her as well as with me. It's therefore only right that she should be able to look after you in the same style that I'm going to be able to from now on.'

'So you still don't think you and Mum can work things out?' asked Reece, looking glum once more.

His dad sighed. 'Look son, if anything, this win makes it less likely. We couldn't get back together now without us both wondering if it was simply for the money. I think we've made our minds up and it's best we leave it like that. At least the money will allow us to do whatever we want with our lives.'

Reece nodded. He was pleased his dad could still show his mum such consideration, but hearing that even winning a fortune couldn't get them back together, saddened him. However, his dad had made a very good point; it would be wrong for him to live with his dad enjoying everything that money could buy, while his mum was living in a caravan.

'So who are the other four?'

'Well me of course,' he said, grinning. 'Seeing as it was my two pounds you spent. Then you, your aunt Debbie, for all she's done for us and of course, Kara.'

Reece leapt off the bed and danced a jig around the room.

'YES! YES!' he cheered, punching the air with his fist.

'Hang on I haven't finished yet. I propose that only the fifteen million is split five ways. I think three million each is more than enough for the five of us to enjoy life. The other one hundred million I'm going to place in trust for your future. This is your win and it's your future that's important to me and I know your mum will feel the same way. I intend to see you get the best education money can buy and if it's true that travel broadens the mind, I'm going to see to it that you have one of the broadest minds in the world.'

Reece's jaw dropped. He wiped the tears welling up in his eyes, but for the first time in days, they were tears of happiness.

'Oh, Dad,' he sobbed. 'Two days ago I thought I might lose you. Yesterday I was still worried you could be paralysed. And today I can't describe how lucky I feel to have you back.'

They hugged each other until his dad reminded him about Kara sitting outside.

'Can I tell her, Dad?' asked Reece, his excitement raising his voice to a squeal.

'Of course you can. But you must tell no one else. Obviously, Kara will need to tell her mum and I shall have to tell your mum and Aunt Debbie. But that's it and I'll be saying the same thing to Kara.'

'I think she'll be okay with that,' Reece said. 'Now can I tell her? *Please!*'

'Bring her in here Reece, so I can see her face. It's not every day a thirteen year old gets told she's become a millionaire.'

Reece went to the door and saw Kara sitting outside, biting her fingernails, something he had never seen her do before.

'Reece, I've been worried sick. Was that the lottery guy who I saw leaving about a quarter of an hour ago?'

'Shh!' he said, beckoning her with his hand. 'Come in here quickly.'

Kara stepped into the room. Reece took her hand and led her to his dad's bedside.

He glanced conspiratorially over his shoulders, before shrieking, 'We've done it! We've won the lottery! All one hundred and fifteen million of it!'

Kara screamed and clasped her mouth with her hands. Reece hurriedly explained to her how his dad had received an email confirmation of the entry and therefore, had been ready to answer Mr Shah's questions. Soon he and Kara were hugging and dancing around the room while his dad grimaced from the pain of laughing at them. Then Reece told her about his dad's plans to divide the money and that she would be getting three million pounds for herself. She screeched her delight and babbled excitedly about buying her mum a new house and a car and taking her and Ethan on holiday

'She's always wanted to go to The Maldives, but it costs a fortune. Now I can't wait to pick up some brochures. Oh my god, I can't believe it. Thank you David, thank you so much!'

David Winner finally asked them to calm down and sit. He was watching the door, worried a nurse might come in to find out what all the noise was about. He repeated to Kara what he had said to Reece about keeping the win totally secret and Kara promised not to tell anyone except her mum.

After another half an hour of elated chatter, Reece could see his dad's eyes straining to stay open. He told him he needed to sleep, if he was going to get out of hospital as quickly as possible to start enjoying his new life. Both Reece and Kara kissed him on the cheek and said goodnight, promising to return to see him in the morning. They forced themselves to walk sensibly past the nurses' desk, even though their smiles looked like they had coat hangers in their mouths.

Outside, the air was like pure oxygen to their heightened senses. They were walking across the hospital gardens when Kara stopped beneath a large tree. She rested her back against the trunk and took both Reece's hands in hers. She pulled him towards her and put her arms around his neck. He held her waist and closed his eyes as she sought his lips with hers. Her mouth was open and he could feel her tongue seeking his. His head swam and he felt his knees shaking uncontrollably. He opened his eyes to see she was watching him and as they separated for air, she was smirking at him.

'Well?' she asked. 'Is my anagram correct or not?' He frowned and Kara appeared to look disappointed. 'You mean you haven't worked it out yet?' she teased. 'Kara Steigers is an anagram of *A **Great** Kisser*.'

'Is it really?' Reece said, trying to arrange the letters in his mind. Then he laughed. 'I'm still not sure,' he said. 'Would you mind doing that again so I can check?'

'Reece Winner, you are welcome to check as many times as you like,' breathed Kara, as she pulled him close once more.

THE END